Gifted

karey white

Gifted

karey white

bonneville books
springville, utah

ISBN 13: 978-1-59955-474-7

Published by Bonneville Books, an imprint of Cedar Fort, Inc., 2373 W. 700 S., Springville, UT 84663
Distributed by Cedar Fort, Inc., www.cedarfort.com

LIBRARY OF CONGRESS CATALOGING-IN-PUBLICATION DATA

White, Karey Lynn, 1964-
 Gifted / Karey Lynn White.
   p. cm.
 Summary: A childless couple adopt a baby girl and realize as she grows
that she possesses the ability to learn phenomenally quickly and to help
others around her learn.
 ISBN 978-1-59955-474-7
 1. Gifted girls--Fiction. 2. Adopted children--Fiction. I. Title.
 PS3623.H57255G54 2010
 813'.6--dc22

                        2010034941

Cover design by Danie Romrell
Cover design © 2011 by Lyle Mortimer
Edited and typeset by Kelley Konzak

The poem on pages 43–44 is from Anna E. Burnham, "A Lost Child" in Edward William Cole, *Cole's Funny Picture Book No. 1*, accessed November 24, 2010, http://www.gutenberg.org/files/30726/30726-8.txt.

Printed in the United States of America

10 9 8 7 6 5 4 3 2 1

Printed on acid-free paper

For Mr. Higginson, Miss Reynolds,
Mr. Bonner, and Mrs. Rasmussen,

Four outstanding English teachers who
helped inspire my love of reading and writing.

Acknowledgments

It's a daunting task to acknowledge the many people who played a role in getting this story into your hands, but I'm determined to do my best.

To my neighbor, whose tragedy broke my heart, kindled my imagination, and inspired my vision of Anna.

To my parents (Lynn and Karen): Thanks, Dad, for helping me love the classics, and Mom, for reading to us every night. Thanks to both of you, who, along with my sisters (Lori, Lisa, and Leslie) and daughter (Veronica), eagerly waited for the daily additions to the story. Your encouraging words and prodding phone calls kept me moving.

To Dad, Nairn, Robert, and Leslie, who pointed out story elements that needed work. To Lori, who called me and said, "Have you heard of Cedar Fort? I think you should send it there."

To the rest of my brothers (Richard, Bruce, John, Spencer, and Mark), my in-laws and nieces and nephews who constantly offered words of encouragement. There's no one in the world with a better family than mine.

To my friends Melanie and McKenzie, who read the first draft, and to Lance, my long lost friend who I found just in the nick of time. Wow, what a blessing you've been!

To the wonderful people at CFI. Jennifer, thank you for caring about Anna and Kelsey and Brent and Susan. From the first time I talked to you, I knew you were on my side. To Kelley, for your hard

Acknowledgments

work and patience. I know the book is better because of you. To Danie, who designed a cover that took my breath away. Thank you all.

To my wonderful kids, Bruce, Veronica, Savannah, and Joseph. What did I ever do to deserve you? You are amazing, and being your mom is my greatest joy. Thank you for your love, support, and goodness. Thanks for being mine.

To Travis: I hit the jackpot when I found you. (Or did you find me?) However it happened, I'm genuinely blessed. You encourage me, you brag about me, you stick up for me. I love you.

And finally, to my Father in Heaven, for loving me and blessing me with a creative itch that has to be scratched and for putting all these wonderful people in my life.

—

Prologue

Guardian Angel: noun. 1. An angel believed to protect a particular person, as from danger or error. 2. A person who looks after or is concerned with the welfare of another.

Merriam-Webster Dictionary

Guardian Spirit: A supernatural being that protects people or places. Belief in guardian spirits is found worldwide and has a long history. Many faiths teach that each person has a guardian spirit or angel who watches over them. In Islam there are believed to be two such angels, one on either shoulder. In many branches of Christianity it is believed that at birth everyone is given a guardian angel to whom they can turn in times of stress or temptation.

Encarta Encyclopedia

"I have spoken here of heavenly help, of angels dispatched to bless us in time of need. But when we speak of those who are instruments in the hand of God, we are reminded that not all angels are from the other side of the veil. Some of them we walk with and talk with—here, now, every day. . . . Indeed heaven never seems closer than when we see the love of God manifested in the kindness and devotion of people so good and so pure that angelic is the only word that comes to mind."

Elder Jeffrey R. Holland
"The Ministry of Angels," *Ensign*, Nov. 2008, 29–31.

Chapter I

H "ello?"

"Susan Weller?"

"This is Susan." I didn't recognize the woman's voice.

"This is Amanda at Barkley, Stevens & Rollington." I caught my breath and reached behind me, feeling for a chair to catch me. I sat down hard and gripped the edge of the dining room table, reminding myself to breathe. I'd waited thirty-three years for this phone call. Of course, the first twenty-five years I hadn't known I was waiting. I'd just lived each day, unaware that this single telephone call would affect every part of my life—would literally change my world.

"Are you there, Mrs. Weller?"

"Yes, I'm here." I struggled to keep my voice steady.

"Mrs. Weller, I know this is short notice, but Mr. Stevens would like to meet with you and your husband this afternoon, if that's possible."

I swallowed hard. "I think we could do that," I said. Instantly, I knew I had to do better than that. What if she judged me based on the conviction in my voice? I forced my voice to sound surer, stronger. "Of course we can. What time would you like us there?" Thank goodness it was my day off and I was here to answer this long-anticipated phone call.

"Does 4:00 work for you?"

"Yes, that would be fine." I wondered how I was possibly going to wait more than six hours to find out what Mr. Stevens had to tell us. What was six hours after all these years of waiting and hoping, yet it seemed like an eternity.

"Great. I'll put it on Mr. Stevens's schedule. Call if you run into any problems."

"There won't be any problems. We'll be there." I knew nothing would keep us away. Waiting another day was unthinkable.

"Perfect. We'll see you this afternoon."

I sat at the table in a state of shock long after she had hung up. Actually, 4:00 would be good. Brent finished teaching his last math class at 3:10. He could easily get to Mr. Stevens's office by 4:00. I needed to wash my hair. Surely I didn't want to receive this news with my hair in a messy ponytail. Would it be good news? I imagined myself holding a sweet little baby but quickly stopped myself. What if it was bad news? Would they really drag us down to the office to give us bad news? Would they tell us that after four years, they realized they couldn't find us a baby and we needed to move on? Doubts filled my mind. If it was bad news, it really didn't matter how my hair looked. In fact, if I went in looking frazzled and unkempt, they would know they were doing the right thing by drop- ping us. But they could share bad news over the phone or in a letter.

Memories of the monthly heartbreak, the years we'd spent hoping and fasting and praying, and all the frustration, pain, and disappointment had me completely overwhelmed, and thoughts started flooding my mind. Did the car have enough gas to get to Mr. Stevens's office? Maybe I should go fill up now. Or maybe I should wash my hair first.

"If you'd like to make a call, please hang up and dial again." The recorded voice of the operator startled me back to the present. I clicked the off button and dialed Central High.

"Hi, Elsie, this is Susan Weller."

"Hi, Susan."

"Would you put a note in Brent's box to call me during his lunch?"

"Actually, he's here in the office right now. Let me put him on."

"Thanks." I rested my head in my hand. Elsie put me on hold, and Seals and Crofts's "Summer Breeze" began playing. I'd always liked that song, but right now all I wanted was to hear my husband's voice. After an endless verse and chorus, Brent came on the line.

"Hi, hon, what's up?" His voice sounded so good.

"I'm so glad you're there! I thought I'd have to wait until your lunch."

"There's a Mothers Against Drunk Driving assembly right now, so I was making some copies," he said. "Is something wrong?"

"I don't think so. I hope not. Mr. Stevens's office called, and they want us to come in and see them at four today." I took a deep breath and forced myself to speak more slowly. "Can you make it?"

"Sure." He sounded way too calm. "Did they say what they wanted?" His tone was measured and rational. He'd ridden this roller coaster too many times to get his hopes up. He'd learned a long time ago that if he joined me in the optimistic "what ifs" and "whens," my disappointment when things didn't work out was even more crushing. I knew he worried about me, so I tried to maintain my composure, but inside I was filled with hope.

"No, they didn't. But I hope it means there's a baby for us. It's either that or they're dropping us. What else could it be?"

"Well, I guess we'll find out when we get there. I'll have to meet you there. I won't have time to come home first and still be there on time. Is that okay?"

"That's fine," I said.

"Are you sure? I could probably leave a little early and pick you up if you want me to."

"No, no, I'm fine. You don't need to arrange for a substitute. I'll just meet you there."

"Okay." He paused. "I love you, Susan." This was his way of reminding me that no matter what news awaited us, we would be okay. I knew that was true, but I also knew we'd be a lot more okay if Mr. Stevens had found us a baby.

"I love you too," I said. I sat for a moment, staring blankly out the window. Almost without thinking, I went to the kitchen and mixed up a batch of chocolate chip cookies. I think better when my hands are occupied, and I wanted to think—daydream even. And daydreams are always better when accompanied by warm chocolate chip cookies.

Several hours later, with a full tank of gas and clean hair, I pulled into the parking lot of Barkley, Stevens & Rollington. "Darn it," I said. The little clock on the dashboard told me I'd driven way too fast. Here I was, sitting in the parking lot, with twenty-five minutes to spare. I turned the key a half turn and tried to find a song on the radio to distract me. It wasn't easy. Madonna's "Vogue" irritated me. Why would someone bother singing such a pointless song? The grating voice of Michael Bolton singing "How Am I Supposed to Live Without You" made me aware of a headache behind my eyes. Singing shouldn't sound that difficult. I finally left it on Bon Jovi and even joined in halfheartedly on the chorus of "Blaze of Glory" as I waited for Brent. When the song ended, I turned off the radio and closed my eyes.

I'd wanted a baby for so long, I could hardly remember a time when I hadn't felt this hollow ache in my heart. Would it begin to heal today? I started to pray. I pleaded for good news and asked for the courage to go on if the news was bad. Trying to relax, I ran my fingers through my hair and then looked at myself in the rearview mirror. A few minutes later, Brent pulled into a parking space a few cars away. I got out and met him as he opened his door.

"You ready?" he asked, pulling me close and kissing my forehead.

"I guess so." Brent kept his arm around my shoulder as we walked silently into the office building. We quietly rode the elevator up four floors, lost in our own thoughts. I looked at our slightly distorted reflections in the shiny, stainless steel doors of the elevator. We looked like any other couple, and I wondered if we'd look like parents after we talked to Mr. Stevens. At the reception area, we were greeted by a neatly dressed older woman who immediately led us to a conference room. She directed us to two seats at one end of the huge, gleaming table and offered us something to drink. We both declined, but as soon as she left the room, I wished I'd asked for some water. My mouth felt woolly, and my lips were sticking to my teeth.

We'd waited only a few minutes when Mr. Stevens and a young woman entered the conference room. Mr. Stevens wore a gray pin-striped suit and a bright yellow tie with an interesting pattern of tiny bluebirds. His eyes were very blue, his fingers long and elegant. The woman wore a pretty, white blouse with delicate, lacy details that seemed at odds with her spiky, white-blonde hair and heavily lined eyes. Her fingernails were short and bright pink. She sat across the table from us and casually flipped open a notebook, ready to take notes. She was left-handed. Mr. Stevens shook our hands and then sat at the head of the table. He opened a manila file folder, slowly leafing through the pages inside. I felt like a child in the principal's office.

"Thank you for coming on such short notice." His eyes still examined the file before him. We both nodded, not wanting to speak for fear it would delay the news. "I presume your situation remains unchanged?" He raised his eyes from the papers to look directly at us.

"Things are the same," Brent said. I was surprised at the calm confidence in his voice. I was unsure if I could squeak out a single word.

"Very well." Mr. Stevens put on a pair of glasses, adjusting them to sit perfectly halfway down his nose. He picked up the file and turned his attention back to the pages inside. "I have a baby girl in need of a home." He said it as easily as if he were telling us he'd had a tuna sandwich for lunch. He looked at us over the top of the glasses, and I leaned forward.

Looking back at his file, he continued, "There are some unusual circumstances about which you need to be aware. Her parents were both killed in a car accident in New Mexico. The mother lived long enough to deliver a baby girl. The baby was premature and very small, but she seems to be doing well, given her circumstances. She will need to remain in the hospital for a few more weeks." He paused and looked at us again, gauging our reactions. Apparently satisfied with our expressions, his voice took on a kinder tone. "She has no family that can take her, and she needs a home. The doctor says she's a strong little girl, but of course, being born so early, she may have complications about which we're not yet aware. It's important that you realize the implications of a premature birth before you make your decision. Her closest living relative is an elderly great-aunt who feels she can't give the baby what she needs. She looked at your file, among others, and if you're interested, she'd like you to have the baby."

Mr. Stevens removed his glasses and tucked them back in his pocket before leaning back in his chair and making a steeple with his hands. His eyes remained on us the entire time.

I realized I wasn't breathing and probably hadn't been since he'd begun talking. Tears stung my eyes and threatened to spill over. I opened my mouth to speak but couldn't. Brent looked at me questioningly. I nodded. "Of course we want her," he said. "What do we do now?" The tears came, and I brushed them away with the back of my hand at the same time the young woman across from me magically produced a box of Kleenex.

I tried to focus on Mr. Stevens's instructions, but I couldn't. Instead I thought of rocking a baby girl to sleep. I pictured the extra bedroom as a nursery with a closet full of pink dresses. I saw myself playing peekaboo with a laughing baby wearing a pink bow. Thank goodness Brent was there to listen to the details of what was to come. He was listening intently, and I noticed that his knuckles were white as he gripped the arm of his chair. He was finally going to be a dad. She'd be his little princess. The lump in my throat felt enormous.

An hour later, I was in my car, following Brent home. A precious folder full of information sat on the seat beside me. I tried to keep my eyes on the road ahead of me, but they kept drifting to the photograph of a baby wrapped in a white flannel blanket that was paper clipped to the front of the file. At a stoplight, Brent put his arm out the window and motioned for me to pull up beside him. "Let's stop at Dos Hombres," he said, and I nodded gratefully. I hadn't given food a moment's thought, and I couldn't imagine trying to do something as normal as cooking dinner.

As we waited for our carne asada and tamales, we made a list of things that we needed to do. We had less than forty-eight hours until I was expected at St. Vincent hospital in Santa Fe. There was no question I would resign my job at Grand Junction Power Company. We'd always planned on me quitting when we had a baby. I had taken the job thinking it would be a short-term secretarial position, but it had somehow dragged into nearly ten years. I wanted to stay home with our children, so we'd been careful to live in a way that would make that easy. We had used my income for savings and fertility treatments. It wouldn't be a big adjustment for me to quit, and for that I was grateful.

"We need to call our families," Brent said. I added that to the growing list. Our parents would be thrilled when they heard the good news.

The next two days were a flurry of activity. I quit my job and made the necessary preparations for the coming weeks, but I don't really remember doing it. While my body accomplished the necessary tasks each day, my mind was in a hospital nursery in New Mexico. Every job was accompanied by thoughts of holding a sweet baby, singing lullabies, and reading bedtime stories.

I left for Sante Fe at the same time Brent left for school. We said a prayer, and then he kissed me good-bye in the driveway between our two cars. I felt sad that he wasn't coming with me. "I'll be down in a few days," he said, and I nodded.

The seven-hour drive from Grand Junction to Santa Fe was filled with memories of the good and bad times we'd shared these past ten years. I remembered seeing Brent for the first time. He'd arrived late to my college biology class. He was tall and handsome, with short, sandy hair and ridiculous blue eyes, and I knew as I sat there that I wasn't the only girl in the room taking notice of him. He'd seemed completely unconcerned that he was late as he sat in the empty seat next to me. He smiled at me, and my stomach did a flip. When class was over, he leaned over and asked, "So, did I miss anything important?"

I desperately wanted to come up with some witty reply that would make me instantly fascinating to him, but all I could come up with was, "No."

"All right, then. Save me a seat on Wednesday?"

"Sure," I said, probably too eagerly. I felt the color rise in my cheeks. I hoped I wasn't getting all excited over nothing. But when I came to class on Wednesday, he was already there, and he waved me over to the seat next to him. "I saved it for you this time," he said. I pretended to take notes throughout the class, but my mind was occupied with things other than biology. When he saved a seat for me again on Friday, I decided it meant something.

We sat by each other every class after that. He made small talk before and after class, and in time, I untangled my tongue and was able to respond. Eventually, he asked me to dinner, and a year later, we got married. He always said my curly, auburn hair and green eyes were too much to resist, but I like to think it was my witty conversation.

We started our marriage with such well-laid plans. Brent started teaching in Grand Junction just a month after our wedding, and we figured we'd get started right away on a family. For some reason, we never felt the need to have an extended period of alone time before having children. We both wanted children, and we felt ready. But what we got was nine years of alone time while friends and family around us had children. We endured physically painful fertility treatments, including two failed attempts at in vitro. But the emotional pain was far worse. We'd been crushed by disappointment too many times to count, but despite the challenges of those dark times, our love for each other grew. I smiled at the thought of a little girl calling Brent "Daddy."

I took the exit to Santa Fe and checked in at the Santa Fe Plaza Travelodge less than three miles from the hospital. I dropped my suitcases in the teal and mauve southwest-style room, and twenty minutes later, I eagerly walked through the corridors of St. Vincent hospital, on my way to meet our new daughter.

After signing some paperwork and washing my hands, I was given a light-green smock printed with baby bottles and safety pins and was led into the bright, cheerful nursery. I counted three babies, but only one had a pink beanie. I walked to the tiny bassinet with its soft, white flannel blankets. An acrylic canopy enclosed a controlled environment of warmth and extra oxygen. Inside was a tiny baby girl. Since she was already six weeks old, I was surprised by her daintiness. Her skin was pale pink, and her full lips were moving in a barely perceptible sucking motion. Tufts of golden fuzz peeked out from under the little hat. I stood there in wonder, staring at this perfect little baby.

"You can pick her up if you'd like," the nurse beside me said in a quiet, encouraging voice. She carefully raised the canopy, and I reached down and gently picked up the baby—my baby. She felt as light as whipped cream and was surprisingly warm. She fit so perfectly into the crook of my arm that I caught my breath. The nurse guided me to a rocking chair a few feet away, and I sat down, never taking my eyes off the angel in my arms. Tears streamed down my cheeks and soaked into the blanket that wrapped her securely. It was hard to take my eyes off her, but when I finally did, I was astounded at the beauty of the room around me. The speckled black-and-white linoleum looked bright and sparkly. A golden shaft of late afternoon light filtered into the room between the blinds, making a beautiful striped pattern on the floor and wall. The blankets in each of the bassinets looked luxurious and soft. The nurse, standing a few feet away, was beautiful, with intelligent, dark eyes and warm brown skin. Her long, black ponytail was shiny and thick. I looked around the room in awe, surprised that such pretty surroundings were actually in a hospital. Somehow the world looked so different. Could becoming a mom really change the way I saw the world? Oh, what I'd been missing!

Our little Anna was born eleven weeks early and weighed only three pounds, four ounces at birth. By the time I met her, she was up to five pounds, ten ounces—still so small, but the fingers that squeezed my thumb were long, graceful, and surprisingly strong. She had spindly little legs and no bottom at all. I spent hours with her every day in that cozy nursery, and I dreaded the dreariness of the world without her when I was forced to leave the hospital to eat or sleep. The peace and joy I felt upon returning each time were overwhelming.

Brent noticed it too. The first weekend I was there, he flew down to be with his new little family. I picked him up at the airport and described every detail to him on the way to the hospital. If I thought I'd reached my capacity for joy when I held our little Anna, I was wrong. As I watched Brent hold our baby, I thought my heart would burst. Never before had Brent looked so strong and handsome as when he held our tiny girl in his arms. The world was right, and this was what we'd been waiting for. Gone were the fears and disappointments of all those years, replaced with a perfect understanding that all those things had been necessary to bring us to this exquisite joy. The scripture about opposition ran through my mind often, and I felt gratitude for the trials that made this joy so complete. Anna was meant for us. Of that I was certain.

The two days that Brent was with us in Santa Fe were a dream, and it was with a heavy heart that we said good-bye when it came time for him to return home to work. We were eager for the time when the doctor would tell us we could take our Anna home.

Every morning, a doctor would stop by and check on Anna. Usually it was Dr. DeLagonno, a short, stocky man with wavy white hair. He was a happy man who obviously enjoyed his job. He came each day with a smile, a twinkle in his eye, and a new little nickname for Anna. He called her a peanut, a ladybug, a Tic Tac, and a button. Three and a half weeks after I'd arrived in Santa Fe, Dr. DeLagonno walked into the nursery, waving a medical chart above his head. "How would you like to take your little buttercup home?" he asked with a smile on his face.

"Really?" I asked from my favorite place, the rocking chair.

"Really," he said. "She's doing great. I'm going to release her the day after tomorrow, so make any arrangements you need to, and you can take your daughter home." He touched Anna's cheek gently with the back of his thick finger, and I felt a rush of gratitude for all the people here who had loved and cared for our baby.

I called Brent with the happy news, and of course, he was thrilled. He'd kept himself busy each day after school, preparing Anna's room. He was impatient for us to get home.

Grandma Anderson—a name I had wanted to call my mom for so long—flew to Santa Fe to help me drive my precious baby home. I picked her up at the airport, and we drove straight to Walmart, where we bought a car seat, some baby clothes, and some snacks for the trip home. We checked out of the hotel and then went to the hospital to pick up Anna. She looked ridiculously small in the car seat, and I took a picture to show Brent.

The drive home took much longer with a baby than when I had traveled the same roads alone three and a half weeks earlier. I didn't mind. It was a treat to stop and feed Anna or change her diaper. Once I even stopped just to look at her. Spring was blooming, so the roads were clear and the landscapes more colorful than when I'd driven to Santa Fe. It seemed that everything around us was growing and blossoming, and the usually dry, brown desert was covered with a pale carpet of green. The sun was warm and gentle, and when it finally slipped below the horizon, the sky looked like dark velvet.

We stayed the night at a moderately priced hotel in Salida, about halfway between Santa Fe and Grand Junction. The room was clean and unexpectedly pretty for a budget hotel. I found it a pleasure to wake up with Anna during the night, happy to trade uninterrupted sleep for a baby. The next morning, we resumed our journey to Anna's new home and her new daddy. The trip was easy, and as we drove into the southern part of Grand Junction, my heart felt like a balloon being blown up bigger and bigger, threatening to explode. I couldn't wait to see Brent and settle into life as a new little family. Grand Junction, like everything else I'd seen since I'd become a mother, looked bright and new. The trees were leafing out, and spring flowers were blooming. The rugged red rocks were fiery and breathtaking under a bright blue sky. Cotton ball clouds floated high above the mesa. I felt like I was seeing this pretty town I'd lived in for nine years for the first time.

"Mom, everything is prettier since Anna came into my life."

Mom smiled. "The world is a new place after you have a baby. A child changes everything."

We pulled into the driveway of our sturdy, brick home—had it always been so cute?—and there was Brent, coming out the front door. The sight of him was like heaven. He greeted me with a hug and a kiss, and then he hugged my mom. Finally, almost reverently, he lifted Anna from the car and carried her into the house.

"Did you paint the whole house?" I asked. Everything looked fresher and nicer than I remembered.

"No, I just painted the baby's room." I left him to hold his daughter and walked to the nursery. The room was a warm shade of yellow. Against the wall was a beautiful white crib with ornate spindles that I'd never seen before. Brent had done well. Everything looked utterly charming. He'd even stocked the crib with pink and yellow bedding. On the wall was a framed cover of an old book of nursery rhymes. I wondered where he'd found such a sweet thing.

Mom stayed until the weekend. She loved holding the baby, but knowing how long I'd waited, she limited her time with Anna and instead occupied herself making a couple of casseroles and two meat loaves, which she froze for later. She shopped for groceries until the kitchen was stocked enough to last for weeks. She washed and put away all the baby clothes and even washed a few windows.

One evening, I overheard her talking to my dad. "She's a

beautiful baby. I can't wait for you to see her this summer. I know. I wish you could have come with us. You're going to adore her. They're so happy. You should see Susan. She's a natural mother, and Brent is so tender." I was pleased that my mother already had such loving feelings for Anna. I was also happy that she thought I was a good mother. It was what I'd always dreamed of, and Mom had been the main reason for that.

She left that weekend, and though I was sad to see her go, it felt wonderful to be our own family—precious little Anna and her mom and dad.

✦

The weeks after we brought Anna home melted into a lovely routine. Brent went to work, looking forward to the summer months when he could spend all the time he wanted with Anna. Evenings were peaceful, happy times spent together. Sunday, we would take our baby to church, and I loved having to get up during sacrament meeting to go change a diaper, just like the mothers I'd envied for all those years.

Anna was gorgeous. She had an angelic face that seemed lit from within. She had an easy smile and was such a calm, peaceful baby. Strangers would stop me and comment on the beauty of our little girl. It seemed that no one could look at Anna without smiling. I marveled at how healthy she was. From her difficult, early entry into life, she seemed to have not only a strength to physically overcome any obstacles but also a difficult-to-describe serenity. Sometimes I'd look into her bright eyes and feel I was looking at someone who knew and understood far more than I did. I supposed all mothers felt these feelings about their children—that they would grow up to be far more than their parents.

I tried to follow the guidelines in baby development books and provide a happy routine for Anna. I found it difficult to be rigid, but I did put forth an effort to establish a regular afternoon nap. I would put her in her crib at about one in the afternoon and try to busy myself with something around the house, but I often found myself standing at the door to her room, looking at her and longing to hold her. Finally, I gave up trying to follow the baby books and instead let her sleep cozily in my arms as I read a book. I'd always been an avid reader, and I loved this time to snuggle with my baby and read wonderful books. I found my mind was sharper and clearer than ever before. I continued to marvel at the amazing changes in me since I'd become a mother. Did all mothers feel this energy and clarity? Had I really been missing out on so much without knowing it? I watched other new mothers and wondered why they looked so tired and worn down. Did their sleep-deprived expressions hide the same focus and clarity I felt? I wasn't sure.

That summer was a delight. Brent's parents came to stay for a week in June, and my parents stayed a week in July. They all doted on their new granddaughter, and I could tell she was going to be spoiled. My sister, Bev, and her family drove over from Portland to see their new niece and cousin for a few days before finishing their summer vacation at the Mesa Verde ruins.

The summer passed far too quickly and ended much sooner than we wanted. Brent went back to the high school. I stayed home. Our lives were happy and complete. I enjoyed a feeling of normalcy that had evaded me for so long. I hadn't realized how much I'd felt like an oddity, even a freak of nature. Women were supposed to become mothers. Women all around me had done it, but I hadn't been able to. All those years, I'd put on a happy face, moving through my life, trying to focus on Brent, my job, church, and anything that would distract me from the painful thoughts that were always in the back of my mind. "You are not a mother." "You might never be a mother." "Maybe you wouldn't be a good mother." "Maybe God doesn't want you to be a mother." Finally, all those horrible thoughts were gone. I was a mother. I was a good mother, and I'd continue to be a good mother. God wanted me to be a mother. I vowed to spend my whole life being the best mother my sweet Anna could possibly have.

Although Anna understandably could have experienced some medical difficulties, she didn't. She was thriving. She was healthy, strong, and happy. Her pink cheeks became chubby and soft, and I couldn't kiss them enough. She learned to crawl at an appropriate age, and not long after that, she took her first tentative steps. Much to my dismay, her first word was "dada." I had to admit it was pretty cute, and Brent was thrilled. I was sure her second word would be "momma," but alas, her second was "bobba," which meant bottle, and then her third word was "babana," which, of course, meant banana. I waited patiently as she learned to say "icky," meaning that she needed a diaper change, and "go," which told us she wanted to take a ride in the car. Finally, her sixth word was "mommm," with a long "m" sound at the end. It was precious, and I forgave her for putting a dirty diaper ahead of me.

At eighteen months, Anna began attending nursery. I was both happy and disappointed that she seemed to be fine without me, and I'd often sneak out of my own class to take a peek at her through the little nursery window.

"She's an absolute delight," Sister Coggins said one Sunday after church. "The children are drawn to her. She seems to bring peace to the chaos." I gave Anna a kiss on the cheek, thankful to have such a special girl.

When Anna turned three, she attended the Sunbeams class. The name fit Anna perfectly. She really was a beam of sunlight wherever she went.

One Monday morning, during breakfast, the phone rang.

"Hello?" I placed a bowl of oatmeal in front of Anna.

"Hi, Susan?"

"Hi, Beth," I said, recognizing the voice of my friend. We'd become friends when we'd both been put on the decoration committee for the ward Christmas party several years earlier.

"Susan, did Anna say anything unusual after church yesterday?"

"Unusual like what?" I asked. Anna always said unusual things.

"Did she tell you anything about the lesson?" The intensity in Beth's voice unnerved me a little.

I hesitated, remembering our visit about her Primary class. "She said they learned about the commandments."

"Well, Jacob didn't just tell us they learned about the commandments. He recited the commandments—all ten of them!" Her enthusiasm was infectious, and I smiled.

"Good job, Jacob," I said as though he could hear me. "That's pretty impressive."

"Susan, that's not all he did. He explained what 'bear false witness' means and even explained that adultery is where 'a mom and a dad act like they're married to a different mom or dad.' I've never heard such a thing. Gail called, and she said that Jessica was telling her the same things during dinner."

"Wow, their teacher must be amazing." I wondered why Anna had just mentioned the commandments and nothing else.

"I think she must be. I never imagined kids could learn these things so quickly. I'm sure she's a great teacher, but these kids must be really smart too."

"I'm sure they are," I agreed. "You know they're just little sponges. I've read that they learn at this age better than at any other age. Makes you wonder why we don't have them learn calculus when they're three. It would sure make high school easier."

Beth laughed. "I almost can't wait for next week to see what they learn. It's pretty cute to see a three-year-old reciting the commandments and describing what they mean."

"I'll have to ask Anna for more details," I said.

"Do. She'll probably surprise you. Well, I'd better be going. Jacob has a doctor appointment this morning."

"Is he okay?" I asked.

"Oh, sure. Just a checkup."

"All right. Thanks for calling, Beth."

"Bye."

I hung up the phone and sat down across the table from Anna, who was almost finished with her oatmeal.

"So, Anna," I started.

"What, Mommy?" she asked, looking up at me with her huge, blue eyes.

"Tell me what you learned in Primary yesterday."

"I learned about Moses and the Ten Commandments."

"Really? Do you remember all of them?"

"Yep." She turned her attention back to her oatmeal.

"Can you tell me what they are?" I asked.

"Yep." She held up one finger. "Thou shalt have no other gods before me." She held up two fingers. "Thou shalt have no gravy image. Shalt not take the Lord's name in vain." At this point she held up four fingers. "Keep the Sabbath day holy." She studied the six fingers she was holding up and said, "Honor your Mommy and Daddy." At this, she held up all ten fingers and looked puzzled. Then she put her hands flat on the table and continued. "Thou shalt not kill, thou shalt not commit 'dultery, thou shalt not steal, thou shalt not bury false witness, and not covet—that means you want someone else's toys."

I smiled, amazed at what I'd just heard. Who knew that Martha Petty was such an amazing teacher? Anna was lucky to have her. And what a smart little girl we had. Anna gave the same commandment speech at dinner, and Brent was appropriately impressed. Again, I felt awed by the gift we'd been given.

Week after week was the same. We'd go to church, and then at Sunday dinner, Anna would tell us about her lesson. On Monday morning, the mother of a child in her class, usually Beth, would call to compare notes. We marveled that our children were learning such incredible things—things that seemed beyond the comprehension of three-year-olds. They learned about Joseph, who was sold into Egypt, and recounted the interpretation of the dreams. They shared the more obscure bible stories of Elijah and the widow who fed him and then had more flour in her cupboard and also of the walls of Jericho tumbling down. Anna told me about Jesus blessing the children in the Book of Mormon and described the blessings as being "so perfect that no one could even write them down."

One Sunday, several weeks later, it was announced in Church that Martha Petty was being released as a Primary teacher. My heart sank until moments later, she was sustained to teach an adult Sunday School class. I was sad that Anna wouldn't have this talented teacher anymore, but another part of me was thrilled at the idea of being able to go to her class myself. If our three-year-olds were learning so much, just imagine how much Brent and I would learn. We looked forward to the following week and went to the class with other parents, eagerly anticipating the scriptural insights we were about to receive.

The class was fine, but I glanced around the room, trying to tell if others were as disappointed as I was. The lesson was just okay. I didn't learn anything I hadn't already known, and it wasn't even particularly interesting. In fact, her delivery was pretty lackluster. Maybe it was just an off week. I looked forward to the next week to see if it would be different. It wasn't. It was just another week with an average lesson, given in an average way. Within a few weeks, I realized it wasn't going to get more insightful. Sister Petty was not a brilliant teacher.

Our children, on the other hand, continued to learn. They continued to come home each week with wonderfully detailed stories and an amazing understanding of the gospel principles they were being taught. We soon decided it must not have been the teacher that was gifted. It was probably our children.

I felt the pride that I'm sure all mothers feel when they discover a special talent or gift in one of their children. I was excited that Anna and her classmates were such great students. What I didn't realize was that before too long, that pride would be overshadowed. In all my daydreams about being a mother, I could never have dreamed of the challenges we'd soon face.

Chapter 2

As days and weeks went by, an uneasy thought took shape in the back of my mind, just beyond my reach. I wasn't sure what it was, but something seemed unusual, not quite as it should be. Why couldn't I move that thought into clear sight and study it? I couldn't share this uneasiness with anyone, even Brent. I imagined this distant thought as a strange and teasing creature, lurking in the shadows of my mind, jumping out to play peekaboo and then vanishing back into the dark corners before I could actually focus on it, and I was left wondering if it was really there at all. It didn't make sense. I had a sweet, healthy, little girl. Brent and I were happier than we'd ever been. Life was comfortable and easy, and I finally had everything I'd dreamed of. So why was there this nagging apprehension in the back of my mind?

Wanting to put my mind at ease, I broached the subject one evening at dinner. "Brent, does something seem wrong to you?" I tried to sound nonchalant. I felt a little foolish even asking since I couldn't wrap my own mind around it.

"Wrong like what?"

"I don't really know. Something just feels strange, like I know something is off, but I can't quite put my finger on it." Brent shot me a concerned look. I smiled quizzically, laid down my fork, and shrugged my shoulders. Anna continued to slurp strings of spaghetti, uninterested in our conversation.

"Are you sick?" he asked.

"I feel fine. I'm not sure what it is. Something just seems . . ." I paused. I didn't know how to describe this feeling. " . . . off?" I knew it sounded crazy, and I was already wishing I'd never brought it up.

"Can you be a little more specific?" he asked.

"I know it sounds nuts, but lately I've felt this nagging feeling that something's not right. I've tried to figure out why I feel this way, but I'm not sure I even know what I'm talking about." I picked up my fork, and Brent looked at me while I continued eating. It was quiet as we ate, and every time I glanced at Brent, he was still staring at me. I felt sillier by the minute and smiled self-consciously, shrugging my shoulders.

After a few minutes of silence, Brent asked quietly, "Is something wrong with . . . ?" He tilted his head toward Anna.

"Oh no. No, no. She's fine," I said. "I really don't know what it is. It's probably not anything at all. Maybe it's the weather or something." It was a lame explanation, but I wanted to somehow end this ridiculous conversation that wasn't accomplishing anything. I was terribly disappointed because I'd hoped that Brent had felt the same thing and that we'd be able to sort it out together. "Don't worry about it," I said. Brent didn't press me to explain any further, and the conversation ended.

But the feeling didn't go away. Sometimes I ignored it and distracted myself by staying busy with other things. A few times I sat down in a quiet place and gave my whole self over to the task of pulling out the hidden thought, but it stubbornly resisted. I started to suspect I was going a little crazy.

Late one evening, I was up by myself, baking cookies for Brent's homeroom class. The house was quiet since Brent and Anna were asleep in bed, and rather than turn on the television or some music, I enjoyed the peace of the late hour. As I scooped spoonfuls of cookie dough, the teasing thought seemed to be knocking on the door of my mind. I wondered if the peace and quiet of the night would finally provide the right setting for lucid thoughts. I felt like there was something right in front of me that I should be noticing but wasn't. As I slowly rolled the dough into little balls, I felt relaxed and unhurried, and I tried to keep my mind empty—maybe I'd been trying too hard to figure this out. I put the last pan of cookies in the oven and sat down at the table. No clear thoughts emerged. Aggravated and weary, I rested my elbows on the table and pressed my hands against the sides of my head, willing myself to figure it out.

"What is it?" I whispered. I realized I wasn't speaking to myself but was offering a desperate prayer. No answer came, and when the timer began beeping, I wiped tears of frustration from my face and took the last cookies out of the oven. I turned out the lights and fell into bed, tired and discouraged.

Sometime during the night, I had a dream. I'd never really remembered my dreams, but the next morning I had a powerful feeling that this one was important. I wanted to remember every detail, so I pulled out my black, leather-bound journal and began to write.

In the dream, I saw Anna as a baby on the day I first met her in the hospital. I stood in the nursery, looking down at her in the clear, little bassinet. Joy filled my heart as I looked at her pretty face. Then, as I stood there, Anna slowly rose out of the bassinet, and the blanket fell away from her. Her eyes opened as she flitted around the room, almost like a fairy or a cherub without wings. As I watched her fly, incredible things happened. Anna extended her arms, and it seemed that color and light were flowing from her tiny hands. She flew to a painting on the wall. Her little baby hands, streaming with beauty, swept in front of the painting, and it became bright and beautiful. Then she flew to the nurse, a rather drab-looking woman, and sweetly touched her hair. Color and splendor flowed out of her hands, and the drabness was replaced with exquisite beauty. The nurse didn't really change, but as the color flowed from Anna's little baby hands, the features took on a radiant loveliness.

I stood there by the empty bassinet, stunned by what I was seeing. I stepped toward Anna, reaching for her, but she escaped my hands. She flew through the open door of the nursery, and I followed her into the hall. As she fluttered down the hall, she left everything around her brighter and more vivid, almost as if she were an angel, changing the world from black and white to color. I followed Anna to the entrance of the hospital. The doors opened, seemingly magically. Anna flew through the open doors, and then they closed behind her. I tried to push the doors back open, wanting to follow her, but they wouldn't budge. I watched Anna through the glass as she flew away and disappeared from my sight.

I closed my journal and put it in the drawer beside my bed. What did this dream mean? Was there something in it to help me understand my strange feelings?

The beauty of the dream was in sharp contrast with the dreariness of the overcast morning, and my morning routine was filled with thoughts of it, so much so that I found myself putting my clean clothes in Brent's drawer. The vision of beauty flowing from Anna's hands filled my mind as I emptied the dishwasher. I closed the dishwasher and leaned against the counter, surveying the room. I thought of the vivid colors of the dream as I looked at my drab and worn-out kitchen. I pictured in my mind how nice it would be to remodel the whole kitchen and get a beautiful new floor and countertops. Of course, I knew that idea was out of reach, and I quickly settled down and considered instead what a difference a nice coat of bright paint on the walls would make. That was a more realistic plan.

I heard Anna rustling around in her room, and soon she walked into the kitchen with a bright pink blouse and four skirts, layered one on top of the other. Instantly my mood lifted and the room seemed brighter. I walked to Anna, picked her up, and gave her a big hug, topped off with a noisy raspberry kiss on her neck. She giggled, and I sat her at the table.

"So, what would my big girl like for breakfast?" I asked.

"Hmm . . ." She tried to decide, even putting her finger up to her mouth as she thought, just like Brent did. "I think I want a pancake with a smiley face."

I laughed. "You know, I was going to make pancakes for you and Daddy on Saturday. How about if you have a smiley face pancake then and today you have something else? Does a scrambled egg sound good?"

She let out a long, dramatic sigh. "I guess that sounds okay."

"Hey, while I make it, why don't you go back to your room and put on just one of those pretty skirts?"

"Mom, I just couldn't decide." She touched each skirt thoughtfully, lifting it off the one below it as she contemplated this difficult decision.

"Which one is your favorite?" I got out the carton of eggs and the frying pan.

"I really like the flowers on this one."

"I like the flowers too."

"But this one is yellow, and yellow is my favorite color."

"Yellow is definitely a good color," I said.

"And purple is my other favorite color." She was struggling with this difficult choice. I turned my head so she wouldn't see my smile.

"Just run and choose. This scrambled egg is going to be done before you get back." Anna slid off the chair and scampered to her room. I cooked the egg and transferred it to the daisy plate—Anna's favorite.

What color should I paint the kitchen? It really needed something. Maybe a nice, light yellow would brighten things up. Or a crisp, clean white. Maybe a new light fixture wouldn't cost too much and would help brighten up the dreary space. I looked around the room, remodeling it in my mind. I imagined dark granite countertops replacing the worn Formica and beautiful hardwood floors instead of tired old linoleum.

"Mommy, can I please wear them all? I don't want to choose," Anna called from her room. I smiled, shaking my head. Oh, what a funny girl. But what harm would it do?

"I guess so, honey. Come on and eat." I heard her running down the hall. She turned the corner, came straight at me with her arms out wide, and hugged my legs tightly.

"Thank you, Mommy."

"You're welcome, sweetheart." I lifted her into the chair and smoothed her soft, golden hair. "Now let's sit down and eat your scrambled egg." I poured her a cup of orange juice, set it in front of her, and looked around the room. And then it hit me like a tidal wave. I stood there, awestruck. This room that had seemed so dreary just moments ago had been transformed. It was suddenly more pleas-ant, even cheery. *Oh, come on, Susan,* I thought, but as I looked around, I knew it definitely looked better. Did this happen all the time? I began digging through my memories to see if it was true. It seemed to be. But how? My analytical mind rebelled at what I was thinking. This realization was ridiculous, impossible even. Maybe I was losing my mind. I was happy to be a mother, grateful for the changes motherhood had brought to my life. But were those changes all normal? Had the clarity and focus and beauty that had come into my life since Anna entered my world been the normal changes that came with motherhood? Or were they something more? I didn't know. A strange feeling of relief flooded over me as I realized that the nagging, teasing thought was out in the open, even if what I was seeing seemed impossible.

I walked into the living room and looked around. It was a nice room, sparingly decorated and comfortable, but it certainly didn't belong in a Home Interiors magazine. "Anna, are you almost finished eating?" I called to the kitchen.

"One more bite," Anna said through a mouthful of eggs.

"When you're finished, could you come in here for a minute?"

"Okay."

I sat down in the big, comfy chair and waited. I felt anxious and foolish. What was I thinking? Surely this was lunacy. I looked around the room, taking in every detail. Soon, I heard her slide off the chair, and a moment later, she was standing in the doorway of the living room.

"What?" She watched me with a puzzled look while I looked the room over. There was no doubt it looked different. It was the same room—same chenille couch, same red chair, same piano. But now everything looked prettier, brighter. It was like someone had filled our living room with sunshine. Every detail was sharp and focused. For a moment I felt like the wind had been knocked out of me. I forced myself to take a deep breath as I looked around the room in amazement.

"What on earth," I said slowly and quietly.

"What's wrong, Mommy?" Anna now stood right in front of me, looking concerned.

"Nothing's wrong, sweetie. Do you want to try a little game? I'm going to go in a room, and then when I call you, you come find me. Okay?"

"Okay," she said. The thought of a game sounded like a great idea. I walked down the hall to my bedroom. I looked at the light green bedspread and the black, wrought iron headboard. I took in the ivory walls and the lamps on the tables. I even looked at my cluttered dresser and the laundry basket of clothes sitting on the chair in the corner. I sat down on the bed, my heart thumping wildly.

"Okay, Anna, come find me." I heard her walk slowly down the hall, probably looking in rooms as she came.

"I found you!" She entered my room, smiling. I looked around. It had happened again. It was still the same room—nothing had changed physically—and yet it had suddenly acquired a new quality. I could see the change, although I didn't understand it.

"Now you're it," she said, playfully poking my leg.

"Maybe I can be it in a few minutes. I'm trying to figure something out, okay?" I smiled brightly, hoping I wasn't scaring her.

"Okay," she said. She folded her arms, and I could tell she was getting bored.

"Now, Anna, you wait here until I call you, okay?"

"All right," Anna said. Her enthusiasm was gone. I walked down the hall to Anna's room. The walls Brent had painted yellow three and a half years ago looked a little duller. *This room could use some new paint too.* The pink princess bedspread was a scrunched-up pile at the foot of the bed. Anna must have kicked off the covers again. Toys and books were strewn on the floor in front of the shelves. A lone skirt was on the floor in front of the closet, apparently having failed to make the grade as she dressed this morning. It was a room that could have belonged to any little girl.

"Anna? Can you come in your room now?" I called.

"Mommy, you just told me where you are. Now it's easy to find you." Anna walked down the hall and came into her room. There it was again, that indefinable difference that almost could have been no difference at all. And yet it was as sure and real as Anna standing there.

"Okay, you wait here for just a minute." I walked to the office Brent and I shared. This room was as nondescript as they come. No efforts at decorating had been attempted in this room. It was all about usefulness. There was a desk with a computer and printer, a chair, and a long table with a sewing machine on one end. Papers were piled around the computer, and there was a stack of fabric on the end of the table. A few toys were scattered in the corner, left there from the last time I had done some sewing and Anna had wanted to be in the room with me. A small television sat on a high shelf, and a file cabinet stood in the corner. This would be the real test. There didn't seem to be much hope of improving this room.

"Anna, can you come to the office now?" I called. Slow footsteps shuffled down the hall, and finally Anna stood in the doorway.

"This isn't a very fun game." Her voice dripped with disappointment as she entered the room.

I smiled at her sad face and looked around me. It had happened again. The room just looked different. There was nothing moved, no tangible change. And yet it looked better. Even this boring office looked good somehow. I looked at Anna for a long time, my mind trying to make sense of what my eyes were telling me. She started to squirm as she looked back at me, but still I gazed at her, wondering.

"I'm sorry, Mommy," she said.

"Sorry for what?" I asked.

"I'm sorry I put another skirt on. But it was all alone, and I didn't want it to feel bad." I looked down and saw that the skirt that had been on the floor in front of her closet had now joined the four others around my daughter's waist. I laughed.

"Its okay, honey. We don't want that skirt to feel bad." I picked Anna up and hugged her tightly to me. For some reason I didn't quite understand, tears were welling up in my eyes. Anna hugged me back, snuggling in close as I carried her into the family room and settled her down on the couch. I turned on the television and found an episode of *Barney and Friends*. Almost immediately Anna started singing along. I sat down beside her, holding her hand, and stared at the television, seeing nothing. I was lost in my own inconceivable thoughts. The whole world really had looked better since Anna came. I had thought it was because I was now a mother. Could it possibly be because of Anna? Not because she was my child, but because she was Anna? Did she have some God-given gift that I'd mistakenly credited to motherhood? Had anyone else noticed? Maybe I was the only one who saw it. Thoughts of the past three years paraded through my mind as Barney ended and *Sesame Street* began.

"Can I watch another one?" Anna looked up at me hopefully. Usually one show was the limit.

"That's fine," I said, distracted. I remembered the beautiful nursery at the hospital in New Mexico, the glistening floor and warm, cozy blankets. I remembered the soft, spring green of the desert carpet and the vivid red of the cliffs as Mom and I drove Anna home. The memories tumbled in one after another, building inside me a certainty that I was right. I couldn't explain it, but I knew I was right. Just like in my dream, everywhere Anna was became somehow better. Bert and Ernie sang a song about sharing as my certainty grew. Somewhere inside me, I had a feeling there was more—much more—and it scared me. There was something very unusual about my Anna.

✦

I wasn't sure what to do with my new knowledge. I wanted to talk to Brent about it, but I didn't want to talk in front of Anna. I hired Sadie, a nice thirteen-year-old neighbor, to watch Anna, and I surprised Brent by telling him we were going out to dinner.

"What's the occasion?" he asked. "Have I forgotten something?" He glanced apprehensively at the calendar on the wall.

"Don't worry. You haven't forgotten anything. I just wanted to go out to dinner with you." I knew I sounded a little too excited. He looked at me, puzzled, but didn't put up a fight. A short time later, we were in the car, and he again tried to get an explanation for the unexpected dinner arrangements. I refused to discuss anything important until we were sitting in our favorite Italian restaurant and I had his full attention. He ordered lasagna, and I ordered chicken linguine, ignoring his wary looks in my direction. When the waiter finally left, I took a deep breath and let it out slowly.

"Susan?" His voice sounded worried. "What's going on?" I'd spent most of the afternoon rehearsing how I would bring this up without sounding like a complete lunatic. I hadn't really figured anything out. Every opening line sounded like I needed to be sent away for a lengthy examination of my head. I still didn't know what to say. I took another deep breath.

"Please, Susan. You're starting to scare me."

"Brent, have you ever noticed how things are different when Anna's around?" It sounded preposterous, even to my ears, and *I* knew exactly what I was talking about. What was he supposed to think?

"What do you mean?" he asked. I thought I could hear a defensive edge in his voice, and my courage faltered. But I couldn't handle today's realization alone, so, determined, I forged on.

"Everything is . . ." I looked for the right word. Nothing seemed to really capture the difference she made. ". . . clearer?" I looked at his face, willing him to know what I was talking about. He looked at me for a long time, and neither of us spoke. After another deep breath, I continued, plowing ahead with what I wanted to say in spite of his silence. "I know it sounds crazy, but when she's in the room, everything looks better somehow. Not like anything is really different—in fact, if you look at each thing, it's in the same place, and nothing's really changed—but somehow it's . . . just different." My voice trailed off. I thought I saw a barely perceptible nod of his head. *Oh, let him know what I'm talking about*, I silently pleaded. Taking courage, I rushed on. "I've just always thought it was because *I* was different. *I've* changed. I'm a mother now, so that's why the world looks better. But last night I had a strange dream about Anna when she was a baby, and then today, it finally dawned on me. I can't believe it hasn't occurred to me before, but today I finally got it. When Anna's in the room, it looks and feels better. When she's not, even if she's just in the other room, it looks and feels . . . normal or something." I was talking too fast. When I finally stopped babbling, I looked back up at Brent, afraid of the expression I might see.

Brent was nodding. I was flooded with relief, and I was surprised to feel tears running down my cheeks. He knew what I was talking about. Maybe I wasn't crazy. I wiped the tears away with my napkin, but they kept coming. I couldn't make them stop. Brent reached over and took my hand.

"Tell me about your dream," he said. He held my hand and listened quietly as I described it in detail. "That's what helped you realize it, isn't it?" I nodded, glancing around the room to be sure no one was listening to this strange conversation. I felt a little crazy even voicing my thoughts.

"I was thinking about the dream this morning, and then Anna came into the kitchen, and it just happened—the way it always does—the way it has since the beginning. The kitchen looked dull and dreary, and then she walked in, and it was suddenly bright and

26

pretty. I can't believe it took me so long to realize it. It seems so obvious now."

We looked at each other without speaking. The relief I'd felt from Brent's understanding was slowly being replaced with concern. I was glad to have someone else understand, but I could tell he was as confused as I was.

"Why?" I finally managed to choke out.

"I don't know." Brent was slowly shaking his head. "It seems like I've known something was different, but I haven't really known how to explain it. So I've just told myself to be thankful that we have such a special little girl. It sounds so crazy. I don't know if I even could have put it into words or had the guts to explain it to anyone. I mean, what do you say? 'My little girl is so amazing that the room changes when she's in it?' 'My daughter makes the world different and beautiful?' "

We were quiet. There was more I needed to say, but I didn't know how. I felt grateful that Brent understood what I'd said so far, but I was afraid to take it any further and tell him of my other realizations. After thinking all day, I knew I was right, but what if he thought I was reading too much into it? He let go of my hand when our food arrived, and we ate in silence. I barely tasted my food as I tried to muster my courage. Finally, I continued. "Honey, there's more." His fork stopped halfway to his mouth, and he quietly laid it back down on his plate, waiting for me to continue.

"I think she's the reason the kids are learning so much in Primary—not because of any teachers and not because all the children are extra bright." I was afraid to see the look in Brent's eyes, so I stared at a crumb of bread on the table.

"But she doesn't even tell us as much as the other kids tell their parents," he said. "We have to ask her about almost everything."

"I know." I looked at Brent's puzzled expression and continued. "Brent, everywhere she goes, things look better. Things are clearer. I understand more if she's there when I'm reading. I think people understand things better when she's around—things they might not quite get when she's not there. I don't know what she does. It seems like she doesn't have to do anything. It seems like she just has to be there."

"Wow!" Brent whispered, pushing his plate aside, his food forgotten. "If that's true, what is it? What's going on? What are we supposed to do with this?" These were the questions I'd been asking myself all afternoon. I'd spent hours pondering and wondering and worrying and praying. I wished I had the answer, but I didn't. I felt like I was floating toward dangerous waters I was ill-equipped to navigate.

"I don't know."

✤

What do you do when you're in the presence of a phenomenon, someone with special and inexplicable gifts? Do you point it out to others? Do you acknowledge those gifts? Do you ignore them? Is there a responsibility to share those gifts with anyone else? Or do you downplay the differences, pretend they aren't there? And what do you do if that marvel is your own sweet little girl, the one who plays with her food and sings herself to sleep, the one with a giggle that sounds like music and ponytails that bounce when she walks? Does her being a phenomenon threaten the happy childhood you want for her? I couldn't even decide if this was a good thing or a bad thing, a blessing or a terrible curse.

Brent and I spent days thinking, quietly discussing, praying, and wrestling over what we were supposed to do. If this gift came from God, was it intended to help others, or was it meant only for Anna, with no expectations? There was no question, Anna was our priority. No matter how gifted she was, we knew we didn't want to do anything that would make her life hard. She had the right to a normal childhood, doing normal things. Anna wasn't even four years old yet. What could she possibly do with her gift at the age of four? Right now she wanted to play dress-up and help bake cookies and sing silly songs. She wouldn't even understand her difference from the rest of the world if we could explain it to her. And who could be sure it was something that would last? Maybe in the coming years, it would disappear, and Anna would be like every other child, outgrowing the gifts much like outgrowing an allergy or a propensity for ear infections.

These nagging thoughts that had eluded me for so long were now front and center. Many times I wished I could go back and push them into the shadows again. I wanted to be blissfully unaware of anything profoundly special or different about Anna. After all, I loved her with or without her gift. This newfound understanding of the power she had scared me. She didn't know she had it, and yet, as her mother, I felt a responsibility to be sure it was treasured and guarded and not something that would hurt her. Every time I thought I had figured out every possible way her life could be affected, something would happen that would stop me short. I felt ill-equipped to be the guardian of this unusual child.

We decided to keep our discovery to ourselves. Brent and I knew we could trust each other, and while I also knew I could trust my mom and my sister, Bev, I realized that the more people who were aware of Anna's gift, the easier it would be for it to affect her life. I didn't want anyone to act differently around her or to treat her like she was a freak. So Brent and I became Anna's line of defense. We tried to talk about and prepare for anything we might have to deal with. As crazy as it seemed, sometimes I wished that Anna wasn't so special. I wanted her to fit in and be like the other children. Then I felt guilty for wanting to wish away one of the things that made her Anna. Truthfully, I wasn't sure what I wanted. The only thing I was sure of was that I wanted Anna to be happy.

Thankfully, Anna was very happy. And why shouldn't she be? She was a healthy, smart, and pretty little girl. Her honey-colored hair hung straight and shiny just below her shoulders. Her eyes had the ability to change from bright blue to gray or green, depending on what she was wearing or even the weather. Her soft skin was fair and seemed to glow. She had a vivid imagination and mothered and taught her stuffed animals and dolls. I noticed that her cheerful disposition naturally drew people to her—a fact that made my heart swell with pride but terrified me for her safety.

Anna had an uncanny understanding of everything she learned, but she didn't share that understanding unless she was asked. One afternoon, snuggled in the big, soft chair, I read her the story of Cinderella. "Did you like that story, Anna?" I asked. Her soft ponytail brushed against my cheek as she nodded her head.

"Yes. It's a perfect story," she answered sincerely and turned back the pages to look at her favorite pictures.

"What do you think is the best part?"

"My best part is that she could talk to the animals, and they helped her."

"Really? When I was a little girl, my favorite part was the beautiful, white dress that the fairy godmother gave her to wear to the ball. I wanted a dress just like it."

Anna turned the page to look at the white dress and then continued turning pages until she found the one she was looking for. "I like the white dress, but I love the dress the animals made for her. The blue ribbon makes it so pretty. It made me really sad that the wicked stepsisters tore that dress."

"Why do you think they did that?"

"Because they wished they were as nice as Cinderella."

"They wanted to be as nice as Cinderella?" I'd never heard this angle before.

"Yes. They weren't nice and Cinderella was, so they hated her."

"Wow," I said. "I always thought that they didn't like her because she was prettier than them, so the prince liked her best."

"Don't you know, Mom? The prince wanted to marry someone nice. He might have liked one of them if they were nice."

"I guess that makes a lot of sense. Maybe someday you'll marry a prince because you're such a nice girl." She looked up at me and smiled.

★

During the summer before Anna turned five, Brent decided to go camping and rock climbing for a few days in the Black Canyon of the Gunnison with Dave and Carl, two other teachers at the high school. I laughed at how excited Brent was. He hadn't done anything like this since the summer before we adopted Anna. I was happy for him to go and enjoy himself, and Anna and I had picked out two "girl movies" to watch while Brent was gone. The guys packed up Dave's truck with what looked like enough gear to last a month. Anna and I waved good-bye as they headed for the mountains.

The afternoon of the second day, I was pushing Anna on the swing in the backyard when the phone rang. I picked up Anna and ran to the phone.

"Hi, Susan?" I didn't recognize the male voice at the other end of the line.

"Yes, this is Susan."

"Good. Susan, this is Dave." Instantly, I felt a sense of panic.

"Dave? Is everything okay? Where's Brent?"

"Don't worry. He's going to be okay." My mind latched onto the "going to," and I started to shake. "He fell. It looks like he might have broken both of his legs. He's being x-rayed right now."

"Where are you?" I asked.

"We're here at the hospital in Montrose. I think you should come down."

"Of course. I'll leave now. When can I talk to him?"

"I'm not sure. He asked me to call you and have you come to the hospital."

"Okay."

"Susan, you might want to bring a change of clothes. He'll probably need surgery, and you may want to stay overnight."

"Okay, thanks, Dave. Tell him I'm on my way." I hung up the phone and ran to my room, where I frantically began throwing clothes into an overnight bag.

The phone rang again. "Dave?" I answered, thinking he must have something else to tell me.

"No, Susan, it's Beth. Who's Dave?"

"Hi, Beth. Dave is one of the teachers Brent works with. Brent was rock climbing in Black Canyon with him and fell. He's hurt, so I'm on my way to Montrose."

"Is it bad?" she asked.

"It sounds bad. His legs are broken. I probably won't be back until tomorrow night."

"What are you going to do with Anna?"

"I was just going to take her with me."

"Don't be silly. Let me keep her while you go. She can play with Jacob. She'll be no trouble, and then you can worry about Brent instead of worrying about a bored little girl at the hospital." I wanted to protest, but what she said made sense. "I'll come over and pick her up. Just put a few clothes together for her. Susan, she'll be just fine. Don't even think about arguing with me," she said. I knew she could sense my reluctance. "I'll be there in ten minutes."

With mixed feelings, I hung up and went to Anna's room. "Anna," I said, interrupting a conversation with her favorite teddy bear and fancy doll, "how would you like to go stay with Jacob's family for a day or two?"

"Are you coming too?" she asked.

"Come here, sweetie, I want to talk to you." I sat down on her bed, and she walked over and stood in front of me. I held both of her hands in mine. "Anna, Daddy fell down while he was camping and hurt his legs, so I need to go help take care of him. It isn't a very fun place, and I think you'd have a much better time if you went and played at Jacob's house and stayed overnight with them. Would you like to do that? I'll call you and talk to you on the phone, and I'll be back tomorrow night. Does that sound okay?"

She shrugged her shoulders. "I guess so," she said.

"Thank you, sweetie. Jacob's mom is going to be here in just a few minutes. Will you go get your toothbrush for me while I pack your jammies and some clothes for tomorrow?"

"Mom, can I take Jupiter with me?" she asked. She walked back into the room holding up her toothbrush.

"That's a great idea. Jupiter can help keep you company." I took the toothbrush and finished packing her bag. She grabbed her stuffed bear, and we walked to my room to finish packing my things. A few minutes later, Beth rang the doorbell. After a hug and a kiss, my little girl was on her way to spend her first night away from me since I'd brought her home from Santa Fe.

The magnitude of leaving Anna with someone else didn't really settle in until I was driving south on Highway 50. It was then that thoughts and concerns filled my mind. Would Beth notice Anna's gift? What would she think if she did? Would she tell anyone? I worried about her reaction and wished I'd just brought Anna with me. What had I been thinking? If I hadn't felt an urgency to get to the hospital before Brent went into surgery, I would have turned around and picked up Anna. But I knew I had to get to the hospital in Montrose. I needed Brent to be okay. I needed Anna to be okay. I had to hope no one would notice anything peculiar during Anna's stay. I turned off the radio and, staring at the road ahead of me, prayed aloud for my family.

I parked in the emergency area of the hospital and made my way through the big, automatic doors by the ambulance entrance. A round and rosy nurse with too much blue eye shadow directed me to a curtained area, where Brent was awaiting surgery. When I stepped behind the privacy curtain, Brent smiled a sheepish, crooked smile. "Hey, honey. How are you?" Dave and Carl, who'd been sitting near Brent's feet, stood up to leave.

"Better than you," I said and kissed him. Then I turned to Dave and Carl. "You don't have to leave."

"Well, at least take this chair," Carl said. He moved it closer to the head of the bed. A minute later, he came back carrying a chair for himself.

"So what happened?" I asked. I glanced at his legs, which were covered by a light sheet.

Brent noticed my gaze. "You probably don't want to look at them right now."

"Okay," I said. Dave was shaking his head, obviously agreeing with Brent that I didn't need to see what was shielded by the sheet.

"We weren't even on the face of the rock yet. We were hiking in, and the trail was right at the edge of a twenty-foot drop." Brent's voice sounded thin and pained. "I had stopped to take some pictures, so I was hurrying to catch up with the others. I must have stepped on a loose rock, 'cause next thing I knew, I was on my way down, praying I wouldn't die."

"Pansy," said Dave. "I thought you knew what you were doing on a mountain." The three of them laughed, but Brent's laugh was shallow and labored.

"Dave and Carl pulled me back up and carried me out."

"Hope we didn't make it worse," Carl said.

"Worse would be if I was still out there," Brent said.

"How bad is it?" I rested my hand on his arm.

"It hurts pretty bad. They've given me something to take the edge off, but it's bad. They're going to put a couple of pins put in my leg. I don't think I'll be rock climbing any time soon. Where's Anna?" he asked.

"She's staying at Beth's until tomorrow night."

"That's good," Dave said. "I was worried the hospital might not let a little girl stay in his room with him. They'll for sure let you." Brent and I exchanged a look that let me know he was having the same concerns I'd been feeling on the drive to Montrose.

"Will she be okay?"

"I hope so," I said. Dave and Carl exchanged a puzzled look, but there was no explanation I could give them, so I ignored it.

A short time later, a doctor who looked like a high school student in a white coat came in and gave us information and instructions about what was going to happen. I kissed Brent, and he squeezed my hand as they wheeled him away for the surgery. Dave and Carl gathered their things and prepared to go home. We moved Brent's gear from Dave's truck to the back of my car. "Thanks for helping him," I said.

"Sure. We'll call you later and check in on him," Dave said. I stood at the door of the hospital and watched them drive away. My stomach growled fiercely, and I realized I hadn't eaten in more than eight hours. I made my way to the hospital cafeteria, where I got a ham sandwich and a yogurt. I took the food to the waiting room, where I choked down half of the soggy sandwich before I gave up and threw it away and started on the yogurt.

Brent was still in surgery when I called Anna to say good night. She seemed happy, and Beth said she was having a great time. The windows were black rectangles when they wheeled Brent into the recovery room. I pulled the blinds and watched a little television while Brent slept. Around 1:00 a.m., they moved Brent to his own hospital room. I pulled out the uncomfortable bed that folded out from a small, wooden cabinet, covered up with a thin, itchy blanket, and tried to sleep. It was a very long night.

The too-young doctor came in the next morning to let us know that things were looking good but Brent wouldn't be able to go home for three or four days. This wasn't going to be easy. I didn't want to leave Brent there, but we both knew that I needed to get Anna. We decided that I'd bring Anna down for a visit each day until Brent was released. That afternoon, I kissed him good-bye and drove back to Grand Junction with an uneasy gnawing in the pit of my stomach.

Chapter 3

"Hi Beth. How did everything go?" I'd driven straight to Beth's from the hospital.

"Great. Come on in." She opened the door wide and then walked in ahead of me. "Anna, your mom's here," she called up the stairs. I followed her into the kitchen. Maybe Beth wouldn't have noticed anything with Anna around. Her home was already a showcase. How could anything make this luxurious house with its granite counters, tile floors, and cherrywood cabinets look even better? "She's such a sweet girl. How's Brent?"

"He did quite a number on himself. He fell about twenty feet and broke his right leg and his left ankle. I think this is going to be a pretty uncomfortable summer for him," I said. We gathered Anna's things.

"That's terrible. Is there anything we can do to help?"

"Not right now. He'll be in the hospital for a few more days, and then we'll see how he does at home."

"Let me know if you need anything. Anna can come over anytime."

"Thanks, Beth. And thanks for watching her. I'm sure she had a lot more fun here than she would have had spending the night at the hospital. Those fold-out beds are torture devices."

"I know. After I had Jacob, Rob said he'd never stay in the hospital with me again. I'd just have to do without him for a few hours while he came home to sleep. The crazy thing is that no one was in the room with me, but he wasn't allowed to sleep in the other bed. They said they'd have to charge us a million dollars or something if he used it."

"I'm definitely going to enjoy my own bed tonight. Did the kids play well together?"

"They got along great, and they seemed to have a lot of fun. It really was no problem at all." A curious look crossed Beth's face as she continued. "Susan," she said, her tone serious, "I wanted to ask you about something. Is there . . ." Before she could finish her sentence, Anna and Jacob came bounding into the kitchen. Anna ran straight for me, and I swooped her up in my arms for a big hug and a kiss. I loved the feel of her little arms around my neck. They reminded me just how much I'd missed her.

"Jacob's mom says you were a good girl," I said.

"I was. I'm a very big girl. I didn't cry even one time," Anna said. I put her down but held onto her hand.

"You were a very good girl," Beth said and touched the tip of her nose. "We want you to come visit us again." Then she turned back to me. "I wanted to ask you about something, but it can wait," she said. She tilted her head toward Anna, letting me know she didn't want to talk about it in front of the children.

"Sure," I said. I was already dreading the rest of this conversation.

"Like I said, Susan, she can come here anytime. I can't believe you were going to take her with you. Don't hesitate to ask. You know we'd love to keep her anytime."

"Thanks, Beth. It was a huge help." I made my way to the front door. She really was a good friend, and for a moment I thought it might actually be nice to talk to her about Anna, but for now I felt relieved that I'd avoided Beth's question, at least for the time being. I put Anna's pink princess bag on the floor of the car and buckled her into the car seat. I waved to Beth as I pulled out of the driveway. She stood at the front door until we'd turned the corner.

"Anna, Daddy says to tell you hello. We're going to go see him tomorrow. Would you like that?"

"Can't we go see him today?" She looked at me pleadingly.

"Not today, sweetie. It would be too late by the time we got there. The doctor says that Daddy has to stay in the hospital for a few more days, so we'll go see him every day until he comes home, okay?"

"Okay," she said. "Is Daddy all right?" I glanced at her worried face in the rearview mirror.

"Daddy's going to be fine. He hurt his legs, so we'll have to take good care of him, but he's going to be fine."

"That's good." She looked relieved.

⋆

In the darkness of the early morning, I was startled awake by Anna, touching my arm. I looked at the clock and saw that it was only 4:30 a.m. "Wake up, Mom," Anna said. "It's tomorrow. Let's go see Daddy."

"Oh, Anna," I said. "It's way too early to go to the hospital. If we go this early, we'll wake Daddy up, and he needs to get his rest so he can get better."

"Oh."

"Why don't you climb in here and snuggle with me." I scooted over and patted the mattress beside me. "When the alarm clock starts beeping, we'll get up and go see Daddy." Anna climbed in and snuggled up on my arm. Within minutes we were both back asleep.

Taking Anna to the hospital in Montrose was surprisingly easy. She walked quietly down the corridors with me, anxious to see her dad. "Anna," Brent said from his hospital bed as we walked into his room. He held out his arms, and Anna scrambled up to sit with him. We spent the afternoon playing "Chutes and Ladders" and "I Spy" and watching television.

"How did it go at Jacob's house?" Brent asked Anna while looking at me over her head. I nodded and smiled in answer to his silent question.

"It went great. We played pirates and princesses," Anna said enthusiastically.

"Pirates and princesses, huh? That sounds like a fun thing to play."

"Jacob wanted to play pirates, and I wanted to play princesses, so we decided the pirate should save the princess. I was on a deserted island with snakes and spiders, and Jacob had to rescue me and take me to my castle."

"What a fun game," Brent said.

"Mom?" Anna turned to me. "Can we invite Jacob to play at our house? My bedroom is a better castle than his. His bedroom isn't pink at all."

"That would be fine, honey. After we get Daddy home from the hospital, you can invite him over to play."

The next couple of days were the same. We drove the sixty miles to Montrose, visited and played games with Brent, and then drove back home. We were all happy when we were finally able to bring Brent home. I borrowed Beth's minivan, and we folded down the seats to make a makeshift bed. It was slow and exhausting for him to situate himself, and he slept most of the way home. He couldn't move much without a lot of pain, so we made a "hospital room" for him in the bedroom. His first few days at home, Anna pretended to be a nurse, bringing him his meals and drinks of water and helping adjust the pillows, but soon the newness wore off, and playing nurse wasn't quite so much fun.

One morning, Anna reminded me that I needed to call Beth and invite Jacob to come and play for the afternoon. After a short pirate and princess encore inside the house, they moved on to bigger and better things—our big backyard. In the back right corner of the yard was a playground with a slide, a swing, and a little lookout tower. The tower made a perfect castle. Anna's wagon became a ship, rescuing Anna from the island of death—the deck. The yard was level from the back door to the fence, but the left side of the yard had a fairly steep slope, too steep to mow, so it was covered with a few bushes and decorative rocks.

I smiled as I listened to the drama and laughter through the back door as I folded clothes. Then the laughter was replaced by tears. Jacob was crying. I ran to the door to see Anna helping Jacob to his feet. Beside him, at the bottom of the little hill, was the green wagon, tipped on its side. "What happened?" I asked.

Jacob was crying much too hard to answer, so Anna filled me in. "We were riding down the hill in the wagon and it crashed really hard," she said. Jacob's leg was a mass of scraped skin and blood from the knee halfway down his shin. A couple of places were gouged pretty badly by the rocks. Blood was running down his leg and soaking into his ankle sock, but he was looking at his hand. I took his hand in mine and gently turned it over, examining the palm. A couple of tiny rocks were stuck in the wide abrasion.

I gently picked him up and carried him into the house, with Anna following. I sat Jacob on the counter by the cupboard with the first aid supplies. I began cleaning the wounds with hydrogen peroxide. Jacob screamed in terror. "Look at this," I said, hoping to calm him. "See how it bubbles?" Anna came closer to look, and Jacob leaned over to look at his leg. "Those bubbles mean it's cleaning all the germs away. Watch this. If I put it over here, where you're not hurt, it won't bubble at all." I poured a little onto his uninjured skin. It looked just like water.

"Wow," Anna said. The amazement in her voice made Jacob curious, and soon his crying turned to quiet little gasps as he watched in wonder.

"Now, look at this. When I put some more on the scrape, it will bubble until the germs are gone. When it doesn't bubble anymore, that means it's all clean." I poured a little more on the wound, and they watched the bubbles.

"That doesn't even hurt," Jacob said, trying not to cry.

"Good. You're being so brave." I finished cleaning his leg and then bandaged it and began cleaning his hand. Now that the kids were quiet, I asked, "What were you two doing?"

"The wicked king had put me on the high mountain, and the pirate came to rescue me," Anna said, as if she faced this kind of peril every day.

"How did you rescue her?" I asked Jacob.

"I took the pirate ship up on the mountain, and then we rode down the hill."

"You rode down the hill in the wagon?" I asked.

"And then it crashed into a bush and tipped over." Jacob's voice began quivering, and tears filled his eyes again as he remembered the painful fall.

"I'm sorry you hurt yourself," I said.

"I'm lucky I didn't get hurt," Anna said enthusiastically.

"Were you in the wagon too?" I asked.

"We were going back to the ocean," she said. I put the last bandage on Jacob's hand and then lifted Anna onto the counter beside him.

"Are you sure you didn't get hurt?" I asked.

"Yep."

I took her hands in mine and looked at the palms. Sure enough, nothing. Then I held her feet and straightened her legs to get a good look at her knees. The white capris she was wearing had dirty stains on both knees, and the left one had two holes where rocks had torn through the fabric. I pushed the capris above her knees and looked in amazement at the smooth, uninjured skin underneath. The pants had ripped clear through, yet there wasn't the slightest scratch on her knees. Once more I had the feeling, as I had so many times over the last few months, that I was on the verge of an important discovery.

I lifted the kids off the counter. "Why don't you two watch a movie, and I'll bring you a snack. We'll let the pirate's hand and leg rest for a little while." They agreed, and together we chose a Barney movie. Anna put a couch pillow beside Jacob so he could rest his hand and then got him a drink of water. She was becoming an experienced little nurse—two patients in just a couple of weeks. When they were settled on the couch with the movie and some snacks, I sat down at the dining room table and stared into the family room at my little girl.

Had she ever been hurt before? I couldn't remember a time when she'd been injured—no scraped knees, no slivers, no smashed fingers. Why had I never realized it before? Had we just had a long run of good luck, or was this a part of my curious child that I didn't understand? Rocks had ripped holes into her pants, and yet nothing had happened to her. I gazed out the dining room window at the steep, rocky slope and the still-overturned wagon and shook my head. I wanted to understand. I wanted an explanation. But where could I go for answers? If I began asking questions, people would notice Anna's unusual qualities, and her anonymity would be gone. Brent didn't have the answers. Prayer and the library hadn't provided me with an explanation. For the thousandth time, I wondered uneasily what we were supposed to do. What was Anna's purpose? Why was she the way she was? I felt lost.

Before we fell asleep that night, Brent and I talked about the strange events of the afternoon. "She's really never been hurt?" he asked.

"I can't think of a single time."

"How is that possible?"

"I have no idea."

"Has she ever been sick?" Brent asked.

"I don't think so. I can't remember her ever having a fever or anything. Even when she got her teeth, she didn't get fussy like other babies. I just thought she was a really good baby."

"She was a good baby," he said.

"How could I have missed this? Wouldn't a normal mother notice something like that? It seems like a pretty big thing." It wasn't the first time I'd wondered if I was as perceptive to Anna as a natural mother would be. The thought that I was missing some special mother's intuition made me terribly sad and even more determined to take care of her and help her have a happy, carefree childhood.

"She's our only child, Susan. We've had no one really to compare her to. You shouldn't feel bad about it."

"I guess," I said. I wanted to be convinced that I wasn't somehow lacking.

We were quiet for such a long time that I thought maybe Brent had fallen asleep. I lay there staring into the darkness, not wanting to sleep until I had a few things clear in my head. The only sound was the soft hum of the ceiling fan as I sorted through the thoughts that were jumbled in my mind. Brent's voice pierced the quiet, startling me. "Should we be talking to someone?" he asked.

"Maybe," I said. "But who?"

Several more minutes of quiet followed, as we both entertained our own private thoughts. I could feel myself beginning to drift off to sleep when I heard Brent sigh and say, "I don't know." The helpless sound in his voice was the last thing I heard before I fell asleep.

We enjoyed the happy atmosphere Anna brought into our family. Of course, Anna amused us with her funny stories, her silly songs, and her clever observations. Like most parents, we thought our child was a prodigy and reveled in her brilliance. I wished that was all Anna was—a bright, happy child with clever things to say. Instead she was something we didn't understand, a bright-eyed, golden-haired mystery.

✷

We had been planning a vacation with Brent's parents in August. We were going to join them in their motor home for a week at the Oregon coast. Now, with Brent an invalid for the summer, they decided to come spend a week with us in Grand Junction. Not nearly as exciting, but Brent and I were both curious to have someone else spend time with Anna. We wanted to see if they noticed anything unusual and, if they did, how they would react. We hoped they might have some brilliant insight that was somehow eluding us. They'd come to visit several times in the years since Anna had joined our family, and we'd gone to Denver to see them as well. But this time they would be with us for a full week instead of just a couple of days, and we'd be at home, without the distraction of activities and sightseeing. Would they notice the things we'd noticed? My mom and dad hadn't, even though they'd seen Anna a few times each year. They were typical grandparents—they thought their granddaughter was beautiful and sweet, but they'd never mentioned noticing anything extraordinary.

At last, the day of their visit arrived. Anna was excited. She would look out the front window every few minutes and report to Brent and me that there was no sign of Grandma and Grandpa yet. When they finally pulled into the driveway, Anna ran through the house, cheering, "They're here! They're here!" She was the first to give Grandpa and Grandma Weller a hug. Of course, Grandpa and Grandma Weller were equally excited to see her. I stood on the porch with Brent, who had hobbled out on his crutches, and watched the reunion. It was obvious that we were not the main attraction.

We decided not to mention anything right away. Even though we were desperate to talk to someone about the situation, we wanted to wait and see if they noticed anything on their own. The first few days were uneventful. We watched movies and played games. Grandma Weller took Anna shopping for a new dress and shared stories and poems at bedtime. One morning, at breakfast, Grandma poured Anna some orange juice. "Thanks, Grandma," Anna said.

"You're welcome, Shiny-eyes." Grandma winked at Anna, and she giggled.

"Grandma, tell my mom why you called me Shiny-eyes."

"I think you should be the one to tell her," Grandma said.

"Okay." She took a deep breath and began. "Because the little girl is lost, and someone asks her what her name is, and she says her name is Shiny-eyes. That's her nickname, and she doesn't even really know what her real name is. Isn't that funny?" She brought her hand to her mouth and laughed.

"It sounds like a funny story, but I'm not sure what you're talking about," I said. Her enthusiasm was catching, and I couldn't help but smile.

"Tell her the story, Grandma. I can't say it all."

"When I was a little girl, my mother used to tell me this poem," Grandma said. She tugged at her earring, a self-conscious habit I'd noticed before. "I told it to Anna last night when I was kissing her good night."

"Are you going to say it for her, Grandma?" Anna prodded. "Please?"

"I guess so," Grandma said. She looked a little embarrassed. She cleared her throat and began:

" 'I'm losted! Can't you find me, please?'
Poor little frightened baby!
The wind had tossed her golden fleece;
The stones had scratched her dimpled knees;
I stooped and lifted her with ease,
And softly whispered, 'Maybe;

" 'Tell me your name, my little maid—
I can't find you without it.'
'My name is Shiny-eyes,' she said.
'Yes, but your last?' She shook her head.
'Up to my house they never said
A single thing about it!'

" 'But, dear,' I said, 'what is your name?'
'Why, didn't you hear me told you?
Just Shiny-eyes!' A bright thought came.
'Yes, when you're good; but when they blame
You, little one—it's not the same
When mother has to scold you?'

" 'My mother never scolds!' she moans,
A little blush ensuing;
' 'Cept when I've been a-throwing stones,
And then she says (the culprit owns),
"Mehitabel Sapphira Jones,
What have you been a-doing!" ' "

"Isn't that a funny story?" Anna said. "Her name was . . ." Anna paused. "I can't even say it. It's such a funny name. I guess that's why they called her Shiny-eyes."

"That is a funny story," I said.

"Grandma said I have shiny eyes too, so she said she was going to call me Shiny-eyes."

"You do have very shiny eyes."

"I really like that name," she said, settling down to her breakfast. "I'm glad I have Shiny-eyes."

And that was that. From then on, Grandma Weller's nickname for Anna was Shiny-eyes. Once in a while, someone else would use the nickname, but after that day, I don't think I ever heard Grandma Weller call her Anna. Anna asked Grandma to write down the poem for me so that I could read it to her when Grandma was gone.

One afternoon, Brent and his dad were playing chess. Anna watched curiously. After a while she said, "Can I play?"

"Sure," Grandpa said and set up the board. He explained how to play as they took turns. "She's catching on pretty quickly," Grandpa commented at dinner.

"Can we play again after dinner?" she asked.

"Sure we can," Grandpa said.

Anna was so excited to play chess with Grandpa that she wanted to take our dishes from the table before we were done eating. When the table was finally clear, Grandpa and Anna set up the chess game. Grandma and Brent decided to watch a silly sitcom, and I mixed up a batch of brownies. I glanced over occasionally and smiled at the cute picture before me. Anna looked so young sitting there with the chess game in front of her. Her brow furrowed as she studied the pieces. Grandpa waited for her to make a move, and then he made a move of his own. "Check," he said. Anna studied the board for a minute and then made another move without speaking. Grandpa took his turn. "Check mate," he said and leaned back in his chair.

"What does that mean?" Anna asked.

"That means I just won the game."

"Oooooh." Anna looked intently at the pieces. "How did you do that, Grandpa?"

Grandpa explained his last couple of moves and what Anna had done that put her king in danger. She nodded her head, her ponytail bobbing up and down, her face concentrating on the game board.

"I get it now," she said, and Grandpa chuckled. "Can we play again?" she asked.

"Only if your mom will let me eat one of those warm brownies," Grandpa said.

"Can he, Mom? Please?" she asked.

"Sure he can. I'll bring one right over." I placed a plate of them on the table and began loading the dishwasher. Grandpa and Anna set up the board for another game. I thumbed through a couple of cookbooks, looking for a chicken enchilada recipe I wanted to make for dinner the next night.

"Well, I'll be," Grandpa said under his breath. I looked over to see what was going on. Grandpa was studying the board carefully.

"It's your turn, Grandpa," Anna reminded him.

"I know, I know. I'm just checking out my options here, little lady. Give me a minute." He continued looking at the board. Finally, he made his move, shaking his head.

"Chick," Anna said.

"I think the word you want is *check*, Anna," Grandpa said. He was smiling, but he was still shaking his head.

"Oh. Check," she said.

Grandpa moved another piece. Anna took her turn. "Check," she said again. Grandpa moved again. Then Anna. "Check." Anna had Grandpa on the run. He moved one more time. Then Anna finished the game. "What am I supposed to say now?" she asked.

"Check mate," Grandpa answered.

"Oh yeah. Check. Mate." She immediately started clapping as Grandpa let out a long whistle.

"What the devil," he said. "I just got beat by a five-year-old."

"I'm only four, Grandpa" Anna announced proudly.

"My, oh my. You're quite the little smarty-pants, aren't you?" He laughed and reached over to tweak her on the nose.

"Can we play again? Please?" Anna pleaded.

"Why don't we let Grandpa have a break and go visit with Daddy for a while," I suggested.

"I think your mom is rescuing me. We'll play again tomorrow, peanut," Grandpa said, lining up the pieces in the felt case. "I'm not sure if my pride could handle another loss tonight."

The next day they played—Grandpa won three, and Anna won two.

"I think you've got yourselves a Garry Kasparov here," Grandpa said and then had to explain to all of us that Garry Kasparov was a famous child chess champion who became one of the best chess players of all time. "She's a mighty smart little girl, that Anna."

"She is pretty amazing," Brent agreed, looking at me. I nodded to let him know that I was okay with him sharing our secret. He started by telling his parents about Anna's Sunday School class.

"She should do great in school. She'll probably be one of those kids that end up in college at age twelve," Grandma said.

"She's brought some amazing changes to our lives. Everything is different now. Do you know what I mean?" I hoped they wouldn't think we sounded delusional. I wanted so much to be able to talk openly about what we knew.

"Children make everything different, don't they?" Grandma said. But she didn't understand. No one did. I'm not sure what it was, but something stopped us from saying more. For some reason, we were afraid to say the words out loud. We longed for someone else to notice and bring it up so we could talk about it. Maybe we even doubted ourselves a little—whether what we'd witnessed was actually true. Maybe Anna was just really smart. Why were we afraid to ask those crazy questions? "Have you noticed that the room looks different when Anna walks in?" "Have you noticed that the grass looks greener when Anna is playing out there?" "Have you noticed that you understand things better if she's with you?" Somehow, we just couldn't say the words aloud to anyone else. So there it ended. Grandma and Grandpa thought Anna was amazing and smart and clever and sweet. But they hadn't yet figured out what we had—that Anna was gifted and special and unusual. We continued to worry alone.

★

Fall came and with it the new school year. Brent returned to school on crutches. The leg we'd thought was the worst was healing well, but the ankle was taking its sweet time and required some extra physical therapy. He graduated from crutches to a walking cast the first week of October. About that time, medical bills began filling the mailbox.

"Susan, Jan told me they're going to hold a fall boutique in the old lumber store in November," Beth said one Saturday morning as we were walking to our cars after aerobics. "We were thinking we could all pitch in and rent a booth. Melinda and I are going in on one together, but you're welcome to join us. It'll only cost you $25.00. It might be nice to make a little Christmas money."

Or a little medical bill money, I thought. "What are you thinking of selling?" I asked.

"I wanted to make those little quiet books for kids. I think Jan is going to sell those little rag dolls she makes, and I'm not sure what Melinda is doing. Knowing her, she'll probably sell a thousand pounds of fudge or something."

"I'm not sure what I'd do." I was a good seamstress, but I couldn't really imagine selling clothes at a boutique.

"Well, it's just an idea, but you know those matching aprons you made for you and Anna last Christmas? Those turned out so cute. I'll bet if you made up a bunch of those, they'd sell like crazy."

"That's not a bad idea," I said. My mind was already planning a trip to the fabric store. "Especially since Thanksgiving and Christmas are right around the corner."

"That's the time people are doing a lot of cooking," she said. "And they were so cute. We all wanted one. I even wanted a little girl to match." She laughed.

"I can't get you a little girl, but I could make some aprons. Sure, count me in."

"Good, I was hoping you'd say yes. We can set up the booth

however we want. We figured since it's four days, each of us could be there one day of the sale, and then it wouldn't be too much work for anybody. If you want, maybe we could watch each other's kids on our two days."

"That's a good idea. I'm sure the kids would enjoy that."

Pleased at the prospect of making a little extra money, I took Anna fabric shopping. She had never been to a fabric store and behaved as if it were an amusement park. She touched the fabrics carefully, pointing out to me the soft ones, the shiny ones, and the furry ones. Anything with flowers became her new favorite. Anna felt like a big girl walking beside me. We found about a dozen that we liked and had them cut. After two trips to the cutting table, we found some thread and trims and returned home.

The next several weeks were spent sewing aprons. Anna watched excitedly at first but soon lost interest and decided to go play instead. Now and then she'd come stand beside me and watch with a curious little "How's it going, Mom?" I'd tell her it was going fine, and she'd return to her playing. By the time the boutique was starting, I had fifty adult aprons and fifty children's aprons ready to sell.

As I starched and pressed the last few aprons, Brent asked, "Do you really think you'll be able to sell them all?"

"I don't know. I guess if they don't sell, I can give them away as gifts for the next ten years." I hung up the last apron, secured it with a couple of pins to keep it from falling off the hanger, and hung it beside the others on the stair rail. I stepped back to survey my weeks of work and smiled with satisfaction. They looked so cute and homey, and I felt really proud of them.

The night before the sale, we left our children home with their dads and organized our space. The old lumber store was being trans-formed before our eyes. The huge space had been divided into a hun-dred smaller shops. As I carried the aprons to our space, I looked around at the creative things people had done. There were fairy wings and skirts, pottery, paintings, baby clothes, all kinds of home décor, including embroidered and stitched pillows. I paused and looked at some intricate birds carved of wood. But my heart sank a little when I saw that there were two other booths selling aprons. I looked at my aprons. They were cute, but seemed a little lost in the smorgasbord of beautiful and clever things.

I put up a double clothes rack along one side of our booth and filled it with my wares. Jan's husband had built shelves along the back wall, and Beth and Jan filled them with cute rag dolls and fun little quiet books. Melinda did just what Jan had expected—and then some. A large baker's rack was filled with fudge, peanut brittle, caramel apples, and chocolate-dipped pretzels, all bagged up and looking way too tempting.

"Okay, Melinda, how am I going to keep my hands off all these goodies?" Jan asked.

"I'm afraid I might spend everything I make on that fudge, especially the ones with all the nuts," I said.

When we were finished, the booth looked cute and ready to go. Each of us was scheduled to work the booth one day—Jan would take Wednesday, I would work Thursday, Beth had Friday, and Melinda would finish up with Saturday. This was the logical choice for Melinda since she had five children and her husband, Shawn would be home all day to take care of them.

The next evening, Jan called each of us to report the sales. "You sold five adult aprons and three children's aprons," she said.

"That's not too bad, I guess."

"It was slower than I expected, but I guess it was a workday. Hopefully Friday and Saturday will be really busy."

"How did everyone else do?" I asked.

"Not too bad. I sold enough dolls today to pay my rent, and then some, so that's pretty good."

"How much candy did you eat?" I asked.

"Only three pieces of fudge," Jan said. "But I did bring a caramel apple home to share. I probably would've eaten more, but I knew I'd have to confess it to you guys. You all saved me a week of workouts." I laughed. "Oh, and several of Beth's books sold. I guess it went okay for a Wednesday."

"We'll see if Thursday is any better," I said.

"I imagine it'll be about like today. Friday and Saturday will probably be the busiest."

It was nearly eleven, and I was just getting into bed when the phone rang. "Hi, Susan. I'm so, so sorry to call so late." It was Beth.

"Hi, Beth. Is everything okay?"

"I'm not sure what to do. Jacob just threw up for the second time tonight, so I thought I should let you know. At first I thought maybe his dinner didn't settle well, but after the second time I'm thinking maybe he's caught something. I wanted to call you. I figured you wouldn't want Anna to be around him."

I couldn't tell her the truth—that there was no chance of Anna getting sick. "Oh, poor little guy."

"I'm really sorry. Maybe Jan or Melinda could watch her. Do you want me to call and check with them?"

"No, that's okay," I said. "I'll just take her with me."

"That's such a pain for you, though. I feel so bad."

"Don't feel bad. It's okay. I'll bring some coloring books for her to play with, and I'm sure she'll be fine. I hope Jacob feels better for Friday so he can come and play with Anna."

"I can't ask you to do that if I'm not even watching Anna."

"Oh, please. Of course he can come. Anna would feel bad if he didn't."

"Thanks, Susan, and I'm really sorry."

I gathered some coloring books and crayons and put them in a bag with some snacks, a blanket, and Jupiter. Anna would be okay entertaining herself for one day.

We arrived at the boutique a little before 10:00 a.m., and I set up a little spot for Anna to play in. I looked around our booth. Everything looked bright and attractive. I thought it might be nice for people to see an apron modeled, so I put on a daisy-covered apron with white trim. It was one of my favorites. Anna chose to wear one that had teddy bears that reminded her of Jupiter. The boutique opened, and we were ready for business. It was pretty slow for the first hour. Only two people came by. I thought I recognized them from a booth on the other side of the room. I colored with Anna while we waited for customers.

"Oh my stars, what a beautiful little girl you are." An attractive older lady with dyed red hair and matching lipstick stopped to look at Anna. "She's such a pretty thing," she said to me.

"Thank you," I said.

"Oh, Pearl, will you look at these. These are just precious." The woman browsed through the rack of aprons.

"I've always loved the frock aprons. Like I've always said, half aprons only keep you half clean," Pearl answered. "Oh my heavens, I've got to get a set of these for Emily and Alexa."

"You're so lucky to have a granddaughter. Now, I love my grandsons, but I don't think they'd much like getting one of these. I never get to buy anything pretty and frilly. I think I'll get one for Kathy, anyway. She loves anything with roses. This one would be perfect for her." The redheaded woman pulled out a white apron with big, pink rose bouquets scattered across it. It was trimmed with pink grosgrain ribbon.

Pearl took down a holiday apron with pumpkin fabric and green rickrack and found a matching child's apron. "You've found some of the prettiest fabrics, dear," she said, turning to me.

"Thanks. I'm glad you like them."

"They're just lovely," she said. "Oh my goodness, I just might have to get this one for me." She laughed a high little laugh that reminded me of our doorbell. "Thirty years I taught school. You'd think I'd be sick of Dick and Jane, but this is just too cute to pass up. Won't the family get a kick out of me wearing this while I cook Thanksgiving dinner?" she asked. She pulled down an apron covered with vintage Dick and Jane images trimmed with red piping. "You should get one too."

"I guess I could. It's not like I need an apron. I haven't really cooked anything for ten years. But they are awfully cute," the lady with red hair said.

"You don't have to actually cook to put one on, you know," Pearl said. "You might just fool them all into thinking you're a gourmet cook if you're wearing this." In the end, they bought five aprons, a quiet book, a doll, and two caramel apples. I smiled as they walked away from the booth chatting about their purchases.

Around lunchtime, business really picked up, and people flowed by at a pretty brisk pace. To my surprise and delight, almost everyone who walked by our booth stopped, commented on how wonderful everything looked, spoke to Anna, and then made multiple purchases. While the rush continued, Anna curled up on her blanket and took a nap. By early afternoon, I had made the connection. Our booth and the ones directly around it were selling like crazy. People were drawn to our area and loved everything they saw. I watched my aprons fly off the rack. By 5:00 p.m. it looked like we might sell out in the next two hours. We came close. I knew that Beth and Jan had only had room to put out part of their things, so they had more books and dolls that they could bring, and of course Melinda could make more goodies, but I had brought my entire inventory of aprons.

When the boutique closed at seven, only three forlorn aprons hung on the rack. As soon as I got home, I called the others and told them about the day's success. Of course they were surprised and thrilled. I left Anna, who wanted to stay home with Brent, and went back to the fabric store before it closed. By the time I dropped into bed at 2:00 a.m., I'd made eight more aprons. I would sew more during the day on Friday.

I was pleased by the success of the day—we really needed the money—but I was afraid it wouldn't continue if Anna wasn't in the booth. If the others knew it was because of Anna, would they want her there every day? Suddenly I realized how tempting it might be to take advantage of Anna's gift for personal gain. It hadn't even occurred to me that Anna's presence might have an effect on the booth's success, but I'd witnessed it all day. I felt a little uncomfortable that we seemed to have profited, however innocently, because she was there with me. Here was one more thing we would have to guard against. It would be so easy to find justifications to exploit Anna for our own interests. Brent and I would have to learn to protect Anna, even from ourselves.

My suspicions proved right. The next two days our sales dropped sharply. We all did well enough, but Thursday had been the most profitable day by far. We were all a little deflated by Friday and Saturday's results. The other women discussed at length their confusion that Thursday could be so much better than Saturday. It defied logic. I listened to them as they tried to figure it out, but I said nothing.

Up to now, Brent and I had not discussed Anna's schooling. Homeschooling was something I'd never imagined doing. My husband was a public school teacher, for heaven's sake. So when Brent asked me if I'd considered teaching Anna at home, I was stunned.

"What did you say?" I asked. I was sure I'd heard him wrong.

"I'm just wondering if it would be better to teach Anna at home."

"Are you serious?" I let the thought sink in. "I don't know. I've never thought about it. What do you think?"

"Maybe we should at least consider it," he said. Once he'd brought it up, I could think of little else. I weighed the pros and cons. On one hand, Anna loved being around other children. She would love school. I couldn't imagine robbing her of that. But on the other hand, I began to realize how exposed she'd be. It might be impossible to hide her peculiarity if she spent so much time away from our protective supervision.

Brent didn't bring up the subject again, but as the months passed and kindergarten drew closer and closer, I tried to imagine what life would be like for her if she didn't go to school. I saw our little girl studying at home all by herself, day after day. I imagined taking her to the park and the museum in an effort to compensate for the exciting experiences we had deprived her of. She would live an isolated life. She wouldn't have an opportunity to make new friends and develop new relationships on her own. She wouldn't have the chance to learn independence. Although I loved having her with me and really wasn't very excited about sending her out into the world, it made me sad when I thought of everything she would miss out on.

Then I imagined Anna if she went to school. I knew she'd make friends, and she'd love learning and playing. She'd be a good student, and her teachers would love her. But wouldn't people begin to notice how different she was? Wouldn't they realize her gifts? Sometimes I had the feeling that other people had already noticed things. The night I'd picked Anna up from Beth's house, she had wanted to tell me something but had been interrupted. Maybe she had discovered our secret. But why hadn't she said anything later? Maybe once Anna had gone, Beth had doubted what she'd seen. A couple of times I'd considered confiding in her. It would be such a relief to share our secret with someone, but every time I thought about actually doing it, something would stop me. It just seemed too risky.

I knew I could teach Anna in kindergarten, and probably clear through elementary school, but then what? I'd be lost when it came to calculus and trigonometry. Biology and chemistry would be impossible. And I couldn't be her whole world. I wanted her to have a normal life. If I kept her at home so she wouldn't find out she was different, that would make her different. The more I thought about it, the more I knew she needed to go to school. We'd figure it out as we went along, but we couldn't hope for her to be a normal, well-adjusted child while treating her like she was strange and different. I was thankful that Brent agreed.

"I'm not sure I ever really thought that we should teach her at home," he said. "I'm just worried about her. I don't want people to treat her like she's weird. Church is one thing, but in school, people will be with her for hours every day, and kids can be pretty cruel." He shook his head, and there was a quiver in his voice. "I just want her to be okay."

"I do too," I said. If only there was someone wiser than ourselves we could turn to for advice.

Chapter 4

Anna could hardly contain her enthusiasm about starting school, and it was so infectious that we almost forgot our concerns. We shopped for school, and she helped pick school clothes like an expert. At the department store, it was her job to cross off each item on the supplies list as it was placed in the cart beside her. I had to point out which word to put the line through, but she didn't mind. She felt like a big girl. I waited as patiently as I could while she spent half an hour trying to decide between a bright pink Sleeping Beauty backpack and a lavender one with sparkly butter-flies. The decision was so difficult that we finally put both backpacks in the cart while we finished shopping. At the check out counter, when a decision had to be made, Sleeping Beauty finally won out. We put a hook in the front closet low enough that Anna could reach it. Every day until school started, she took out her backpack and tried it on, just to "practice getting ready for school."

Anna was in the afternoon kindergarten class, so I'd planned to wake her at about nine, but at 6:30, she was in my room, dressed for school and wearing her backpack. "Oh, honey, it's way too early to go to school. Remember, you're in the afternoon class."

"How long until we go?"

"Quite a while," I said. I wanted to be vague. I knew the actual amount of time would crush her.

"How long in minutes?" she asked.

"A lot of minutes. It's almost six hours."

"How many minutes is six hours?" I smiled at her determination.

"Over three-hundred and fifty minutes. Too long to wear your backpack. Let's put it by the front door, shall we?" I could tell we were in for a long morning. I tried to distract her with breakfast, Sesame Street, and a game of Candyland, but we repeated the same conversation again and again.

"Mom, is it time to go to school yet?"

"No, honey, not yet."

"How many more minutes?"

"I don't think you want me to tell you. It still sounds like a lot."

"Moooom," she said, sighing. "How many more minutes?"

"About 240."

"That's so long. I don't think I can stand it."

"Let's mix up a chocolate cake, and then you can have a piece of cake and milk when you get out of school. I'll even let you lick the beaters."

"Is it time to go to school now?" she asked. We had just put the cake batter in the oven. What would I do now to keep her entertained?

"Not yet."

She put her hands on her hips and stomped her foot. "Is it ever going to be time to go to school?"

When the time finally arrived, she strapped on her backpack and waited for me at the front door. When I joined her, she took my hand and nearly dragged me the three blocks to Kaiser Elementary. The warm and sunny weather perfectly matched Anna's mood. We walked through the gate to the kindergarten entrance and stood in line with the other children and their parents. Brightly colored smiley faces were painted on the concrete leading to the door, and Anna quickly claimed a yellow one. The kindergarten room was cheerful and exciting. Giant block letters lined the top of the walls, picture books filled a large bookshelf, and primary-colored tables were surrounded by little chairs. Built in the corner was a little log cabin, big enough for children to play inside. Cubbies labeled with each child's name lined the back wall. It was a happy and cheerful room—a five-year-old child's dream. I thought back to my year of kindergarten. I couldn't remember the room looking this exciting.

Miss Simmons, Anna's kindergarten teacher, was young and energetic. She had long blonde hair tied up in a high ponytail and looked more like a junior high student than a teacher. She stood at the door and introduced herself. She shook each child's hand as they walked in and complimented cute tennis shoes, neat backpacks, and happy smiles. The children were going to love her.

"Students? Parents?" she said after the bell rang. "I am so excited to be here today." She was cheerful and animated. "This is my first year of teaching kindergarten, and I can tell from meeting all of you that this is going to be a great class. You look so smart and grown up. This is just so exciting!" She clapped her hands. The children looked up at her, enraptured. The parents lining the walls smiled to themselves and at each other. I thought back to grouchy Mrs. Adamson, my kindergarten teacher, and wished I'd had a teacher like Miss Simmons. After a few minutes of general information, the parents were excused, and I said good-bye to Anna, kissing the top of her head. At the door, I looked back and blew her a kiss. She blew one back before she turned her attention to Miss Simmons. It was time for me to go.

I thought I had prepared myself for this event. Brent and I had spent so much time discussing how things would be for Anna at school, what things we might need to be prepared for, and how we would answer probing questions, that I'd spent no time at all thinking about Anna going to kindergarten in its most basic way. Now I was just a mom leaving her little girl at school. As I left the school for the walk home, the tears started to fall. I saw a few other mothers visiting in the parking lot, but I didn't want anyone to see me cry, so I didn't join them. I cried most of the way home and then sat down in the big, comfy chair with a box of Kleenex and cried a little more. These weren't tears of concern for Anna's gift. I was crying because my little girl had started school—not the little girl with the extraordinary power to change things around her, just my sweet little girl, my Anna.

The afternoon dragged on for me just as the morning had for Anna. I felt lonely without her. I busied myself with housework and started dinner. I frosted the chocolate cake we'd baked. I folded and put away the clothes and then read a book until it was finally time to walk back to the school. I couldn't wait to see Anna, to ask her about her day and what she'd learned. I was anxious to see how much she liked her teacher and if she'd made any new friends. Beth was waiting for Jacob just outside the door, and we visited for a few minutes before the bell rang. Jacob had been quite nervous about going to school, so Beth was glad he and Anna were in the same class and was thrilled with the kind, new teacher.

Anna threw her arms around me as soon as she walked out the door, and then she turned back and waved good-bye to Miss Simmons. We held hands as we made our way through the crowded halls and out of the school. Once we'd reached the sidewalk, I said, "So tell me about your first day of school." That was the only prompting she needed. All the way home she talked about her teacher, her new friends, and the great things they'd learned. She told me how high she and Kelsey had swung on the swings during their recess and about the pretty yellow table she sat at with three other children. Then she sang me a song about the days of the week.

"And Mom, I have a special note for you. It's on the most beautiful blue paper. It's in my backpack. Wanna see?" She stopped in the middle of the sidewalk, took off her backpack, and retrieved it for me.

"Back to School Night, Thursday night," I read aloud.

"And guess what we get to do? We get to paste a picture of ourselves on a paper cup so you'll know where my seat is. And you get to sit at my seat too," she said.

"That sounds great!" I smiled at her enthusiasm. She made it sound as exciting as a trip to the amusement park.

The next few days of school were much like the first day except that I managed not to cry on my way back home. Each afternoon Anna filled us in on the glorious details of the day. She did her homework, which was to write a page of uppercase and lowercase letters, practice her numbers, and follow along as Brent or I read to her for ten minutes from *Old Hat, New Hat* or *The Foot Book* (or whatever book was her favorite at the moment). She usually wanted the stories to go on much longer than ten minutes.

On Thursday evening, we left Anna home with a sitter and went to Back to School Night. Anna desperately wanted to come with us and was only appeased when Natalie, the sitter, asked her if she wanted to play princess.

In the crowded classroom, we joined other parents in search of their child's picture. We soon found the yellow table and the cup with Anna's picture on it. The grin on Anna's face made me laugh. I sat down in her chair and Brent pulled a chair from the reading circle and sat slightly behind me. I glanced around at the other paper cups, looking for the names of the children Anna had mentioned. Jacob and Kelsey's cups were on the table next to us. Soon Beth came in and sat down at Jacob's paper cup. She nodded and waved. No one ever came to sit at Kelsey's cup.

Miss Simmons walked into the room and stood at her desk, where she picked up some papers and began handing a stack to each table. "Is she really old enough to be a school teacher?" Brent whispered in my ear. Her hair was down that night, which made her look even younger than she had the first time I'd seen her. She stood at the front of the room, cleared her throat, and smiled.

"Parents, thank you for coming tonight. I'm Miss Simmons, for those of you who haven't met me yet. I'm very excited about school this year. Your children are a pleasure to work with. Of course, this is my first year teaching, so I don't have any other classes to compare them to, but I'm amazed at how quickly they're learning and how wonderful they are." Her voice was a little shaky, and her notes shook in her hand. I thought she must be more comfortable with the children than she was with their parents. "I'm going to start with the paper on top and then work through," she said. "If you want to follow along, that would be great, and then you can take this home with you for future reference. Please stop me if you have any questions."

Miss Simmons explained her philosophy of teaching, told us about the weekly newsletter, and described the homework we could expect. Another sheet listed the three field trips she had planned for the year—a trip to the grocery store, a trip to a bank, and an excursion to the local fire station. She explained the procedure to follow if our child was absent and then pointed out a sheet on the door where parents could sign up to volunteer. "Does anyone have any questions?" she asked. A couple of parents raised their hands, and Miss

Simmons answered their questions.

"I believe that kindergarten is a time for children to learn to love school. I don't want them to feel worried or slow or uncomfortable. If children absolutely love kindergarten, they'll have a much better chance of doing well through the rest of their schooling."

She straightened her papers, laid them on her desk, and nervously clasped her hands together. "Really, you should all be so proud of your children. I'm thinking I might have to adjust the homework a little as we go along. I almost feel bad sending home pages of letters for them to write since it seems that all the children in the class already know how to write their alphabet, but we'll just hurry through that part and then move on. They're such bright children. They've picked things up much faster than I expected them to. And that means we'll get to do more exciting things. I can tell we're going to have a great year. Are there any other questions?" There were none, so she pointed to the volunteer sheet on the door. "Thank you for coming. Be sure to sign the volunteer sheet, and please come see me anytime before or after school if you have any questions or concerns."

I looked at Brent as we stood up, and I could tell we were wondering the same thing. Did the children all know the alphabet before school started, or were they learning quickly because Anna was there? We had our suspicions, though we might never know for certain. I paused at the door and signed the volunteer sheet—my job would be to help with an art project twice a month.

We said hello to several people we knew but didn't stop to visit as we made our way out of the school. The sun was low in the sky, and our long shadows made us look about fifteen feet tall. I saw Brent smile as he opened the car door.

"What are you thinking?" I asked him over the car.

"That it isn't a bad thing if they're learning quickly because of Anna. I'd imagine most parents would appreciate a little extra help for their kids."

"That's true," I said. "As long as they don't connect it with her, I guess it's all right." I thought for a moment. "Is there any way they could make the connection?"

Brent got in his side of the car, and I settled into my seat. "I doubt it," he said. "It's too unbelievable. Even if someone suspected the truth, they'd be too embarrassed to tell anyone. She's our daughter, and we didn't figure it out immediately." He chuckled to himself, and I thought of Beth. Now and then I'd see her staring thoughtfully at Anna. If only I knew what she was thinking.

★

Over time, I grew accustomed to the miraculous things that happened when Anna was around. I forgot how different our lives were, and sometimes I even forgot there was anything remarkable going on. In fact, as the school year progressed, nothing out of the ordinary happened. I helped out regularly with the art projects, and I'd often hear Miss Simmons comment on how smart the class was, but no one said anything to me that caused me concern. Anna was just one bright child in a class of bright children. Life seemed normal. Brent taught school, I did laundry and cooked dinner, we helped Anna with homework, and we went to church. It seemed to me that we appeared to be just like every other family.

For Thanksgiving that year, we drove to Flagstaff to be with my family. Bev and Dan also came with their kids, Chester and Max. We all stayed at Dad and Mom's for three days of food, good company, and no distractions. Thanksgiving dinner was excellent. The turkey was tender and juicy, the pies were as delicious as ever, and the kids played for hours without fighting. In the afternoon, the guys watched the Tennessee Oilers beat the Dallas Cowboys while Mom and Bev and I worked on a really difficult one-thousand-piece puzzle of the New York skyline. It was so nice to spend time relaxing with family. For a little while, our daily cares seemed small and far away.

"I don't think Chester and Max have ever gone this long without fighting before," Bev said. She studied a piece of the sky, turned it around, and fitted it into the puzzle. Chester was seven, and Max was four, just enough of an age difference to make Max a real trial for his big brother. "Usually Max would be driving Chester crazy by now."

"I can't believe how big they are," I said. "You and Dan should move to Grand Junction. Then we wouldn't have trouble recognizing them when we see them."

"Now there's an idea," Mom said. "If you and Dan moved to Grand Junction, maybe Dad and I would too. Then we could all be closer to each other." Mom hated that I'd moved to Grand Junction and Bev had ended up in Portland. It meant separate trips to see us, and though Bev and I had both told Mom to move closer to one of us, she couldn't bring herself to choose. Mom had always tried to treat us fairly, and to move closer to one daughter would seem too much like favoritism. So she and Dad stayed in Flagstaff by themselves, visiting each of us a couple of times a year and waiting for us to come see them.

"You know, Brent could teach school in Portland, and you *know* our weather is nicer than yours. I think you should all move our direction," she said with a laugh. We both knew it was unlikely that either of us would settle in the other's hometown. Mom let out a dramatic sigh, and we all laughed.

That evening, we put the kids to bed, made a big bowl of buttered popcorn, and sat down to watch a movie. Dan and Brent wanted to watch *Independence Day*, but since they got to watch their football game, they agreed to let the women choose the movie. After a short discussion, we turned on *Fools Rush In*, a predictable but entertaining romantic comedy. At one point in the movie, the star-crossed couple argues heatedly on a bridge in a downpour. I sensed someone was behind me and turned to see Anna sitting on the stairs in her white nightgown, her elbows on her knees, her chin resting in her hands. Tears were streaming down her face, and her bottom lip quivered.

"Anna, what's wrong?" I asked. I got up and went to her. She let out a little sob as she tried to speak but couldn't get any words out. I picked her up. She buried her head in my shoulder and hugged me tightly as she shook with the force of her sobs.

"Do you want us to pause the movie?" Dad asked.

"No, that's okay. I've seen it," I said. I walked with Anna into the quiet darkness of the living room and sat down in the corner of the couch. Only a faint shaft of light shone from the hallway. I held her close and rubbed her back until she had settled down enough to talk. "Hey, sweetie, can you tell me what's wrong?"

She wiped her eyes. "What was wrong with them?"

"What was wrong with who?" I asked. I wondered if something might be wrong with Chester and Max.

"That boy and girl in the rain. Why do they hate each other?" Her lip quivered, and her voice broke.

It took me a moment to realize that she was talking about the couple in the movie. "Oh, they don't hate each other. They just had a disagreement."

"They sounded like they hate each other," she said.

"They were just really upset. Lots of people sound like that when they have a disagreement, but it doesn't mean they hate each other." I pulled her close and hugged her. She rested quietly for a minute.

"I'm glad you and Daddy don't talk like that."

"Sometimes we do. When I think things should be one way and Daddy thinks they should be another way, sometimes we get upset with each other."

"You never talk like that." She shook her head against my shoulder. "I didn't like it when they talked mean. It made me really sad." I kissed the top of her head.

"I'm sorry you feel sad. But, Anna, they're people in a movie. They're not real. They were just pretending to be upset." Anna was quiet for a minute or two.

"Are they really happy?" she asked.

"I'll bet the real people are happy. They were just pretending to be angry for the movie."

This seemed to satisfy her, and I felt her slowly relax against me. I continued to rub her back as I held her, and soon her steady breathing told me she'd fallen asleep. I sat there holding her for several minutes, amused at her reaction to a silly movie. Had she never seen a movie with a heated argument before? I couldn't think of any, and I smugly congratulated myself on this bit of good parenting, glad we only allowed her to watch children's programs. I couldn't think of a single show she might have seen that had arguing in it. Surely that explained her reaction to the people on the bridge.

But what about Brent and me? She had to have heard us have a disagreement. I thought back over the last few years, trying to think of an argument Brent and I would have had that Anna might have witnessed. I couldn't think of any. Not a single argument. I could remember several from before we adopted Anna. Once we had argued when Brent had bought a new stereo for the car without talking to me about it first. Another time a misunderstanding about a doctor's appointment had escalated into a ridiculous shouting match. They had all been stupid things. But what about more recently? What had we fought about in the last few years?

I couldn't think of anything. Nothing at all. It annoyed me that my memory was so bad. I carried Anna back to bed and tucked her in. Chester had kicked off his blankets, so I covered him back up before rejoining the other adults in the family room. The movie was over, and they were talking about real estate in Las Vegas, a subject inspired by the movie.

"What was wrong, Susan?" Brent asked.

"Did she have a bad dream?" Mom said.

"No, she was upset by the argument on the bridge. She was sad for that couple because she thought they hated each other."

"The couple from the movie?" Dan asked.

"Yes," I said.

"Really?" Bev asked. I nodded.

"Is that all? You look like something's bothering you," Brent said. I sat down beside him, and he held my hand.

I wondered if I was losing my mind. I turned to Brent. "Have we had an argument or a disagreement in the last few years?"

He laughed. "I'm sure we have. Why?"

"Anna said she'd never heard us talk like that, and I'm sure we have, but I really can't remember a time."

"You had a pretty good one that time you came to visit us," Dan said.

"Yeah, remember?" Bev was trying to be helpful. "It was about which day you were going to the coast or something."

"Yeah, I remember that," I said. I was embarrassed that they still remembered the ridiculous argument. "When was that?"

"Well, it was a while ago. We didn't have Max yet," Bev said. "I'm pretty sure I wasn't even pregnant with him yet."

"You weren't, because we were going to ride the dune buggies, and you wouldn't have done that if you were pregnant," I said.

"Actually, I think Chester was only about one," Bev added, "so you didn't have Anna yet."

"It was just the two of us," Brent said. "I think we adopted Anna that next spring."

"Help me think," I said. I knew I sounded silly, but I didn't care. I needed to get to the bottom of this. "When was our last argument?"

"Your mom and I try hard to forget ours," Dad said. "Are you sure you don't want to just forget yours too? Be glad you can't remember. It's one of the few benefits of getting older."

"It's not that I'm dying to relive old fights." Now I was feeling stupid. "I just can't remember if we've had an argument that Anna would have seen. I guess it just seems strange to me that I can't remember a single one."

"Well, I think we can safely bet that you've had some kind of argument in the last five and a half years," Dan said. Everyone laughed, but I noticed that Brent hadn't said anything for a while. I looked at him, and his expression surprised me. He met my eyes, and I thought we were suspecting the same thing.

"I'm dying of thirst," he said. He stood up and gathered the popcorn bowls. "Does anyone else need a drink of water?"

"I'd take one," Mom said.

"Thanks, Brent," Bev said and handed him her popcorn bowl. "I'd like one too."

"I'll help you," I said.

In the kitchen, Brent deposited the popcorn bowls in the sink and turned to me. "We haven't had any kind of argument or disagreement since we got Anna," he said without a hint of uncertainty.

"We haven't, have we?" I said. "Did you ever realize that before tonight?"

"I've never thought about it." He leaned against the counter and folded his arms. "Has Anna ever had an argument with anyone?"

"I don't think so. In fact, every time anyone says anything about Anna and their kids, they always say, 'they got along so well.' Brent, she was really upset by the movie. She was crying pretty hard, and she was sure the people were really upset."

"Wow." He shook his head. "She has such a soft heart. She must be quite a little diplomat if she somehow keeps everyone she plays with from arguing." He smiled.

"I can't believe we haven't had any arguments for the last five years. And I can't believe we haven't noticed." I laughed. "How unobservant are we?"

"I guess we just took it for granted," he said. We filled the glasses with water and went back to the others. We sat down and joined the conversation, glad they had moved on to a new subject. We didn't tell them our discovery.

*

I thought a lot about this new revelation over the next few weeks. I paid special attention to what was going on when Anna played with other children. Maybe she was just a great peacemaker and helped smooth things over. I soon realized that there was nothing to smooth over. There were no disagreements, no tense moments. Everyone just got along. I kept an eye on Anna at church too. I asked her if there were ever any fights on the playground at school, and she said there weren't. Curiosity overcame me one day, and I decided to do an experiment. Anna was playing on the floor with some paper dolls. I turned on the television and flipped through the channels in search of some kind of contention or discord. I found a soap opera in which a couple was having a heated argument. I left it there and watched Anna. Within seconds, she'd turned her attention from her paper dolls to the television. Her happy face immediately clouded over, and she furrowed her brow. After about a minute, she turned to me and said, "Mom, I really don't think we should watch this."

"Really?" I said. She came and stood beside me. She looked intently at the television and gripped my arm tightly with her little hand. Her distraught expression broke my heart.

"Please turn it off, Mom. I don't like it." I quickly changed the channel, feeling ashamed at the distress I had purposely caused her.

One Sunday, Brent and I were in a Sunday School class in which the teacher led a discussion about the Sermon on the Mount and how each of the beatitudes was a special gift. When the discussion turned to "blessed are the peacemakers," Brent squeezed my hand. We definitely recognized this gift in our little girl.

*

One warm Saturday the following spring, Brent was working in the front yard. He was trying to repair one of the sprinkler heads that had broken over the winter. "Hey, Susan, I need to go get a part," he said from the front door.

"Okay," I said. I'd been doing laundry most of the morning.

"Anna wants to go with me." She'd been "helping" him outdoors. I really didn't blame her. It was a sunny, spring day, the nicest we'd had that year. I wanted to play outside too. "Why don't I take her with me, and you come meet us at the park in half an hour. We can let her play for a while," he said.

"Sure," I said. "I'll finish up this load and meet you over there." Brent loaded a happy Anna into the car, and I folded and put away the rest of the towels. I decided I'd walk and enjoy the warm sunshine. I grabbed the book I was reading in case I had to wait for Brent and Anna and headed to the park. It really was a nice day. The sun was shining, the leaves were a new and soft green, and the air felt warm and clean. I took a deep breath and enjoyed the smell of the neighbor's first lawn-mowing of the year. I smiled. Spring was my favorite season, and days like this were the reason why.

There were a few kids playing at the park when I arrived. A mother sitting on a blanket smiled and said hi. She had rolled her pants up to her knees and her short shirt sleeves onto her shoulders to get as much sun as possible. I sat down on a metal bench and rested my hands on the seat beside me. I enjoyed the contrast between the cool breeze on my face and arms and the sun-warmed metal. A little strawberry blonde girl laughed while her brother pushed her higher and higher on a swing. After a couple of minutes, I opened my book and began to read.

I'd read only a few pages when I was interrupted by the sound of yelling on the other side of the playground. I glanced up and saw half a dozen teenage boys gathered around two other boys who were yelling at each other. A couple of boys were standing on the merry-go-round to get a better view. A few curse words were exchanged. I tried to ignore them and continue reading my book, but within about thirty seconds, the ruckus had gotten noticeably louder, and now it appeared that three or four more teenagers were involved. The mother on the blanket quickly gathered her young daughter and the remains of their lunch and left. I wanted to leave too, but Brent would be here with Anna any minute. If the commotion was still going on when they arrived, I'd just get in the car, and we could drive to a different park.

"What do you think you're doing?" one of the boys yelled at another, adding a derogatory name and a curse word.

"What do you think?" another yelled back. They postured and moved around each other menacingly. A moment later, one of the boys on the merry-go-round jumped into the middle of the fray, ducked his head, and charged. I didn't have a clear view of what was happening—a slide and some of the boys' bodies partially blocked my view—but I could tell that someone ended up on the ground for just a moment before he quickly jumped back up.

I wasn't sure what to do. The skirmish was escalating. As I glanced around the playground, I saw the strawberry-blonde children walking across the lawn, and I hoped they were going home. I was now alone with this group of fighting boys. Would they notice if I got up and left? Should I try to stop the fight before someone really got hurt? Although I wanted to break it up, I was afraid to approach the hostile group by myself. I held my book as if I were reading, grateful that they couldn't see my eyes as I watched them behind my dark glasses. I glanced at my watch. Brent and Anna should have been here by now. What was taking them so long?

The shouting rose and fell a few times. Then there were two boys on the ground, one on top of the other. A couple of kids in the circle were kicking dirt at the fighting boys. The language and threats were getting worse. I needed to get out of here. These weren't little boys, and it seemed to be getting out of control. As much as I wanted to try to stop what was happening, I knew I was outnumbered and unequipped to resolve this on my own. I felt very uncomfortable and even a little scared. I glanced toward the parking lot and saw Brent's blue car in a parking space. In front of it, I saw Anna running toward me as fast as she could.

"Momma, we stopped and got you an ice cream cone." She squealed with delight and held up her bright orange ice cream to show me. Behind her several paces was Brent with an ice cream cone in each hand. I quickly stood to go toward them, anxious to get all of us away from there as quickly as possible. But I wasn't the only one Anna's voice had reached. Quiet settled over the playground, and the eyes of the teenagers moved from me to Anna and back to me.

"That sounds great, Anna." I walked quickly toward her and took her hand to guide her back to the car.

"We got you rocky road 'cause that's your favorite. I got orange 'cause it's my favorite. See?" She held up her cone as she looked around the playground. She stopped when she saw the group of young people a short distance away. Her eyes were wide and serious as she looked at them. I turned to look at the boys, worried that Anna would be upset by the fight. I was surprised to see that the two who had been on the ground were now separated and sitting apart from each other. One brushed the dirt off his jeans. The other looked back at Anna.

"Hope you're in the mood for ice cream," Brent said. His words drifted off as he looked curiously from Anna to me to the silent group of teenagers.

"Thanks," I said. I felt very conspicuous as I took the ice cream cone from his hand. I looked back at the teenagers. Several of them were talking quietly. A couple of them watched us warily. Two had already left the group and were walking away across the lawn. One of the fighting boys stood, offered his hand to the other, and helped him to his feet. Both of them glanced sheepishly in our direction as the group dispersed.

"No hard feelings, man," I heard the taller of the two fighters say to the other as they walked away.

"Dude, forget about it," the other boy said.

Within a couple of minutes, Brent, Anna, and I were alone on the playground. Anna turned to Brent. "Can I go play now? My ice cream is almost gone."

"Sure you can," he said.

Brent and I sat on the bench and finished our cones. I quietly watched Anna and replayed the last several minutes over again in my mind. Brent seemed lost in thought. "What was that all about?" he finally asked. "What was going on here?"

"They were yelling and fighting, and then they just stopped when you guys got here," I said. "Brent, they were actually fighting. On the ground. And yelling and cursing. And they just quit the second you got here."

"I must have looked pretty intimidating," Brent said. He laughed and then stopped when I didn't laugh with him. "I'm sure it wasn't any big deal. You know how boys mess around and wrestle."

"No, Brent." I turned to face him. "They were calling each other horrible names, and they were swearing. They were shoving each other and wrestling on the ground. They were so angry, I was actually afraid. And they just quit when you . . ." I paused. "When Anna got here," I finished. Brent didn't try to explain it away again. We sat there watching Anna, trying to make sense of what had just happened.

"So it's not just that she gets along with people. People get along with each other when they're around her," Brent said matter-of-factly, finally breaking the silence. I shrugged my shoulders but didn't say anything. What could I say? Just when we thought we had Anna and her gifts figured out, we'd discover something new. What did this mean? Suddenly I felt like I couldn't get my breath, like there was something heavy and cumbersome sitting on my heart. What had happened wasn't a bad thing, and yet I felt as if I was drowning. I was worried about people noticing Anna's peculiarities and making her feel different and insecure. I just wanted her to have a normal life, a life like mine and Bev's had been when we were growing up. Like Chester and Max's were now. But Anna wasn't normal. She would never be just like the other kids, and there was nothing I could do about it. I knew that. If I could just know what I was supposed to do with my special little girl and her abilities, I could get my head above water and handle it. But what was I supposed to do? Where would I find the wisdom to protect and advise the little blonde mystery that was my daughter?

Anna was six years old now. Was she starting to realize she was different? Did she notice the unusual things that happened around her? Did she feel different, or did she think she was just like the children around her? I desperately wanted to know what she knew and how she felt, but fear kept me from asking her. I didn't want to put ideas in her head or point out things that she might never have realized before. I didn't want to be responsible for altering the way she saw herself.

Kindergarten was nearly over. Anna's class had exceeded everyone's expectations. Every student in the class was reading at a second grade level or better. They not only knew their numbers, but they were already doing addition and subtraction. A reporter had even come to the school and written an article about Miss Simmons's kindergarten class, calling Miss Simmons a "remarkable and gifted teacher." Brent and I had read the article and smiled, relieved that Miss Simmons was getting the credit for these accomplishments. No one seemed to suspect who was really behind the class's high performance. We were starting to hope that maybe no one ever would.

I pondered Anna's gifts often. As I did, my thoughts often led me to contemplate my responsibility to help her handle her gift appropriately. I felt that somewhere, somehow, there was a God-given purpose to these gifts, and if that was true, how were we to know what that purpose was? Was she supposed to do something great? Would the gift need to be channeled or used in some way? Would the meaning of it ever be revealed to us, or would Brent and I be left to figure it out on our own?

One afternoon, I received a call from the secretary at the adoption agency asking if Brent and I could come to the office for a meeting. We felt uneasy but agreed.

"Don't look so nervous," Mr. Stephens said as he shook our hands. "There's nothing to be worried about. I'm sorry if we've had your blood pressure up all day. Come on in and have a seat." I breathed a little easier at his encouraging words, and we followed Mr. Stephens into his book-lined office. "Please sit down," he said.

"Your daughter's only known biological relative passed away a few months ago. In settling her affairs, her attorney found two letters she'd written—one to you and one to your daughter. The one to your daughter says it's to be opened on her eighteenth birthday. Of course, you're under no obligation to give this to her then or at any time. You're her legal parents, and this can be handled at your discretion." He handed me two pink envelopes. On the front of each was the shaky handwriting of an elderly woman. On one was written "Our Sweet Baby on Her 18th Birthday," and on the other was "Our Baby's Parents."

"As I said, you're free to handle this as you see fit."

"What do we do?" I asked. We were sitting in the parking lot outside Mr. Stevens's office. Brent hadn't started the car yet.

"What do you want to do?" Brent asked. I quietly fidgeted with the envelopes. "There might be some answers in there."

"I know. I was thinking the same thing. Of course I think we should read ours," I said, and Brent nodded. I carefully opened the envelope, keeping it as neat as possible. I took a deep breath. In the same shaky hand was a single-page letter. I began reading aloud.

> *To Our Baby's Parents,*
>
> *Thank you for taking our baby girl and giving her a home. I felt so burdened about her future until I saw your adoption file. I knew you were the right people to share her life.*
>
> *Angela (your baby's birth mother) was my sister's only child. She was a delightful girl and would have been a wonderful mother. She was so happy to be having a baby and shared with me during her pregnancy that she had a feeling her baby was going to be very special. I'm sure that has proven to be the case.*
>
> *I would ask that you give this letter to your daughter on her 18th birthday. I do not wish to disrupt the happy course of your lives, but I believe she may have some questions about herself that the letter might help explain.*
>
> *I thank you for protecting and loving this sweet child.*
>
> *Sincerely,*
>
> *Mrs. Beatrice Parker*

"Her great-aunt knew something," Brent said. I nodded. "Maybe her birth mother too."

"I wish we could just open it and see what it says." I turned the thicker envelope over and over in my hands. One word from Brent and I know I'd have opened it. After all, Mr. Stephens had said it was up to us how to handle it. I wanted to know what questions Mrs. Parker thought Anna might want answered. But Brent was quiet, and I knew we wouldn't open it. We took the letter home and filed it away with our birth certificates and other important papers. It looked as though, at least until Anna's eighteenth birthday, we'd be left to wonder and muddle through on our own.

Chapter 5

From Anna's journal:

Today Mary said I'm magic. I told her I'm not, but she didn't believe me. She just turned around after recess and said she can tell I'm magic. She wanted me to show her how I do it. I don't know what she means. I wish I was magic. If I had magic powers, I'd turn yucky peas into green M&Ms.

★

"Mom, can I invite Kelsey over to play after school?" Anna asked one morning between mouthfuls of Cheerios. "She was sad yesterday, and I think she would be happy if she could come and play."

"Why was she sad yesterday?" I asked.

"She doesn't have very many friends."

"I wonder why," I said. "She seems like a nice girl."

"She's very nice. Some of the kids just say they don't want to play with her 'cause they say she wears boy clothes and they're dirty."

I knew what the kids were talking about. Ever since first grade had started, I'd gone into Mrs. Rawlie's classroom twice a week to do timed readings with the children. It looked like Kelsey was wearing an older boy's hand-me-downs, and they were usually dirty and disheveled. But she was a sweet girl, very quiet and respectful.

"I think inviting her over to play is a great idea." I was happy that Anna had noticed a lonely little girl and wanted to do something for her. I pulled out the school directory, found Kelsey Davies's phone number, and dialed. I smiled across the sunlit table at Anna, and she smiled back brightly. A woman answered the phone. "Hello, is this Kelsey's mom?" I asked.

"Her mom don't live here," the woman answered.

"Oh, is her father there?"

"Stan! Phone!" The woman's voice was loud and sharp as she yelled directly into the mouthpiece. I winced and held the receiver away from my ear a few inches.

A man's voice came on the line. "Yello."

"Hello, is this Kelsey's father?" I asked.

"Shore is," he said.

"This is Susan Weller. My daughter, Anna, goes to school with Kelsey."

"Uh-huh." He sounded bored and distracted.

"We were wondering if Kelsey could come home with Anna after school and play for a while?"

"If Kelsey wants to, it's okay by me."

"All right." I felt suddenly awkward. I didn't know if I should offer more information about myself and where we lived or leave it as it was. He didn't seem to care. "I'll plan on picking them both up after school, and then we'll bring her home around six, if that's okay."

"That'll be fine." We said good-bye. I'd expected him to ask for an address or maybe want to meet me, but he hadn't. I tried not to jump to any conclusions about the kind of parent he was, but it irritated me that he'd be so unconcerned about the after-school whereabouts of his little girl.

After school I parked at the curb in my usual spot and waited for Anna and Kelsey. I smiled as the bell rang and the quiet, empty schoolyard filled with children and noise. Soon I saw Anna and her friend walk out of the first grade door. As I watched them come toward the car, I was surprised at the contrast between the two girls. Anna had on jeans, a long-sleeved pink T-shirt and a denim vest with pink buttons. Her honey-blonde pigtails bounced as she walked, and she had a bright, happy expression on her face. Kelsey was a full head taller than Anna. Her long, brown hair was stringy and uncombed.

Her brown T-shirt had a red dinosaur on the front. It looked like a boy's shirt. It was tucked into a pair of too-large camouflage pants that were rolled up at the bottom and held up by a pink, sparkly belt—a necessity, not a fashion statement. It was chilly outside, and a brisk breeze was blowing. Kelsey's skinny, bare arms were wrapped tightly around herself to ward off the cold. A worn, black backpack was slung over one shoulder. The other strap was torn loose and dragging at her side. When she took it off to get in the car, I saw that there were red and yellow racecars on it.

"Hi, Mom." Anna gave me a big smile. "It's a good thing you drove, 'cause Kelsey doesn't have a jacket."

"I can see that. How are you, Kelsey?" I asked and smiled at her.

"I'm fine." Her voice was quiet, and she didn't meet my eyes.

"It's pretty chilly out there. Did you forget your jacket?"

She continued to keep her eyes lowered, and I had to strain to hear her. "I just have a winter coat, and Starr said I didn't need to wear it out before it even gets to be winter."

"Well, I'm sure we can find something for you to wear if you and Anna want to play outside." I turned the heater up in the car and adjusted the vent so it would reach the backseat before I eased the car into the street. I listened to the girls talk as we drove the few blocks home. Their personalities were so different—Anna cheerful and talkative, Kelsey shy and soft-spoken.

The girls had a great time. They played princess with Anna's dress up clothes and built a castle in her room with chairs and blankets. I cut up apples and cheese, and they ate a feast in the grand dining room. While they played, I went to the basement and rummaged through a few boxes of clothes until I found a zip-up sweatshirt that Grandma Weller had given to Anna on her last birthday. I held it up to look at it. It was still too large for Anna but would probably fit Kelsey just right. It was light pink with a rhinestone star on the front. I carried it upstairs and draped it over a chair in the dining room. When it was time to take Kelsey home, I called Anna to the dining room while Kelsey gathered her backpack and the pictures they'd colored.

"Do you remember this sweatshirt Grandma gave you?" I asked.

"It was too big," she said.

"I know. I think it might still be too big for you, but I think it would fit Kelsey."

"Then we should give it to her." Anna smiled brightly, excited by her good idea.

"Well, since it's yours, why don't you give it to her," I said.

"Okay." She took the soft, pink sweatshirt and headed back to her bedroom. A few minutes later, Kelsey came into the kitchen, wearing the sweatshirt, with the backpack slung over one shoulder. She ran her fingers lightly over the rhinestone star.

"It's just your size," I said.

"Anna said I could have it." Kelsey's voice sounded panicky, and her eyes looked afraid, as though maybe she'd done something wrong.

"I know. I'm glad it fits you. That can keep you warm until it's time to wear your winter coat." I felt a tug at my heart. It made me sad that she seemed so afraid.

"Thank you," she said softly. "It's really pretty. I've never had a pink jacket before."

I gave her a little pat on the back. "You're welcome."

I'd written Kelsey's address from the directory on a slip of paper. I knew the street she lived on. It wasn't too far from ours, but as I looked back and forth from the paper to the numbers on the houses, we got farther and farther away from the area I was familiar with. We left a section of small, tidy homes and moved into an area of businesses. I began to wonder if I had written down the right address. "Kelsey, is this the right way to your house?" I asked.

"It's down there a little farther." She pointed down the road ahead of us. We passed a few older businesses—a taxidermist, a pawn shop, and a couple of bars. After the second bar, we came to three little, rundown houses. There were no numbers to be seen on any of them. The first one had the windows boarded up. "It's that one right there." Kelsey pointed at the third house. On the other side of the house was an empty lot, full of weeds and trash. Beyond that was an old, deserted gas station, the pumps looking rusty and ancient.

Kelsey's house was tiny. It was hard for me to picture a family living in such a cramped space. The walls were covered with gray imitation brick that was peeling away like old wallpaper. The empty frame of a screen door swung in front of a front door of weathered, unpainted wood. A broken front window had been repaired with tape and cardboard. A chain-link fence surrounded the weedy, little yard and a large, dirty dog barked wildly and jumped up against the front fence as we pulled the car up beside it. The dog threw itself against the fence, which had been deformed by the dog's repeated attacks so that it bulged grotesquely. I wondered how long it would take to make a bulge like that. There was no driveway, so I pulled up behind an old green and white Chevy pickup outside the fence. A crumbling sidewalk lined with dirt and weeds led from the front gate to the door. To the left of the sidewalk, several dozen empty beer bottles lay scattered around a few pieces of broken-down, plastic lawn furniture. I had planned to go to the door and introduce myself, but as I watched the dog's frenzied behavior, I knew I wasn't courageous or reckless enough to take on the crazed animal. I was afraid for Kelsey to go near the wild dog, but she seemed to be used to it.

Kelsey climbed out of the car. "Thank you for inviting me," she said. She picked up her backpack and headed for the door.

"You're welcome. You'll have to come again sometime," I said. I waited in front of the house as she opened the gate. The dog jumped wildly in the air beside her as she walked to the front door. She tried to turn the doorknob, but it was locked, so she knocked and waited. She turned to wave at us, and we waved back. After a minute or so, an older boy opened the door and Kelsey went inside. I turned the car around and headed home.

I tried to concentrate on Anna's enthusiastic descriptions of the play date, but it was hard to focus. I was proud of Anna for befriending this poor girl, but I was also worried. I felt guilty for that concern. I didn't want to be a snob. Kelsey seemed to be a sweet girl, but she was from a home very different from Anna's.

"I feel bad, Brent," I told him that night when Anna was in bed. "I'd never let Anna go play at her house."

"Then they'll just have to play here." He seemed far less concerned than I was. But then, he hadn't seen what I'd seen.

"What if they invite her over to play? What do I say?"

"You just invite her over here. It may not even be a problem. Kids at this age have all kinds of friends. Don't worry so much. They may not even want to play together again."

"That's true, I guess."

That proved not to be the case, but it turned out that I didn't need to worry about what I'd say if Anna was invited to Kelsey's house. She never was. But Kelsey became a regular visitor at our house. She came over at least once a week after school. I didn't want to hurt her father's pride and make him angry, but I decided I wanted to do something to improve her situation each time she came. One week, I repaired the strap on her backpack. Another time, we organized her schoolwork into folders, so she wouldn't have a backpack full of loose papers. On one visit, we played beauty shop and washed and brushed the girls' hair. I wanted to trim Kelsey's hair but worried that I might be overstepping my bounds, so instead, we put it in two long braids that she wore to school for the next four days.

I found myself looking at the sale racks for clothes that would fit Kelsey and gave her a few new things to wear. I always told her that they were too big for Anna so she would have an excuse for accepting them if anyone asked. I don't think anyone did. I started to get the feeling that no one noticed Kelsey at her house. No one minded her coming to our house, and it didn't seem to matter at all if she checked in or stayed late. After a few calls to get permission for Kelsey to stay to dinner, her dad said, "You know you don't need to call about this every time. I don't care if she eats with you. I'm giving my okay right now for her to eat with you any time you want her to eat with you." I stopped calling and just fed her whenever she came over.

As time went on, Kelsey grew to trust us, and she wasn't so shy. She'd join in during dinner conversation, tell us about her day at school, and every once in a while she'd even crack a joke. We'd laugh, and she'd look down at her plate with a smile.

As Kelsey became more comfortable with our family, we came to learn more about hers. "So, Kelsey," I said one evening at dinner. "How old is your brother?"

"He's thirteen." She ate a big bite of mashed potatoes.

"Do you know what grade he's in?" Brent asked.

"I don't know. I know he's in junior high. He hates school. He says he wants to drop out as soon as he can, but Starr told my dad that if Dusty drops out of school, Dad should kick him out of the house. So Dad told Dusty to go ahead and drop out if he wants to. That'd give us more room at home. That made Dusty feel bad."

"Does Starr live with you?" I asked.

"Uh-huh." She nodded. "She's my dad's girlfriend."

"Has she lived with you a long time?" I wanted to know more, but I didn't want to make Kelsey feel uncomfortable.

"She moved in the day after Mom left."

"Really," I said. Brent raised his eyebrows. "When was that?"

"A long time ago. I was really little." She took a bite of chicken, unaware or unconcerned that she was revealing family secrets. "Mom moved to Denver 'cause she said Dad was mean and she couldn't live with him for one more minute."

"Do you go visit her?" I asked.

"No. Dad says she doesn't want to see us anymore." She said it with no emotion, and my heart broke for her. What seemed unbearably tragic to me was just an unremarkable fact of life for this young girl. I knew I needed to change the subject. I didn't want to cry in front of the girls.

"Hey, you know what?" I said. "I'm going to take Anna to get her hair trimmed tomorrow after school. Would you like to get yours trimmed too?"

"Really?" Kelsey's eyes grew wide with excitement.

"Sure. But we need to make sure it's okay with your dad. Do you want to call him and see?"

"I sure do," she said. We finished dinner, and Kelsey excitedly called her dad as I cleared the table. Of course, he didn't care, so Anna and Kelsey sat down at the table to sketch out ideas for their new haircuts.

At the salon the next day, the two girls buried their heads in a style book and tried to find their perfect cuts. An hour later, they both walked out with short bobs.

"I guess you won't be wearing pigtails for a while," I said.

"That's okay. I like this," Anna said. She swung her head back and forth, flipping her hair.

"I didn't know I was so pretty," Kelsey said. She quietly stroked her own hair. "Feel how soft it is." She leaned over so that Anna could feel the smooth texture of her hair.

"You haven't had your hair cut for a long time, have you Kelsey?" I asked.

"I don't think I've ever had my hair cut before," she said. The girls loved their haircuts, and I was glad that Kelsey's hair wouldn't look so straggly and stringy.

It didn't take long to realize that Anna and Kelsey's friendship was no passing phase. They were best friends, and I was no longer uncomfortable about it. I didn't need to worry about Anna going to Kelsey's house. She was never invited, and that was fine with me. I liked Kelsey and was happy to think that maybe we were helping her in some small way. And we all enjoyed having her around.

✦

One morning in November, Beth called and wanted to know if she could stop by for a few minutes that afternoon. "Of course," I said, but the serious tone in her voice made me nervous, and for the first time in many months, I remembered the look on her face when I'd picked Anna up after Brent's accident.

When she arrived, we sat down and exchanged a few pleasantries. I dreaded what was coming, but I wanted to get it over with once and for all. Finally she got to the point. "I just don't know what to think, and I wanted your opinion." She twisted her wedding ring around and around on her finger, something I'd seen her do many times when she was about to give a talk in church or teach a lesson. She seemed hesitant to continue, and I became even more apprehensive.

"Beth, is something wrong?" I asked.

"I think so, but I'm not sure what it is or even how to tell you." She continued to twist her ring.

"What is it?" I asked.

Beth let out a long sigh and then continued. "It's Jacob. He's really struggling in school this year, and I don't understand it. He did so well last year with Miss Simmons, but this year he's just having a really hard time. How is Anna doing?"

I chose my words carefully. "She's doing fine."

80

"I've talked to a few parents, and it seems that several of the kids that were in Miss Simmons' class last year are really falling behind this year. I don't know if Mrs. Henderson is a bad teacher or what, but I've been thinking about putting Jacob in Mrs. Rawlie's class after Christmas. I've heard she's a great teacher. I wanted to ask you what you think of her."

I was very uncomfortable with this conversation. I hadn't seen this coming. I'd never expected that the other first grade teacher would be blamed for the children not learning as quickly. It was one thing for Miss Simmons to get accolades because of Anna, but this was different. It just wasn't fair for a teacher to be criticized for her teaching when her teaching wasn't at fault. "I think Mrs. Rawlie is a good teacher," I said, "but I've heard good things about Mrs. Henderson too."

"But Susan, last year Jacob, Alli, Sam, and Mason were all learning so much faster than they are this year. They're all in Mrs. Henderson's class, and they're all struggling." Beth leaned forward in her chair. "But the kids that went to Mrs. Rawlie's class seem to be doing just fine, from what I can tell. I haven't heard a single complaint, and I've heard several of the parents talk about how great their kids are doing. Ben's mom said Mrs. Rawlie's a great teacher."

I didn't know what to say. "I'm sure Mrs. Henderson is a good teacher too." I knew I sounded idiotic. Beth stared at me, her hands finally still, and I didn't know what else to say. I knew the children in Mrs. Rawlie's class were doing better than the other children. They were reading third grade chapter books and were doing double and triple digit addition and subtraction. I could imagine Mrs. Henderson's frustration as she watched the other class move ahead quickly while the children in her class were average.

Beth sat back in the chair, deflated. "You know, Susan, we're friends," she said. I could hear a slight tremor in her voice. "You could at least pretend to care about my dilemma."

"I do care. Of course I care. I just don't know what to say about it," I said. I felt terrible that I'd hurt her feelings.

"Do you think I should try to change him to the other class or not?" Her voice was stronger. She was challenging me.

"If you think that would help, maybe you should," I said. I hated myself for saying the words. I felt like a lousy friend, and I felt like I was betraying Mrs. Henderson, even though I didn't know her. She seemed like a nice lady who was trying hard. It even occurred to me that maybe I should have Anna transferred to her class, but what reason could I possibly give? And that would focus more attention on Anna than we wanted. Then I remembered that if I moved Anna, she'd no longer be with Kelsey. She wouldn't like that at all. I didn't know what to say. I wished I could talk to Brent before I said anything else. He could help me figure out how to handle this. But Brent wasn't there, and Beth was looking at me, wanting me to be a caring friend. I wanted to be a good friend, but I knew too much to be able to have this conversation without feeling like I was a liar. I took a deep breath and let it out slowly.

"Beth, of course you should do what you think is best for Jacob. That's what any good parent does. I'm just not sure if Mrs. Rawlie is a better teacher than Mrs. Henderson, and I'd hate for you to move him and then regret it later. That's all."

"I'm sorry, Susan. I didn't mean to put you on the spot. It's just that I can't figure out why Jacob's having such a hard time. The only difference I can see between the kids that are struggling and those that are doing great is that some went to Mrs. Rawlie and some went to Mrs. Henderson. I don't know what to think." Of course, I knew what the difference really was, and as much as I wanted to discourage Beth from drawing the wrong conclusion, I knew I couldn't do it without upsetting her. But if she did have Jacob change classes—if any of the parents switched their children to the other class—it would reflect badly on Mrs. Henderson. When the children's school performance suddenly improved, it would look like Mrs. Henderson really was a bad teacher. I felt sick to my stomach.

"Thanks, Susan." Beth stood up to leave. "I just needed to talk to someone about it. You're a good friend, and since Anna's in the same grade, I just . . ." Her voice trailed off, and she gave me a hug. I blinked hard to hold back my tears. I felt like a terrible person. I wasn't sure how all of this was going to play out, but I knew it wouldn't end well. I leaned against the front door and listened to Beth's car start and pull out of the driveway. The sound hadn't completely faded before the tears were sliding down my cheeks.

"Brent, what are we going to do?" I asked him that night after Anna was in bed. My conversation with Beth had worried me the rest of the day. Brent had looked troubled when I'd told him of Beth's visit, and his expression gave me no comfort now. I'd hoped he'd know what to do. I'd been counting on that all day. But he looked just as lost as I felt. Completely overwhelmed by the enormity of the situation, I broke down and started to cry again. For the thousandth time, I wondered if we were doing what we were supposed to be doing with Anna. I thought of Mrs. Henderson as I'd seen her just last week, lining the first graders up for lunch, patient and cheerful. I wanted to protect her from the storm of injustice that was heading her way.

Brent put his arms around me and held me close while I cried. "I don't know what to do," I said between sobs.

"I don't either. I never realized Anna's gift would have a bad effect on anyone else," he said. "I just don't know what we can do to fix it."

✦

We did nothing. Not because we didn't want to, but because we had no idea what to do. After the Christmas break, Jacob and a little girl named Alexa transferred from Mrs. Henderson's class to Mrs. Rawlie's. Of course, none of the parents wanted to take their child out of Mrs. Rawlie's class. We didn't want to call attention to Anna by taking her out of one class and putting her in another, and we didn't want to separate her from Kelsey. My heart ached when I thought about what was going to happen.

Almost immediately, Jacob and Alexa began to improve, and in just a few weeks, they had caught up with the rest of the class. Beth was thrilled. She told everyone about Jacob's wonderful new teacher and the difference she had made. She even thanked me for helping her make the decision to change Jacob to Mrs. Rawlie's class. I smiled and congratulated her, but I did it with a heavy heart because of what I knew.

I continued to volunteer each week in Mrs. Rawlie's class, but every time I'd see Mrs. Henderson in the hall or look into her class and see her there teaching, a wave of guilt would come over me. A couple of times I left the school with tears of helplessness and frustration burning my eyes. I couldn't stand it anymore. I had to do something.

One afternoon, after I'd finished reading with Mrs. Rawlie's class, I walked by Mrs. Henderson's open door. I glanced inside and saw her explaining subtraction problems on the chalkboard. I kept walking, my heart breaking, until I reached the front door of the school. I stood at the door for several seconds, an idea taking shape. Then I turned around and walked purposefully back to Mrs. Henderson's classroom. I knocked on the open door, and she turned and looked at me, a question on her face.

"Could I talk to you for just a minute?" I asked. I smiled at the twenty-four curious young faces that had turned to look at me.

"See if you can figure this one out," Mrs. Henderson said to the students. She walked to the door. "What can I help you with?" Up close her face looked tired and worried. I couldn't help feeling that some of her sadness was the result of the trials she had faced that year, trials I had inadvertently contributed to.

"Mrs. Henderson, I'm Susan Weller. I was just wondering if you could use an extra volunteer to read with your class or help them with math. I'd love to come in and help one day a week with anything you need. Anything at all."

She seemed confused and maybe a little defensive, but she quickly responded. "Do you have a child in my class?" she asked.

"I don't. My daughter is in Mrs. Rawlie's class. I just have some extra time each week and thought maybe you could use me." I knew this was an unusual offer, and when I saw confusion on her face, I wondered if I'd made a mistake. I didn't want to make her feel worse.

"Well, sure, we can always use an extra volunteer." I smiled and let out the breath I'd been unconsciously holding. The rest of the school year, I spent one afternoon a week helping Mrs. Henderson's class. She really was a good teacher. I watched her work patiently and kindly with the children. She expressed her appreciation to me several times, but I knew that what I was doing was more for me than for anyone else. It did make me feel a little better, even though I felt sad at how unfair it all was for this good woman.

✴

In March, Mrs. Rawlie's class had a special "Dads and Donuts" party. The children in the class were invited to bring their fathers to school for the morning. Each child would read a book to their father and then the fathers would spotlight each of the children. Brent took the morning off to be with Anna. Mrs. Rawlie asked if I would come and help serve the juice and donuts.

I stood at a table in the back of the room, where I filled cups with orange juice and arranged sprinkled donuts on plates. I watched as the room filled up with children and their fathers. Of course, a few of the dads couldn't come, and I saw a couple of children had arrived with what looked like a grandfather. Abbott Brower came with an uncle because his dad was in the military, and a little girl named Chloe brought her mom. The children settled in around the room to read their fathers a story. I watched for Kelsey, anxious to see what Stan Davies looked like. Just before the bell rang, Kelsey walked in alone and stopped to talk to Mrs. Rawlie. Mrs. Rawlie leaned toward Kelsey, listened carefully, and then stood up and surveyed the room. Brent had been watching the same thing, and I saw him motion toward Mrs. Rawlie, inviting Kelsey to come join him and Anna. Mrs. Rawlie nodded appreciatively as Kelsey sat down by Brent.

After they'd read a book together, Brent, Anna, and Kelsey came back for donuts and juice. "How was your book?" I asked.

"It was great," Anna said. "It's my favorite book. You know the one about feeling silly and all those funny moods."

"I like that one too." I handed her a napkin. "Did your dad have to work this morning?" I asked Kelsey.

"No. He said I should ride the bus, and he'd come when he finished getting ready. He's probably just a little late." She looked toward the door.

"She's just sitting with us until he comes." Brent sounded convincing, although I could tell by the look he gave me that he had his doubts about Kelsey's father showing up. They returned to their seats, and each father was invited to share something about his child.

I watched as the dads or their substitutes stood and shared interesting facts about their children. The children loved it. They hung on every word as they looked up at their dads. Kelsey twisted her hair around her finger as she craned her neck and watched the door, hoping her father would come.

The boy and his father next to Anna stood. "This is Ryan," the man said. "He loves sports. We like to go out in the yard and throw the baseball or football. He has a pretty good arm on him. He's also very fast. Sometimes he beats his older brother when they race, and he's almost two years older than Ryan." Ryan beamed as they sat back down.

Brent and Anna stood when it was their turn. Brent held Anna's hand while he spoke, and she looked up at her dad with adoring eyes. "This is my daughter, Anna. She's a very special girl. She is cheerful all the time and always wants the people around her to be happy. One of her favorite things is to help her mom make cookies, and she makes the most delicious chocolate chip cookies you've ever tasted. We love having Anna in our family." They sat down, and he kissed the back of her hand before he let it go. She smiled and scooted back in her chair happily, thrilled with the nice things her Dad had said. Kelsey was next. She was watching the door with a worried expression.

"Kelsey, do you think your father might still make it?" Mrs. Rawlie asked.

"He said he'd come," Kelsey said, a hint of desperation in her voice.

"Then we'll go on to Ben and come back to you in a few minutes," she said.

"Okay." Kelsey let out a sigh of relief. I got angry as I watched Kelsey check the door for her father. He wasn't coming, of that I was sure. She was practically sitting on the edge of her seat as she waited for the father who'd said he'd be there, while he probably had no intention of coming. Once again, I tried to stop myself from judging Mr. Davies harshly. After all, I'd never even met the man. But that was part of the problem. Kelsey had been to our home dozens of times, and I'd still never met her father. I couldn't fathom such a lack of interest. I tried to convince myself that maybe he had planned to come and something really had come up. But inside I didn't believe it.

The rest of the fathers introduced their children, and Mrs. Rawlie looked back at Kelsey, unsure what to do. At that moment,

I thought my heart would burst with love for Brent as he stood and pulled Kelsey to her feet. Then he put his hand on her shoulder. "This is Kelsey," he started. "I'm not actually her father, but since he can't make it this morning, I'd be proud to introduce her. One of the great things about Kelsey is that she has really good manners. She always says please and thank you and she's always willing to pitch in and help with anything that needs doing. Kelsey is a smart girl and loves to read. She is a wonderful young lady, and we're very glad she's our friend." He squeezed her shoulder when he finished, and they sat back down. Kelsey sat back in her chair, a smile on her face. She wasn't worried anymore. Mrs. Rawlie smiled at Brent appreciatively. So did I.

When the party was over, Brent left for the high school, and I finished cleaning up with Garrett's mother. Stan Davies never came.

Chapter 6

From Anna's journal:

Today we had a spelling test. Miss Winters said she was giving us 4th grade words because we're so good at spelling. Everyone got them all right. She said she's never heard of that before. She kept shaking her head and smiling at us.

✦

Second grade brought with it more of the same anxieties. Who would end up in Anna's class? What difficulties might we encounter? I tried not to spend too much time worrying about the things I couldn't control. While there were some concerns that were always close to the surface, we knew we were blessed with a very happy little girl. That was the most important thing.

We were happy that Anna and Kelsey were in the same class, and I breathed a little sigh of relief that Jacob had also been assigned to Miss Winters.

In October, the school held a talent show. Anna was looking at the audition form for the talent show when she asked, "Mom, do I have a talent?"

"Of course, you do. Everyone has a talent."

"What could I do in a talent show?" she asked.

"Well, you can sing."

"I don't really want to sing. That would be too embarrassing."

"But you have a really pretty voice," I said.

"I really don't want to sing, not in front of everyone. I'd be too scared." She had a look of panic in her eyes.

"You could draw a picture."

"Well, I don't think so," she said. "I don't think I'll do a talent," she said after a few more minutes.

"Are you sure? I'm sure we can think of something," I said.

"I'll just watch the talent show this year, and maybe it will give me an idea about what talent I want to learn for next year."

"All right. That's probably a good idea."

Several days later, I pulled up to the curb after school to wait for Anna. I smiled as she ran to the car much faster than usual, a huge smile on her face. "Mom, I've picked my talent," she said.

"Really? What did you decide?" I tried not to laugh at her enthusiasm.

"I want to play the piano."

"That's a great idea," I said. Bev and I had taken piano lessons as children, but neither of us had enough patience to put in the necessary practice time. Bev complained first and loudest and was allowed to quit after only one year. I lasted two and a half years—not long enough to be any good but long enough to be the recipient of the family piano when my parents moved to a smaller house. I was pleased that the lonely piano in our front room would finally get some attention.

"Mom, you should have seen it. A girl from fifth grade played the piano in the talent show," Anna said. "Her fingers were moving so fast you could hardly see them, and it sounded so good. Everybody clapped and clapped, and some people even stood up. Can I play the piano? Please?"

"If you take piano lessons, you have to practice every day," I said. Strange how I heard my mother's voice instead of my own.

"That's okay. I want to practice every day. I want to practice ten times a day."

"I'll talk to Dad and see what he thinks." I hoped her enthusiasm would last longer than mine had.

That night, I talked to Brent about piano lessons.

"You know, we might run into some of the same problems we've faced in everything else. If she learns it as quickly as she learns everything else, it might raise a few eyebrows."

"They'll just think she's a piano prodigy," I said. I'd already thought that through. "And piano lessons will be private, so a lot of other kids won't be affected. It will just be Anna. Besides, we can't tell her no on things like this. It's normal for kids to take piano lessons and play soccer or dance. Are we going to tell her she can't do any of these normal things because she might be really good at them?"

Brent laughed. "I'm not saying she can't take piano lessons. I just think we need to have our eyes open when we jump into things like this."

"My eyes are open. If she wants to play piano, I think we should let her."

Brent agreed, and the next day I made some phone calls in search of a piano teacher. What started out as an exciting prospect turned out to be very discouraging. In fact, I began to get more and more annoyed with myself that I hadn't taken piano lessons seriously. There was a terrible shortage of piano teachers, and most that I found weren't taking any new students.

"I'm sorry, I'm completely full. I even have a couple of kids on a waiting list," the fifth piano teacher I called told me.

"Is there anyone you could refer me to?" I asked.

"You know, you might want to give Mildred Thompson a call," she said. "I don't know if she teaches anymore, but if she does, she might have an opening." She gave me the phone number, which I immediately dialed.

"Hello." The woman who answered the phone sounded very old.

"Hi. Is this Mildred Thompson?"

"Why, yes it is."

"My name is Susan Weller. I was told you might be willing to give my daughter piano lessons."

"Well, dear, I actually retired from teaching piano several years ago." Her voice had a charming, singsong quality.

"I see," I said, disappointed. "Is there anyone you could recommend? My daughter wants to take piano lessons, and I'm having a terrible time finding a teacher."

"Oh dear. That's too bad." I could tell she meant it. "How old is your daughter?"

"She's seven. She'll be eight in a few months."

"Hmm." Mildred was quiet for a moment. "You know, dear, I could probably teach her. The truth is, I miss teaching, and I don't think one student would be too difficult. You know, there was a time when I had sixty-five students. But that was a long time ago. Oh my, that was a lot of students, wasn't it?" She sounded as if she were just now realizing it herself. "Does she read, dear?"

"She does. She's actually a very good reader."

"That's good. It's much easier for them if they know how to read. I always recommend that they be able to read pretty well before they start piano. If you start a child before that, it can be quite confusing for them, and then they don't enjoy it. And if they don't enjoy it, they'll never be very good. Can you bring her on Thursday after school?"

"I sure can. Thank you so much, Mrs. Thompson," I said.

"Oh please, dear, call me Mildred."

"All right. Thanks, Mildred."

⁂

Anna was thrilled when I gave her the good news. Several times in the next few days she sat down at the piano and composed her own pieces as she "practiced" the piano.

Thursday came, and we drove to Mildred's home after school. It was a small, white house in an older section of town. The street was neat and tidy with big shade trees in every front yard. Along her small driveway was a fence overgrown with grapevines. It took a couple of minutes for her to answer her front door. Mildred extended her gnarled hand when we introduced ourselves. "Why don't you come in and join us for the lesson," she said. I took a seat in an old recliner and watched Anna take her first piano lesson.

Mildred was a stooped, round woman with hair the color of rain clouds. Her living room was filled with trinkets, knickknacks, and sheet music. Music books were stacked on chairs and tables. The top of her grand piano was covered with pictures and cards. An organ sat in one corner of the room, covered with piles of still more music.

An enormous, old cat lazily slept on a pillow under the piano. On the wall hung certificates, a bachelors of music, a masters of music, and a doctorate degree in music. It was clear Mildred knew what she was doing. We'd hit the jackpot.

Anna was a model student. She paid close attention to everything Mildred told her. Toward the end of the lesson, Mildred played a song for Anna, a catchy piece with a quick tempo that had Anna clapping at the end. I found it amazing that those old, knotted fingers could move so easily over the piano keys. After the lesson, Mildred and I talked for a few minutes while Anna played with the cat. I'd guessed her to be in her seventies and was surprised to find out that she was actually ninety-two years old. She had taught high school choir and orchestra for more than fifty years and had taught private piano lessons for nearly seventy years. She had stopped giving private lessons only four years ago but seemed happy to have a student again. She tugged on a lock of Anna's hair as we left and reminded her to be sure to practice what she'd learned today. "Perfect practice makes perfect music," she said as we walked out the front door.

"I think she's going to be just what Anna needs," I told Brent that evening. "But I don't know how long she'll be around to teach. She's ninety-two years old."

Brent let out a whistle. "I guess we should just be glad to have her as long as we do," he said.

Unlike Bev and me, Anna threw herself into piano lessons with real enthusiasm. She willingly practiced every day. When it was time to leave for school in the morning, I'd find her by the sound of her small fingers plinking away at the piano keys. I started waking her up fifteen minutes earlier so she could practice before school. Most days, she was hardly in the door before her backpack was on the floor beside the piano bench and she was practicing her assignment. She learned quickly, as we'd suspected she would, and each week Mildred was astonished at her progress.

A lovely friendship blossomed between Anna and this charming old lady, and Anna looked forward to her lessons each week. She always asked if we could take Mildred a plate of cookies or a little bag of Enstrom's toffee, Mildred's favorite treat. I could tell that Mildred looked forward to the lessons just as much as Anna did. She always wore a little red lipstick, slightly smeared, which was out of place with her housedresses, but I figured it meant she was ready to greet company.

One afternoon, when Kelsey had come to play, Anna excitedly performed a new piano piece for her. I listened from the kitchen as Kelsey encouraged her to play another song and then another. Kelsey was a very appreciative audience and clapped enthusiastically after each song.

I turned on the television and watched the news while I prepared dinner. When it was time to sit down and eat, I called up the stairs for Anna and Kelsey to come to dinner. "We're in here," Anna said, and I stepped around the corner into the living room. There sat Kelsey on the piano bench. Anna sat beside her on a chair. "We're having a piano lesson," Anna said.

"You're teaching Kelsey how to play the piano?" I asked.

"Yes, but she doesn't have a piano to practice on at her house, so she'll have to practice when she comes here," Anna said.

"Is that okay?" Kelsey asked.

"Of course it is," I said. "I guess that just means you'll have to come over more often." Kelsey and Anna looked at each other and grinned.

I'm not sure why I was surprised at what took place in the coming months. I should have expected it. Anna's piano playing progressed quickly, surprising Mildred, who said she'd never seen anyone pick it up so fast in all her years of teaching. I smiled to myself as I realized how amazed she would be if she knew that Kelsey was learning almost as fast as Anna—with limited practice time and with Anna as her teacher.

One day in February, while I was mixing up a batch of biscuits, the phone rang. "Mrs. Weller, this is Miss Winters at the school." I was instantly concerned.

"Hi, is everything okay?"

"Yes, everything's fine. I just had a quick question. This morning we had music appreciation, and the music teacher asked the children if any of them played a musical instrument. Anna raised her hand and said she takes piano lessons, so Mrs. Crowley asked her if she'd like to play something for the class. She played an impressive little song, and then Mrs. Crowley asked if there was anyone else. Kelsey Davies surprised us all by raising her hand and saying she played the piano too. Then she played a song. I asked her when she started taking piano lessons, and she told me that Anna is teaching her. I figured she must be confused. Is she taking lessons from you?"

Oh boy, I thought, smiling. "I don't actually play the piano well enough to teach lessons. Anna is studying with a really good piano teacher, and after her lesson, she teaches Kelsey what she's learned." I cringed as I said it, knowing how outlandish it sounded. I was glad Miss Winters couldn't see my face. I hated having to tell her what was going on, but I couldn't lie about it.

"Wow," she said. After an awkward pause, she continued, "Well, I didn't mean to bother you, but I wanted to check because I do have parents ask me on occasion if I know of any piano teachers, and I was going to refer them to you." She laughed a nervous little laugh, and I wished at that moment that I could read her mind. "I'm sure the mothers would think I was crazy if I referred them to Anna."

"They probably would," I said.

"Well, I guess I should go. My lunch break is almost over."

"Thank you for calling," I said, and I stifled a giggle as I hung up.

From Anna's journal:

> *I think there's something wrong with me. Mom and Dad thought I was in bed, but I was really getting a drink, and I heard them talking in the bedroom. I heard Dad say it isn't my fault that I'm different. I didn't know what he meant, so I stood by the door and listened. Mom sounded like she was crying, and Dad was telling her everything will be okay. Mom said she doesn't know what to do. She said she wishes she understood why I have to be different. How am I different? I don't know if it's bad, but if it makes Mom cry, how can it be good? I wanted to ask them, but I felt too scared.*

Kelsey came after school about three nights a week, and sometimes she'd come over on Saturday, as well. I found it hard to believe that her family didn't want her at home more, but I guess they didn't mind if other people helped their daughter with her homework, gave her piano lessons, and fed her dinner, so long as it didn't put them out or cost them anything. Occasionally, I'd speak with her father, but most of the time it was Starr who answered the phone and gave her permission. When we drove Kelsey home, we seldom saw anyone there, though sometimes her older brother would be in the yard with friends. They'd be sitting on the broken-down plastic chairs, usually smoking. Strangely, I still hadn't ever seen her father.

During the summer after second grade, Grandpa and Grandma Weller drove from Denver in their motor home and picked us up. We'd been planning to take a trip with them ever since the summer of Brent's accident, but for one reason or another, it had never happened. This year, we were going to Disneyland. But we made the mistake of telling Anna about the trip several months in advance. I'd forgotten that when you're young, months feel like years. The only thing that dampened her excitement was that Kelsey wouldn't be coming with us. "Mom, please, please, please, please can we take Kelsey to Disneyland?" Anna begged for the twentieth time. "I'm sure she'd be really good."

"I'm sure she would, Anna, and I wish we could, but Dad and I don't think her parents would like the idea." I felt a pang of guilt when we said good-bye to Kelsey the night before we left. I wished I felt comfortable enough to ask her father to let her come with us, but in spite of their willingness to have Kelsey spend so much time at our house, something made me feel that Mr. Davies wouldn't be too pleased about sending his daughter to California with strangers.

We had a wonderful time. Brent and his dad took turns driving the motor home. We watched movies, and Grandpa and Anna played chess. In a small town in California, Brent and Grandpa Weller took Anna to the park while Grandma Weller and I spent a couple of hours in a little quilt shop. We stopped at a campground with a heated swimming pool and ate roasted marshmallows until we thought we'd be sick.

Brent had gone to Disneyland as a child, but this was the first time for Anna and me. We stayed at an RV park half an hour from Disneyland. We spent three days taking pictures with Mickey and

Minnie, riding the rides, and enjoying the parades. Anna insisted that we ride "It's a Small World" until we could sing it in all the different languages. Brent and Grandpa gave up after six rides, but Grandma, Anna, and I had memorized the entire song by the end of the third day. Anna loved the parades, and we had to see every parade every day we were there. Each morning we caught the first shuttle to Disneyland and each evening we caught the last shuttle back to the RV park.

On the first day, Anna searched for just the right present to take home to Kelsey. "We don't have to pick it out today, Anna," I told her. "We're going to be here for three days." I soon realized, though, that we wouldn't really enjoy the park until she'd found Kelsey's gift, so Anna and I visited several gift shops in the park on a quest for the perfect gift. Nothing was quite right, and we were soon referred to the largest Disney shop near the entrance. We looked at dolls and snow globes, hats and princess dresses. "Anna, you really need to choose. We can't stay in here all day."

"I know, but I just don't know what to get her," she said. "It has to be just right."

"I think Kelsey will be happy with anything you choose," I said. Finally, she decided to get her a Belle doll because it had brown hair like Kelsey's and a beautiful yellow dress. The clerk packaged it carefully for traveling, and we finally left the store. We were now free to enjoy the park. It was an exciting few days.

We were exhausted as we rode the shuttle back to the motor home on our last evening. I looked at Anna, who had fallen asleep with her head on my lap, and smiled. The warm day finally cooled down, and even though it had been a delightful day, my feet hurt and most of the passengers on the shuttle had a blank too-much-happiest-place-on-earth expression on their faces. I looked back from the shuttle as the lights on Cinderella's castle receded into the distance. It had been fun, but I was relieved that we would be heading home in the morning and not back to the park. "You Ain't Never Had a Friend Like Me" played over the speakers on the shuttle, and a couple of tired guests chatted quietly. Anna stirred, and I looked down at her, surprised to find her big, blue eyes open and fixed on me. I smiled at her, and she smiled back.

"Mom, next time we come, can we pretty please bring Kelsey? She's never seen anything so wonderful in her whole life."

Touched by her thoughtfulness, I nodded my head. "Next time we come, we'll ask her dad," I said. Satisfied, Anna closed her eyes and fell peacefully back to sleep.

Two days later, I watched Anna give Kelsey the doll. She handed it over carefully, as if it were the most precious of possessions, and Kelsey tenderly held it in her arms. She carried it around with her all afternoon. She adjusted the yellow dress and stroked the long, dark hair. Kelsey loved her doll. Anna had definitely picked the perfect gift. That evening, as I watched her carry the doll into that little, rundown house, I felt happy that she'd have something pretty to look at in her room.

★

In August, we received the letter telling us that Anna's third grade teacher would be Mrs. Bateman. An hour later, we picked up Kelsey for a play date.

"Who's your teacher?" Anna asked, excitedly.

"Mrs. Black," Kelsey answered, and I watched Anna's face fall in the rearview mirror. "Who's yours?" Kelsey asked. She nervously studied Anna's expression.

"Mrs. Bateman," she said quietly.

"Oh," Kelsey said, and the two girls sat silently in the backseat. When I pulled into our driveway and put the car in park, I turned around to look at the girls. They were holding hands and both had tears in their eyes.

I smiled and tried to muster a happy voice. "It'll be okay, girls," I said. Neither girl could manage a smile in return, and neither of them believed it would be okay.

"I think we should call and talk to the principal," Brent said when I told him they had different teachers. I was surprised. As a teacher, Brent was especially sensitive to the challenges of school authorities and knew that parents often made unreasonable demands. I was surprised that he had suggested this.

"What would we tell him?" I asked.

"We'll tell him about Kelsey. Anna will be okay wherever they put her, but Kelsey . . ." He paused and gathered his thoughts. "Kelsey needs to be with Anna," he said. "We'll go talk to him together."

I don't think the principal, Mr. Giles, would have given us the time of day if Brent hadn't been a teacher at the high school. He looked at us, puzzled, and then asked us why we wanted to have one of the girls moved. "You know, they're both excellent teachers," he said. He sounded defensive, and I wondered if it had anything to do with the difficulties Anna had unknowingly caused in the first and second grades.

"It has nothing to do with the teachers," I assured him. "It's Kelsey. You can put them in either class. We'd just like them to be together."

"Kelsey's not even your child," he said, "and I'm not in the practice of rearranging classes to accommodate friendships."

"You're right. Kelsey's not our child," Brent said, "but she comes to our house at least three times a week, and Susan is the only adult who helps her with homework and reading. We don't know everything about her home life, but we do know she spends a lot of time with us, and I'm afraid if they're not in the same class, her schoolwork will suffer."

"I see," Mr. Giles said. He thoughtfully rested his arms on the table, tapping his fingers together in a little pyramid. "Do Kelsey's parents know you're requesting this change?"

"Her mother isn't around. We haven't spoken to her father about it, but we're pretty sure he doesn't care what class she's in." I could tell Brent had chosen his words carefully. He didn't want to badmouth Mr. Davies, but it was important that Mr. Giles understand at least a part of Kelsey's situation.

We waited quietly for a few moments while Mr. Giles mulled it over, and then Brent continued. "We just want to be sure Kelsey is okay, and if they aren't in the same class, it will be much harder. They're good students and won't be disruptive. Please think about it." Brent stood, took my hand, and pulled me to my feet. I was terribly disappointed that we'd failed. As we walked to the door, I tried to blink back the tears, but they stubbornly filled my eyes and slid down my cheeks.

"Mr. and Mrs. Weller?" I quickly brushed the tears away with the back of my hand as we turned around. "I appreciate your concern for

Kelsey. We are aware of some of the challenges she faces." He paused and studied his tapping fingers. I held my breath. "I'm going to move Kelsey to Mrs. Bateman's class, but I'm going to request that you please keep this information private. For some reason, it seems that the last few years it has been nearly impossible to keep parents happy with their children's assigned teachers. I've had to get pretty strict about moving children around, so even though I understand your concern for Kelsey, and I want to help out, I don't want other parents to think that they can request teacher changes for frivolous reasons, and that includes friendships."

"We understand," Brent said. "We won't mention it to anyone. And thank you."

"Very well," Mr. Giles said. Brent stepped back and shook his hand. "I'll have Miss Standish send a letter informing Kelsey's family of the change."

★

At the end of August, Anna and Kelsey started the third grade with Mrs. Bateman. I had a bad feeling when Beth told me Jacob was in Mrs. Black's class, but I knew there was nothing I could do. That year, I volunteered to be the classroom parent representative for the PTA. This meant I had monthly meetings with the PTA presidency and the other classroom representatives. The meetings were usually rather dull and uneventful. Most discussions revolved around things like fund-raisers, teacher recognition, and the weekly birthday table, so I was surprised when I walked into the school library for November's meeting and saw the large number of people already seated. I sat down on a metal folding chair about halfway back and waited for the meeting to begin. As I thumbed through my notebook, I overheard unsettling bits of conversations that were taking place around me.

"If we can't get competent teachers, maybe we should take our kids out of the school and send them somewhere else. What would they do then?" one mother said.

"What is it about this group of kids? It seems like every year one class excels and the other class struggles. I don't understand."

My stomach tightened up in knots, and I had an overwhelming urge to get up and leave. *Not again*, I thought. Would this never end?

"Hi, Susan," Beth said. She sat down next to me.

"Hi, Beth. I didn't expect to see you here."

"There are some problems with Mrs. Black, so I wanted to be here," she said. She looked around the room.

"What kind of problems?" I suspected I already knew what they were, though I hadn't heard anything until that day.

"I'm just not sure if she's a very good teacher, which makes me sad. She's a really sweet lady, but the kids just aren't learning very well."

"That's too bad," I said. I felt a little short of breath. The PTA president stood to call the meeting to order. The treasurer gave a report on the fall fund-raiser. The head of the committee over the Christmas program sent around a sign-up sheet for volunteers to help with programs and decorations. Then the PTA president stood. She took a deep breath and let it out slowly, appearing to stall for a moment before finally speaking. "A few concerns have been brought to our attention, and I can see from the number of parents we have here that this matter is far-reaching. I've asked the principal to be here to help address this issue. Jane Atherton was the first to bring this to our attention, and she has asked if she could take a few minutes, so I'll turn the time over to you, Jane."

I didn't know Jane Atherton. I'd seen her at school activities a few times but had never spoken to her. She was a large woman with a friendly, cheerful face, so the harshness of her tone and words surprised me. "Some of us have third grade students in Mrs. Black's class, and we're very frustrated with the poor job she is doing. Our kids are bright kids with good grades to prove it, and they're just not learning. The other class is significantly further along in math. The children in Mrs. Black's class haven't even passed off all their times tables yet. These kids just aren't getting it, and the obvious thing they have in common is Mrs. Black. Our kids deserve to have a competent teacher." I winced as Mrs. Atherton sat down.

"Are there other parents with these same feelings?" the PTA president asked. A low rumble of voices filled the room. Several parents raised their hands to show their agreement. One of them was Beth. "This is a difficult situation," the PTA president continued. "Mr. Giles will now field some of your questions. Hopefully we can get this resolved. Mr. Giles?" Mr. Giles stood, and the PTA president quickly returned to her seat. She seemed uncomfortable with what was happening and happy for someone else to take over.

Mr. Giles cleared his throat and straightened his jacket uncomfortably before he began. "First, I'd like to make one thing clear. We are very interested in what each of you has to say, but this matter needs to be handled in an orderly and respectful way. Mrs. Black has been teaching here for more than ten years, and there have never been any complaints about her before. She has a spotless record. Her teaching has never before been called into question. Nevertheless, we intend to investigate this situation thoroughly. We want to find solutions, but it would be unfair and indecent to cast aspersions on Mrs. Black without solid proof of any wrongdoing. Now, I'd like to encourage those of you who want to share your concerns to do so. Then, I'd ask for your patience as we try to figure out what to do." Several hands went up, and Mr. Giles pointed to a tall man with a neatly trimmed goatee on the front row. He stood.

"Mr. Giles, I don't want to be unfair to Mrs. Black, but it seems that in the four years that Mason has been at this school, it's always either hot or cold. He's either learning like crazy and way above average, or he's falling behind. I know we can't blame that all on Mrs. Black, since he's had other teachers in other grades, but I would like to have an explanation. I just don't get it." He sat down, shaking his head, and Mr. Giles pointed to a woman toward the back.

"He's right. In kindergarten and first grade, Ashley was getting excellent grades. But in second and third, her grades have been average, even below average in some subjects. The only thing we can figure is that certain teachers must be better. But when we talk to the school about putting our children in the classes with the best teachers, we get told no. What are we supposed to do?" Several people around the room nodded their heads in agreement, and I wondered how many times Mr. Giles had been approached with requests to change classes. A wave of relief flooded through me as I realized how lucky we were that he'd allowed Anna and Kelsey to be together. Then I felt guilty. The problems these teachers and poor Mr. Giles were facing were because of Anna, and there was no fair way to fix them.

Three more parents voiced their concerns, and then Mr. Giles nodded to Beth. She stood up, and I felt uncomfortable as every eye in the room turned in our direction. I looked at my hands and nervously capped and uncapped my pen. I said a silent prayer for Mrs. Black and endured my feelings of guilt.

"Mr. Giles," Beth began. "I don't know what the answer is. I have a twelve-year-old son, and his education has gone pretty smoothly. He's an average student, but he's stayed an average student. Jacob's education has been such a roller coaster. One year is great and he loves school, and then he has a hard year. He loves Mrs. Black. She's a very nice lady, but something isn't working. It's hard for the kids to feel smart and then stupid and then smart and then stupid." Beth paused, and when she spoke again, her voice trembled with emotion. My heart ached for the pain and frustration of these parents, who wanted what was best for their children and for Mrs. Black, who had done nothing wrong and yet was the object of such withering criticism. "I don't even know if it's Mrs. Black's fault," Beth continued. "I'm just confused and want some sort of explanation."

"I think we understand your concerns now," Mr. Giles said. "I share your confusion. We've looked at this group of children and their records since kindergarten, and it is difficult to find an explanation for the inconsistent performance." At this revelation, my guilt began to turn to panic. If they had studied these classes, how long would it be before they figured out the common denominator in all the classes that did well? "One thing I will say, it doesn't appear to be a failure in teaching. As you've said yourselves, the same child does extremely well one year and performs only adequately the next, and it certainly doesn't seem reasonable to believe that we have one good and one bad teacher in every grade. Please remember that the children you suspect are falling behind are actually performing very normally. Just know that we want to get to the bottom of this problem as quickly and fairly as possible, but right now we are as confused as you are. I would urge anyone with any ideas regarding this matter to please make an appointment with me so we can discuss possible solutions at our next meeting. In the meantime, please be patient with our teachers. I've spoken to Mrs. Black, and she's just as puzzled and concerned as all of you are. She's anxious to work with you parents to help your children, so don't hesitate to speak with her. But, please, let's be productive and helpful to each other. Groundless attacks on the characters of good teachers won't do anything to remedy the problem. Thank you for your attendance here today." Mr. Giles left the room, and the PTA president concluded the meeting. Around me, parents talked and commiserated.

"You've sure been lucky," Beth said to me.

"What do you mean?" I felt guilty as I realized I was trying to sound confused.

"Anna's had good teachers every year. She's never been in one of the struggling classes, has she?" My guilty conscience made Beth's voice sound accusatory to my ears.

"I guess she hasn't," I said. For a brief, terrifying moment, I thought Beth was going to follow this line of thinking to the correct conclusion. If Beth figured out the difference Anna made, who would she tell? Visions of Anna as the rope in a tug-of-war being pulled apart by frustrated parents and teachers flashed through my mind.

"How have you lucked out? Have you ever requested a teacher?"

"Not for Anna," I said.

"Maybe I just need to make sure Jacob is in Anna's class." Beth laughed halfheartedly. "She must be charmed."

"Jacob's a smart boy. I'm sure he's going to be fine, Beth." I tried to reassure her. I didn't want her to think I was brushing her off or that I lacked concern for her plight. The last thing I needed was to get on Beth's bad side now or to arouse her suspicions.

"He does fine. It isn't that he's failing or anything. It's just such a big difference from year to year that it doesn't make sense, and it's confusing for him. If Anna was going through it, you'd understand better."

"I'm sure I would. I'm sorry it's been hard." I meant it. I was sorry for every single child that was suffering from this. I was sorry for every parent that was confused and every teacher that was being blamed. I hated that I knew why and could do nothing about it. I understood the situation far better than Beth or anyone else could imagine. I had the answers. If I had to, I could explain everything. But at what cost?

✦

"Brent, we have to do something," I said. I'd just told him about the PTA meeting as we were getting ready for bed. "I don't know what, but we have to do something. You should have seen that room full of parents. They're confused and worried about their kids, and I don't blame them. Just think how we'd feel if Anna was going through the same thing."

"What do you think we should do? I'd do something if I had any reasonable ideas."

"Maybe we should go explain the whole thing to the principal."

"Explain what? That our daughter has an amazing ability to make those around her learn? First of all, he wouldn't believe us. How many parents think their kids are amazing? He'd just think we were delusional and arrogant. And what difference would it make if he did believe us? There would still be a class she's in and a class she's not in."

"Maybe we should take her out of school," I said quietly. The thought made me sick.

"We could. But that wouldn't be fair to her."

"I'm afraid they're going to figure it out. We need an old-fashioned, one-room school where all the kids are thrown in together." I smiled wryly. "At least she'd be helping the whole school."

"Now you're onto something," Brent said. "All we have to do is find a one-room school with a wood-burning stove. Then everything will be fine."

"Is there a school with only one class per grade that we could put her in? At least then there wouldn't be all these comparisons."

"We can't afford a private school, Susan. You know that."

"We can't afford to sit here and do nothing either. We've stood by and watched confused parents blame innocent teachers for their children's perfectly normal learning struggles. We've done nothing because of Anna, but how long can we do nothing? It doesn't seem right. What if one of these teachers ends up losing her job? What then? I couldn't live with that."

"We'll look crazy if we say something, and I don't think they'd believe us anyway," Brent said.

"They're going to figure it out eventually. Mr. Giles said today that they've gone over this class's records since they started kindergarten. They haven't found a common denominator, but it's only a matter of time. I imagine it will become more obvious every year."

Brent leaned his head on the frame of the bathroom door as he brushed his teeth. When he finished, he sat down on the bed and stared at the wall for several minutes. I didn't know what to say. I could tell he was worried, and I longed to be able to ease his mind, to tell him that everything was going to turn out fine. But I didn't know how it could turn out fine. Doing nothing wasn't working. Innocent people were paying the price for our silence. Finally, he lay down and covered up. "We just have to pray harder," he said, taking my hand. "Dear Father, please help us know what we should do." I was so surprised at Brent's spontaneous vocal plea for help that I remained silent. But somehow, as we lay there in the dark, holding hands, I felt comforted. Maybe we'd figure this out after all.

Chapter 7

From Anna's journal:

A strange thing happened today at Sarah's birthday party. We were playing a game where one person had to go out in the hall for a minute, and then when they come back in they had to ask questions and figure out what everyone was doing that was the same. It's called Psychiatrist. It was a fun game. But then when it was my turn, I came back in and started asking questions and Sarah said, "Can you go back out for a minute?" I went back out, and when I came back in, she said, "See?" to everyone else.

I said, "See what?" and Ellie said to go back out, so I did. When I came back in, they all started nodding and someone said, "Wow." Then Sarah said, "I told you." Sarah wouldn't tell me what they were talking about, and we kept playing the game, but it wasn't as much fun. I felt really uncomfortable.

After the party, I asked Kelsey what they were talking about. At first she said it was no big deal, but when I kept asking her, she said they noticed that things look different when I'm there. I didn't know what she was talking about. Then she said, "You know, when you're there, things look cleaner and prettier." I didn't know that happened. That must be one of the strange things about me. I don't think I like it. I don't want people to think I'm different. I wonder if that's why people look at me funny sometimes. I wonder if it happens all the time.

★

It had never been a secret that Anna was adopted. We'd told her the story of how she came into our family many times, and she loved to hear about it. "Tell me again about the pretty nurse with the long, black hair," she'd say, or "Tell me about the time you first saw me." She delighted in every detail.

One day Anna came into the kitchen and sat down at the counter with a thoughtful look on her face. "What's up?" I asked.

"I was just thinking about something, and I had an idea," she said. "What did you have to do to adopt me?"

"Well, we had to visit a lawyer and fill out papers. Someone had to come visit our house and make sure it was a safe place for a baby. Then we had to wait a long time until someone chose us to be parents." I wasn't sure where she was going with this, so I wasn't sure how much to tell her.

"Would you have to do that to adopt someone else? You know, after you've already adopted one kid?" She rested her chin in her hands, and I could tell by her serious expression that this would require a serious answer.

"Well, I'm not sure. Probably. It's been a long time since we adopted you, so they would probably make us start all over."

"I was thinking you could adopt another kid," Anna said. "Will they let us?"

"They might. You know, we were able to adopt you because your other dad and mom died in a car wreck, and your relative chose us. We might be able to start over, but someone else would have to choose us. Why are you asking about this?"

"Because I want you to adopt Kelsey."

"I think that is such a nice idea, but I don't think that will work, honey. Kelsey has a dad, and I think he probably wants to keep her," I said.

"He doesn't act like he wants to keep her. He always tells her to go sit on her bed and stay there."

"I'm sure he doesn't say that all the time."

"Well, he does a lot. She told me. And he yells at her and makes her cry. And sometimes he gets really mad and breaks things. I don't think he even loves her."

"It would be great for you to have Kelsey for a sister, but you can't adopt someone who has parents unless they give their permission. And I don't think Mr. Davies would do that." Anna's chin quivered. She pursed her lips tightly and tried to remain composed. I reached across the counter and held her hand. She squeezed mine back, and it felt like she was squeezing my heart as well. I knew how she felt. I'd often thought how nice it would be if Kelsey could live with us, but right now, Anna needed to understand. "You know, Kelsey is here a lot. Lots of parents wouldn't let their child come over as much as she does, so we should probably try to be happy with that. Don't you think so?"

"I know she comes over a lot, but then we have to take her home to those mean people, and I don't want her to have to go home. I just want her to be able to stay here. We'd take better care of her than he does, and we love her more."

"I'm sorry, honey. It just isn't that simple." How do you explain something like this to a nine-year-old, especially when the nine-year-old was right? "We'd all love it if Kelsey was in our family, but we just need to be happy she's here with us as much as she is." I walked around the counter and put my arm around her. "You're sure a good friend to be so concerned about her. Kelsey is very, very lucky to have a friend like you."

"I just wish I could help her," she said in a whisper.

"I know. I wish we could too. Just keep being her friend, okay?"

Anna breathed a heavy sigh and wiped the tears from her eyes, but she didn't smile. "Of course I will."

Meanwhile I was desperate to resolve the problem at Anna's school. I felt like I was on a mission. I had to find a way to make things right. Either we would have to take Anna out of school and teach her at home, which I was loath to do, or we'd have to find some other solution. We could no longer just sit back and allow students, teachers, and parents to suffer because of Anna's uniqueness.

I decided to find out everything I could about children with unusual gifts. Surely Anna wasn't the only child ever born with these extraordinary abilities, but since I'd hit a dead end with her biological family, I'd have to start from scratch. The best place to start seemed to be the library of Mesa State College. I found several articles and a couple of books, but none of them described any cases like Anna's. In fact, most of the cases sounded ridiculous to me. Of course, I realized if someone read about Anna, they'd probably think it sounded ridiculous. One account told of a five-year-old child who solved complicated math equations on the bedroom wall each night while she slept. Another told of a ten-year-old German boy who dreamed he was on a safari in Kenya and woke up able to speak Swahili fluently. But I was determined to keep looking. I became a regular at the library. I went there day after day. I searched the Internet and the stacks for anything I thought might prove useful. I even found camps for psychic children with "counselors" who could help us channel Anna's gifts in productive ways. There was a man who said he could help Anna predict changes in the stock market and make us rich. Of course, he wanted a piece of those profits.

I became familiar with some of the library staff. One of them, a woman by the name of Katherine, offered to help me with my research. It was tricky because I couldn't explain exactly what I was looking for, so I just described Anna as gifted. I knew that was a woefully inadequate description, but I couldn't come up with more without divulging what we'd now spent years trying to conceal.

One afternoon, as I was searching on the computer, Katherine hurried over. She seemed excited. She sat down beside me. "I heard about something you might be interested in. I was at my sister's house on Friday night, and she told me about a gifted program. Some teachers started it this school year at Meadow Hill Elementary. Jenny knows a girl who's been accepted into the program, and she really likes it, and her parents love it." Katherine reached into her pocket and pulled out a slip of paper. "I wrote down some information for you." She handed me a yellow sticky note.

"That's great," I said.

"Jenny said to talk to Norma Beasman." Katherine pointed at the name on the paper. "She's the director of the program. Jenny said the kids have to apply and get accepted. They have to take some kind of entrance exam, and the board looks at the applicant's past grades. She didn't know if there are any openings, but she said to go talk to her. I wrote down her number for you."

"Thanks, Katherine." Although I knew this wasn't going to help us understand Anna's gifts, I was filled with hope. This might be a solution to the immediate problem. Two days later, I was in the office of Norma Beasman, discussing Anna's grades and accomplishments.

"It sounds like she'd be a perfect candidate for the school. What grade is she in?"

"She's in third grade."

"What a lucky break. That is actually the only class that has an opening," Mrs. Beasman said. "When were you hoping to have her start?"

"Would it be possible to start her after Christmas?"

"Our term ends on January 12, so it would probably be best if she started the week after that. We could give her the entrance exam before Christmas. All we need from you now are copies of her report cards, and we can begin processing her application. And just so you know, we require the parents of all our students to volunteer forty hours at the school per year. Are you able to do that?" she asked.

"I do at least that much now," I said. "Of course that would be fine."

"Good, we'll call you to set up the testing." Mrs. Beasman crossed her hands on her desk and smiled at me. I was being politely dismissed.

I knew I was pushing my luck, but I had to try. "Is there any possibility that there might be two openings?"

"In the same grade?"

"Yes. Anna's friend is an equally good student, and it would be nice if she could come, as well."

"I don't have any other openings right now, but we could put her on the waiting list so she'd be first in line if a spot opened up. I'd need to look over her grades, and she'd have to take the entrance exam, of course. If her parents are interested in the program, they would have to comply with the volunteer requirements too." She pulled a second set of application papers out of a file for me. "What is her name?"

"Her name is Kelsey Davies, and her parents are very busy people. If they gave permission for her to come to the school, would it be okay if I did the volunteer hours for her too?"

Mrs. Beasman looked at me suspiciously. She'd probably never heard of such an arrangement. She stared at me for so long that I shifted uncomfortably in my seat. Finally, she spoke. "I suppose that would be acceptable. But we'd need them to come in or send us a signed letter requesting her admittance. It's extremely irregular, but I suppose it would work."

I left the meeting feeling both relief and nervousness. Of course, this would solve the problems we were worried about, and once Anna was no longer at Kaiser, the comparisons and accusations would eventually die down. With only one class per grade in the gifted program, there would be no comparisons, and because it was the gifted program, the children would be expected to excel. But what about Kelsey? I couldn't bear the thought of leaving her behind. I knew we faced an uphill battle. We'd never even met Stan Davies before, and now we were supposed to convince him to write a letter requesting admittance for Kelsey into the gifted program at a different school. He probably didn't even realize she was smart or that she could play the piano. I'd never seen any sign that he cared about her schooling at all. Would he even be willing to cooperate if they found room for Kelsey?

Brent suggested we invite Kelsey's father to stop by our house to discuss the alternative school. I listened nervously as Brent made the phone call. Stan grudgingly accepted after he asked Brent what trouble the little punk had gotten herself into. Brent assured him Kelsey was not in trouble, and they arranged for him to come at six o'clock the following evening.

All day long I worried. I made bread pudding, hoping a little good food might soften him up. Kelsey and Anna came home from school, did homework, and practiced piano before they disappeared to play. I hoped they'd stay occupied and not listen in on the conversation. I was afraid of what Kelsey might hear.

By a quarter after six, I was sure that Stan Davies wasn't going to show. I was a bundle of nerves and wanted to pace the floor, but I forced myself to sit with Brent in the living room and talk while we waited. I nervously braided and unbraided the fringe on an afghan.

"What do we do if he won't agree to this?" I asked. "We can't just abandon Kelsey."

"Just think positively. This will be good for Kelsey. He'll see that."

"Will he think we're trying to take over her life? What if he gets defensive?" Stan had always been so unpleasant on the phone that I couldn't really picture him giving his permission without a fight.

"Let's just wait and see what he says." Brent opened the newspaper, and I continued to braid the fringe. This time I left the braids and made my way around the afghan in an effort to soothe my frayed nerves. Mr. Davies had me completely intimidated, and I felt like he held way too much power over the girls' situation for someone who seemed so detached and uninterested.

"He's probably not even going to show up," I said at 6:30. "He'll probably blow us off and then expect us to bring Kelsey home, like every other day." I could hear the bitterness in my voice, but I didn't care. In all the time we'd known Kelsey, I hadn't seen Stan show any concern for her education. Did he care about her future at all?

"Susan, we have no choice but to be patient and see what happens. If he doesn't come, we'll have to talk to him at his house." I envied Brent's apparent calmness.

At ten minutes before seven, Mr. Davies's old pickup pulled noisily into the driveway. I wiped my sweaty palms on my pants, said my hundredth prayer of the day, and laid the afghan over the arm of the couch. Brent greeted him at the door. Starr was with him. They stepped into the room, and with them came the smell of old cigarettes and cheap perfume.

I shouldn't have been surprised at how tall Stan was. After all, Kelsey was a tall girl. I felt even more intimidated as I looked up at him. He had to be about six foot six, but he was lanky and bony. He probably weighed less than two hundred pounds. The tight-fitting western jeans and cowboy boots he wore made him look even taller. In spite of the cool November weather, the sleeves of his western shirt were rolled up above his elbows, revealing tattoo-covered forearms and hands. A tattooed deck of cards peeked out from under his shirt collar. His dirty hair was a lifeless, sandy brown and hung over his ears and forehead. I wondered if Kelsey's mother was a brunette since Kelsey's hair was so dark.

Starr looked like a frightened animal. Her eyes darted nervously, and she carefully avoided any eye contact. She looked uncomfortable in her high-heeled ankle boots. Her legs were pale and bare under her frighteningly short denim miniskirt. She wore a tight, cropped jacket with a matted gray collar of fake fur. Her bleached blonde hair reminded me of Farrah Fawcett's except for the two inches of dark roots and the dry, split ends.

Brent invited them in and asked them to have a seat. They sat together on the couch, and we each took a chair opposite them. Starr shifted uncomfortably, trying to adjust her skirt so as not to show her underwear. Then she unzipped her little jacket and revealed bright pink bra straps under the tight little white tank top she wore. One wing of a butterfly tattoo was visible on her wrist.

"So what's this all about?" Stan seemed unconcerned that he'd made us wait almost an hour. He draped an arm across the back of the couch and rested a boot on his other knee. It was clear he knew he held all the cards in whatever game we'd invited him over to play.

"Well," Brent said, "I'm sure you know our girls have been best friends now for more than two years."

"Uh-huh," Stan said. He already sounded bored.

"They're both very bright girls, get excellent grades, and are very talented. We've been looking into sending Anna to the gifted program over at Meadow Hill, and we were hoping you'd agree to send Kelsey there with her."

"Gifted, huh? Is that what we call a good student these days?"

"The school only accepts children with excellent grades who pass the entrance exam," I tried to keep my voice steady. "Anna is going to take the exam next month. Kelsey could take it then too, if you gave your permission."

"I don't know about that. Right now, Kelsey can ride the bus if you don't pick her up after school. Is there a bus from our house to Meadow Hill?"

"I don't think so, but I'll be driving Anna, and I'd be more than happy to give Kelsey a ride too." I was glad my voice sounded a little stronger. So much was riding on this. We had to make him see the light. "I think Kelsey would really like it, and of course, something like this looks great on a college application."

"Kelsey won't be going to college. Ain't got no money for that nonsense." He said it like it was already decided, and I had to bite my tongue. Did he think Kelsey would have no say about her future? How could he be so ready to throw away an opportunity for his own daughter?

Starr opened her mouth as if she had something to say and then changed her mind. She nervously picked at her chipped, red fingernail polish. After another minute, she spoke so softly it was hard for me to hear from just a few feet away. "It wouldn't hurt for her to have that option. 'Specially if she got a scholarship or something." She didn't look at Stan.

He didn't acknowledge that she had said anything. He went on. "How much do they wanna rob me to pay for this *gifted* school?" He said "gifted" like it was a curse word.

Brent answered. "Actually, they don't charge anything." Stan looked from me to Brent suspiciously, and I forced myself to hold his gaze.

"Now, you don't expect me to believe that, do you?" he said slowly. "Nobody does nothin' for nothin'."

"They don't require any money because it's part of the public school system. All they ask is that parents volunteer some time at the school."

"Well then, I guess that won't be happ'nin'. Got way too much to do to go to some fancy pants school and do their job for 'em. That's what them teachers are being paid for." He slapped both legs with his hands and leaned forward as if to get up. He was ready to go. Starr took her cue and slid to the edge of the couch. I felt panic rising in my chest. "Guess we better grab Kelsey and git goin'," he said. As far as he was concerned, the matter was closed. I said a quick, silent prayer.

"Mr. Davies." The firmness in my voice surprised me. "Kelsey and Anna are good friends. Please hear us out. I know you're busy. I'm a stay-at-home mom, and I have plenty of free time. I'm more than willing to fulfill the volunteer requirements for both Anna and Kelsey. I already explained to the director that you're a busy man and that I'd like to do the volunteer time for you, and she agreed that that would be fine. Kelsey is smart. She gets straight A's. I don't mind driving her back and forth to school—I'll be taking Anna there anyway. If it will make things easier for you, Kelsey can come home with us every night so you won't have to worry about her while you're working, and then we can bring her home after you get home from work. Please let her go with Anna." I hated to beg, but I had no choice. I loved Kelsey and knew how important this would be for both girls. Anna loved Kelsey, and it would break her heart if she had to leave her behind. If I had to beg, I'd beg.

Starr reached over and put her hand on Stan's arm. "It wouldn't hurt anything, would it?" she asked.

Stan shrugged her hand off his arm. He seemed to be thinking it over.

"We've got some dessert if you'd like, and we could talk about this a little more. Do you have any other questions?" Brent asked.

"I don't need no dessert," he said to us. "I could use a beer," he added under his breath.

"Would you like some dessert?" I asked Starr.

"She don't need none either," Stan said before Starr could answer for herself.

"No, thank you." She shook her head.

Stan just sat there with his hands on his knees, looking right at me. I met his gaze. I refused to look away first, in spite of the awkwardness I felt. I wasn't sure what I was doing, but I knew I couldn't back down. He needed to think of Kelsey. After an uncomfortable pause, he finally spoke. "I guess it wouldn't hurt nothin'. Maybe it'll keep her from droppin' out. What do I need to do?" he asked.

Brent explained the letter that needed to be written and pulled out some paper we had ready. Mr. Davies scrawled out a brief message:

> To Whom It May Concern:
> Kelsey Davies has my permission to go to the gifted school.
> Stan Davies

"That good enough?" he asked.

"That should be fine," Brent said. "If they need anything else, we'll call you."

"Well, where is she?" he bellowed as he stood up. "We gotta go." I went to call Kelsey, and a few minutes later, we watched her leave with them. I collapsed into my chair, my breath ragged.

"What's wrong, Mom?" Anna asked.

"Nothing, honey," I said.

"Let's go have some bread pudding, Anna." Brent guided her into the kitchen. "Mom's okay. She's just had a hard day."

I picked up the box of Kleenex from the table, curled up in my big chair, and cried—cried with relief for Anna, cried for joy that the girls would be together. And I also cried with a broken heart for Kelsey's sad life.

✦

The girls passed the entrance exam, and I ignored Mrs. Beasman's look of disapproval when I gave her Stan Davies's letter. She'd see how wonderful Kelsey was, and Kelsey wasn't responsible for her father's bad behavior or lack of concern. I just hoped that an opening for Kelsey would come up soon. I hoped they wouldn't be separated for long.

That problem was solved during Christmas break. "I have some good news," Mrs. Beasman told me over the phone. "One of our student's father is being transferred to Seattle, so we have an opening for Kelsey. She can start the same time as Anna."

"Oh, thank you." I felt a wave of relief flood over me. I knew this was a blessing and an answer to our prayers.

✦

From Anna's journal:

I'm moving to another school. Kelsey is coming too. Mom and Dad are really happy about it and keep saying it's an answer to their prayers, but I'm scared. Kaiser's the only school I've ever gone to. I like it there, and I know everybody. I'm afraid the kids at the new school will think I'm weird. Sometimes I feel like I'm different from other kids. I don't want to go to a new school where everybody thinks I'm strange. I'm really glad Kelsey is coming to the new school with me. I don't know what I'd do if she wasn't. I'm going to miss Mrs. Bateman. She's really nice. And I'll miss Jacob and Allison and Mara and Jane and Alex. I'm going to miss too many people to name them all. I wanted to tell Mom that I didn't want to go, but she's so happy about it that I didn't want to make her feel bad.

✦

Transferring Anna and Kelsey to Meadow Hill proved to be the solution we'd needed. I hadn't realized how stressful things had been until I no longer had to worry about teachers and other students and their parents. Now that the children were free to excel without being compared to others, I realized what a burden had been lifted from us. Brent and I felt more relaxed. It was such a blessing.

The girls thrived at their new school. The entire class progressed at an astonishing pace, and no one complained or worried. It was a gifted program with bright students, so no one questioned the speed of their learning. It was wonderful. The girls came home almost every day and excitedly told me stories of the things they were learning and the experiences they were having. They loved the school, and they were thrilled that Kelsey got to come home with Anna every day. We asked Mildred if she'd like a second piano student, and soon both girls were taking official piano lessons. Mildred asked if she could enter them in a piano festival, and both girls scored superior ratings.

Kelsey truly became a part of our family. She and Anna were more like sisters than best friends—until we'd take her home each evening and watch her walk past the savagely barking dog and into the sad, dilapidated house.

Spring came, with its longer days and balmy weather. One warm evening, Anna and I drove Kelsey home, rolling down the windows and enjoying the warm evening air on the way. We pulled in front of the house and watched Kelsey walk through the fence and to the front door.

"Bye, Anna and Susan," Kelsey called from the front door. We'd given up the formality of Mr. and Mrs. Weller a long time ago.

"Bye, Kelsey." We watched her walk inside, and then I turned the car around and started for home.

"Uh-oh," Anna said a few minutes later. "Kelsey left her backpack."

"We can give it to her in the morning," I said.

"She wanted to study the spelling words before she went to bed tonight. We have a test tomorrow."

I turned the car around and drove back. The dog barked and smashed into the fence. Only the screenless porch door was closed, so I was sure that they'd hear the dog's racket. I stood at the gate with Kelsey's backpack and hoped someone would come outside so I wouldn't have to fight off that canine fiend. I paused with my hand on the gate as screaming voices from inside filtered into the yard. It sounded like Stan and Starr. I wasn't sure what I should do. Dealing with the dog was bad enough, but interrupting a fight wasn't something I wanted to do. As I turned back toward the car, I heard the sound of shattering glass. Now I was really torn. I wanted to get away from there, but I hated to leave Kelsey in that madhouse. Should I try to get her out, or would I make things worse if I interrupted them right now? I was just two steps from the car door when Stan flung the screen door open.

"What are you barking at?" he yelled at the dog. I turned back to the house. Stan's eyes were fixed on me.

"Hi, Mr. Davies." My voice shook a little. "I'm just dropping off Kelsey's backpack."

He leaned into the house. "Kelsey?" he yelled. "Get your butt out here and get your backpack." A moment later, Kelsey hurried past him and took the backpack. Before she could get back inside the front gate, Starr was at the door.

"Whatcha screaming at her for? She's not the one you're mad at."

Screaming and cursing continued as the fight moved from inside the house to the front yard. I just wanted to go home, but I couldn't leave Kelsey standing by the front gate. I worried if I offered to take her with me that Stan would get angrier. His anger scared me, but what about Kelsey? As I struggled with what to do, I realized it had suddenly gotten quiet. I looked from Stan to Starr to see what had caused the sudden silence and saw that they were looking at my car. I turned, and there was Anna, her window down, looking back at them. She was quiet and unafraid, and her eyes moved from Stan to Starr and back to Stan again. I was struck by her calm beauty as she looked directly at them. I remembered the park and held my breath.

Finally, Starr turned to Stan. "It's going to be okay," she said in a quiet voice.

"I guess so," he answered. "But you gotta help me. You know I can't take care of everything on my own."

"We'll do it together," she said.

I stood there, dumbfounded.

"Thanks for bringing her backpack," Stan said. His voice was civil, almost friendly.

"You're welcome," I said. "We'll see you in the morning, Kelsey."

"Okay. Bye." She said this to me, but all the while she stared at her father with what might have been shock or amazement.

I got in the car and turned it toward home. "Are you okay, Anna?" I asked.

"Uh-huh." I glanced over my shoulder at her. She was staring out the window, her hair blowing. Was she aware of the little miracle that had just happened?

"What are you thinking about?" I wanted to give her a chance to talk about it. She didn't answer immediately.

"I'm glad they stopped fighting. Now Kelsey can study for spelling."

"Me too," I said.

When I told Brent what had happened, he just shook his head. Then he smiled and said, "We should have had Anna in the room with us when we were trying to convince Stan that Kelsey should go to Meadow Hill." We both laughed.

After church that next Sunday afternoon, Brent and I were watching golf, and Anna was lying on her stomach, drawing. Suddenly she said, "Why am I weird?" She put down her pencil and sat up, cross-legged.

"What do you mean?" I asked.

"Am I weird because I'm adopted?" She had a very serious look on her face. Brent turned off the television, and we joined Anna on the floor.

"Anna, you're not weird. Lots of kids are adopted. They're still just regular kids," he said.

"But . . . I'm not like everybody else."

I sensed she was talking about something much deeper than her adoption. "Anna, tell me what you mean when you say 'weird.' " Her face was serious, and something inside told me we were heading into uncharted waters.

"Well . . ." she hesitated. "Sometimes . . ." Her voice trailed off, leaving the thought unspoken.

"Go ahead," Brent said. "You can tell us anything."

Anna looked at us for a moment and then took a deep breath. "Weird things happen sometimes." She paused again, and we waited for her to continue. "You know, like what happened with Kelsey's dad the other night."

"What did that feel like?" I asked.

"I was just looking out the window, and then they stopped screaming and looked at me all funny."

"Did that feel weird?" I asked. I so wanted to know how she experienced the world and whether she was aware of her gifts.

"Nobody fights around me," she said matter-of-factly. "Even at school, if any kids are ever fighting, they stop when they see me, and then they just stare at me. Why do they stop fighting?"

"I don't know, honey. I think you have a gift for being a peacemaker," Brent said. "Look, I'll show you." Brent got his Bible and then sat back down on the floor. "Scoot over here, and let's read this," he said. He flipped through the pages until he found what he was looking for. "Right here in the Bible, Jesus is talking to the people. He's telling them important things, and he says, 'Blessed are the peacemakers, for they shall be called the children of God.' That is a very special gift, Anna, to be a peacemaker. A special gift that I think you have."

She looked at Brent. "Do you have a gift?"

"I'm sure I do. I think Heavenly Father gave us all gifts. I'm not sure my gift is as obvious as yours, but I think we all have them."

Anna thought for a minute. "I think your gift is that you work hard."

Brent laughed. "That's a good gift. I like that one."

Anna turned to me. "What's your gift, Mom?"

"Well, you and Dad are my best gifts."

"I think your gift is being nice. You're nice to me, and you're nice to Kelsey, even though she's not your own little girl." It was quiet for a minute as she thought. "Do I have any other gifts?" she asked. Brent and I looked at each other. How much should we reveal to Anna? She was so young. Her gifts were huge and complicated. We didn't want to overwhelm her.

"Anna," Brent said, "You do have other gifts, very special gifts. You're a very special girl."

She sat up on her knees, eager to hear more. "What are they?" she asked.

"I think some of your gifts are too big for a little girl to understand," I said. I reached out and held her hand. "You just concentrate on being a happy girl, and someday you'll understand the rest of your gifts."

Anna looked disappointed but didn't push the subject. I knew that someday we'd have to help her understand just how special she was, but for now, being a peacemaker was enough for her to think about.

✦

Fourth grade was blissfully normal. Anna and Kelsey loved school and excelled in everything they did. They had a wonderful teacher, Miss DeAngelo, who encouraged them to write stories and poetry. She gave each of them a journal to write in. Anna's was covered with lilacs, and each page had a lilac in the corner. Kelsey's was covered with daisies. The girls loved them, and many days they'd come home from school, sit down at the table, and write. They kept me busy as I read their short stories and poems. One day, Kelsey shyly handed me a poem. "I wrote this for you," she said. I took the paper and sat down at the counter to read.

> It's dark, and I'm scared as I sit in my room.
> I wrap up in my blanket and look out at the moon.
>
> The night is so long, and I want it to go.
> I wait for the morning; the night is so slow.
>
> Then up comes the sun; now I feel warm.
> You make me feel happy and push out the storm.
>
> So when the night's cold, and I look at the moon,
> I just have to remember that you'll be there soon.

"That's beautiful, Kelsey," I said over the lump in my throat. I reached out and gave her a hug. "When did you write that?"

"Last night," she said as she tightly hugged me back.

✦

Miss DeAngelo was especially pleased with Kelsey's writing and entered one of her poems in a national poetry contest that spring. Kelsey took first place and received a $400 savings bond for college and a beautiful certificate with gold trim. She excitedly showed me her certificate and then called her dad to tell him about the prize.

"Dad, guess what? I wrote a really good poem about rain and it won a contest. I got a $400 scholarship," she said. I watched her out of the corner of my eye. She paused while he answered. I hoped he'd say something encouraging. "No, I don't have the money. Miss DeAngelo said it's a savings bond that stays in the bank, and I can't take it out until I'm eighteen, 'cause it's for college." Her voice sounded a little less excited. "No, Miss DeAngelo said I'll get it for sure," she said. There was a long pause. "Okay, bye." Her smile was gone, and her shoulders sagged.

"Kelsey, I'm so proud of you. That's a huge accomplishment. I hope you know how great you are," I told her. She smiled as she touched the gold trim on her certificate and then carefully put it back into her backpack.

✦

One afternoon in April, I carried a stack of folded towels to the linen closet. The door to Anna's room was ajar, and as I put the towels on the shelf, I thought I heard crying. Then I heard Anna's soft voice, "It's okay, Kelsey. It will be okay. Please don't be sad."

"What am I going to do?" I heard Kelsey ask.

"Don't worry about it. You'll be okay. I'll take care of you. No matter what. I promise."

"Is everything okay, girls?" I opened the door a little wider and poked my head inside the room. They were sitting on the floor. Kelsey's elbows were on her knees and her chin rested in her hands. Anna was on her knees beside Kelsey, her hand on Kelsey's back. Anna looked at me sadly as Kelsey picked up a paper that was unfolded on the floor in front of her and held it up toward me. I stepped inside the room and took the paper.

Hey Little Sis,

Sorry I had to leave. You know how it is around here. I can't stand it anymore. At least Dad likes you better. I'll be gone when you get home from school.

I'll try to check in on you sometimes and make sure you're okay. I might go find Mom. If I do, I'll come get you, and we'll go live with her.

Don't miss me too much.

Dusty

"When did you get this?" I asked.

"I found it in the bottom of my backpack," she said through her tears. "He must've put it in there last night."

"He didn't tell you he was going to leave?" I asked.

"He said he was, but he says that all the time." I sat down on the floor beside her. "Dad's just so mean to him." She started sobbing again, and I put my arm around her. She toppled over and laid her head on my legs. I stroked her hair and tucked it behind her ear and then wiped away her tears.

"Is he mean to you?" I asked. I dreaded the answer, but I needed to know.

"He yells at me. But he isn't mean to me like he is to Dusty." I quietly rubbed her back.

"You're going to miss him, aren't you?" I said after a minute or two of quiet.

"Yes," she said simply. I thought my heart would break. I looked at Anna. Her sweet face that always betrayed her every emotion registered the anguish she felt for her friend. I reached over and held her hand. We sat there quietly for a few minutes as Kelsey cried herself out.

"How old is Dusty now?" I asked.

"He's sixteen." Her voice was wooden, like all the hope had been drained from her thin body.

"Maybe he can find your mom, and he'll be happy there," I said.

"If he does, I don't want to go live with her. I hardly even remember her, and I don't want to move far away from here," Kelsey said. I had no idea what to say to her. I wanted to offer some kind of comfort, but how could I know what would be best for her brother or her?

Finally, aware that I couldn't offer promises of a happy ending for any of them, I said, "We'll just have to hope everything turns out for the best. We'll all pray for him, okay?" I wondered why I didn't promise Kelsey the same things Anna had. Why couldn't I be as hopeful and encouraging as my young daughter? Was it because I was older and wiser, or was it because I lacked Anna's faith and conviction?

"Okay," Kelsey said. She sat up. I picked up the note that was sitting beside me on the floor and handed it to her. She folded it up and put it in the pocket of her backpack. "Can we have a prayer now?" she asked.

"Of course we can," I assured her.

"Will you say it?" She was looking at Anna.

Anna smiled and nodded. We held hands, and Anna prayed. She prayed that Dusty would be safe. She prayed that Kelsey wouldn't miss him too much. She prayed that Kelsey's father would be nice to her, and she prayed that no matter what happened, Kelsey would be okay. It was the sweet prayer of a good friend. When she was finished, we all stood up.

"Are you okay?" I asked her, and she nodded her head. "Come here, you two," I said and held my arms out. "I think we need a big hug." We hugged each other, and both girls giggled a little as I squeezed them tightly, rocking back and forth dramatically. "I love you, Anna," I said.

"I love you too, Mom."

I gave Kelsey an extra squeeze. "And I love you, Kelsey."

After a moment she spoke very softly. "I love you too."

Chapter 8

From Anna's journal:

I was wrong about the new school. I thought I wouldn't like it as much as Kaiser, but I do. I like it a lot. I'm learning so many neat things. I'm really good at math, and I really like numbers. Sometimes I sit and think about numbers and make up story problems in my head. Kelsey thinks that's crazy, but I like to look at math problems and figure them out.

There's only been one thing I haven't liked about Meadow Hill. There's a teacher named Miss Drake that teaches one of the fifth grade classes. Every day at lunch, she watches me. She just watches me from the time I walk into the lunchroom until I leave. She sits at a table with a couple of other teachers, and I can feel her looking at me. I don't think she's mean. If I look at her, she smiles, but she keeps watching me. I wonder why. Maybe she can tell there's something strange about me. Maybe she sees things change or she's noticed that no one fights around me. I wish I could ask her why she looks at me, but I'd die of embarrassment if I did, and she'd probably just smile and say she wasn't looking at me.

I know there are strange things about me, but I don't understand them. If I try to figure them out, I just get frustrated, so I've decided not to think about it very much anymore. I just hope no one thinks I'm a freak. I just want to be a normal girl.

The gifted program at Meadow Hill was a godsend. Anna and Kelsey had never been happier. They continued to learn and get excellent grades. When they were in the sixth grade, the school chose the top four students from the fourth, fifth, and sixth grades to go to the state capitol in Denver for a special two-day conference. They would attend a session of the state legislature as guests, where they would answer questions about the gifted program. A representative from Grand Junction would give them a tour of the state capitol and then take them out for lunch. The students would also get to stay in a hotel. The next morning they would visit an art museum and a science center before coming back home.

Anna and Kelsey were the top two students in their class, so they were chosen to go. They excitedly told me all the details of the trip, which was only going to cost the girls forty dollars each. I listened to them chatter about what they were going to wear when they spoke to the legislature.

I thought we should pay Kelsey's forty dollars, and Brent agreed. All Stan Davies would have to do was sign a permission slip, so we didn't think there'd be a problem. He probably wouldn't even look at what he was signing.

We were wrong about that. The next morning, Kelsey had red-rimmed and puffy eyes when I picked her up for school. "What's wrong, Kelsey? Aren't you feeling well?" I asked. She silently buckled her seatbelt. I glanced at her in the rearview mirror and saw that her chin was quivering. She reached up and put her hand on her chin, trying to control the shaking. She swallowed hard in an effort to compose herself but was still unable to speak. I reached over the seat and took her hand.

Finally, she let out a sob, and the words spilled out. "I can't go." Her shoulders shook as she cried. Anna reached over and put her arm around her.

"Why not?" Anna asked.

"Dad says I can't," she said between sobs. "He says he doesn't have the money, and when I told him he wouldn't have to pay anything, he said we wouldn't take charity and it's bad enough I go to some fancy pants school. He wouldn't sign my permission slip, even though I begged him and promised him I'd wash the dishes for the rest of my life."

"My dad and mom will talk to him," Anna said. "They'll change his mind. Don't worry." I didn't know what to say. Of course, I wanted to talk to Kelsey's father and change his mind, but I felt we were pushing him pretty close to his limit. Would we make things worse by trying to change his mind? I didn't want him to pull Kelsey out of Meadow Hill with only six months of the program left. Next year the girls would be starting junior high at a regular public school. But what if he pulled Kelsey out of the gifted program now? I knew we were walking a tightrope, and I didn't dare make any promises.

Instead of pulling up to the curb to drop off the girls as I usually did, I pulled the car into a parking stall and got out. I opened the back door where Kelsey was sitting and took her hand as she got out of the car. "Listen," I said. I wiped her eyes and took her by the shoulders. "I'm going to talk to Brent, and we'll try to figure out what to do, but you need to go have a good day. Don't worry about this. No matter what happens, everything is going to be okay." She nodded, and I hugged her good-bye. Then I hugged Anna. "Don't you worry about it either." I smoothed her hair and kissed her on the forehead. I stood by the car and watched as they walked into the school. Neither of them spoke.

That night, Brent called Mr. Davies.

"Hi, Stan, this is Brent Weller," he said. He stopped talking, and his hopeful expression changed to one of disappointment. He could tell it wasn't going to work. Brent listened to Mr. Davies rant and only tried to respond occasionally. "No, we aren't trying to take over your job as parent." Again, he listened. I could hear Stan yelling, although I couldn't make out his words. Brent's elbow rested on the table, his hand on his forehead. He breathed deeply as he patiently maintained his composure, and I knew it had been the right choice for him to call Stan. I wouldn't have been able to control my emotions or my temper. "Look, Stan, I've got some work I need done in my classroom, and I'd sure be grateful if Kelsey would help me out with it. It would be worth forty dollars to me, that's for sure." Again he listened. "Well, you let us know if you change your mind. Kelsey's a good student, and it was an honor for her to be chosen." Stan was speaking again, but quieter now. I couldn't hear him at all. "Okay then, good-bye."

Brent laid the phone down on the table and shook his head sadly. "He's not going to budge, and I don't dare push him anymore."

"What did he say when you said she could work for the money?" I asked. Brent hesitated. He didn't want to tell me. "Brent, what did he say?"

"He said if Kelsey can make forty bucks working for me, maybe she should give the forty bucks to him to help pay for all the stuff he has to buy her."

"Are you kidding?" I was furious. What could he possibly be talking about? He hardly paid for anything. Kelsey ate dinner with us almost every night. Most of her clothes were things we'd paid for. I was the one volunteering at the school so she could go there. When she needed school supplies or shampoo or money for a field trip, we were the ones who took care of that. "I think there are a few things I'd like to say to him," I said. My blood was boiling as I reached for the phone. I'd kept a lot of things to myself over the past few years that I now wanted to set him straight on.

Brent grabbed my hand before I could dial. "We have to keep a cool head, Susan. If we push him too hard, he'll pull Kelsey back and Anna will lose her best friend. This trip isn't worth that." I sat down hard in a chair beside Brent. I knew he was right, but it made me sad to think of Kelsey missing out on such an amazing opportunity because of her father's stubbornness.

"It isn't fair." I pounded the table with my fist. Unfortunately, all that accomplished was make my hand hurt.

"We need to tell the girls," Brent said. "And we need to be calm. We've got to be careful not to make Stan out to be a villain."

"But he is a villain." I knew I sounded like a sullen child, but I didn't care.

"Susan, I know you're upset, but Kelsey has to go back home to him every night."

"I know," I said. "That's what kills me."

"We have to help him understand. We can't push him too hard. We both know that. If we make him mad, he'll pull the plug on everything, and Kelsey's the one who will suffer." Brent put his hand on my arm. "Okay?" He studied my face and waited for a response.

"You're right," I said at last.

"Are you okay? I know it's hard, Susan, but we've got to handle this right." Brent was looking at me closely, and I felt guilty. He already had to deal with Stan Davies, he didn't need another out-of-control person to worry about. I nodded, and he called the girls into the kitchen. "Kelsey, I talked to your dad about the trip, and he doesn't think you should go." His voice was gentle, and he gave Kelsey's shoulder a squeeze.

"You can change his mind though, can't you, Dad?" Anna asked. She looked from Brent to Kelsey and back at Brent.

"I could try. But Stan feels pretty strongly about it. I think we have to support your dad on this, even if we don't understand and we're disappointed."

Anna let out a huff of indignation. "That's not fair. She worked hard, and she should get to go."

"It's okay," Kelsey said. Her voice was soft, and she reached over and patted Anna's arm.

"We don't want to make him angry, Anna," I said. "If he gets angry, he might not let Kelsey go to Meadow Hill. Even though it makes us sad, we just have to accept it and move on." Somehow I managed to keep my voice calm, even though I wanted to scream. It was wrong that Brent and I had to defend the actions of someone like Stan Davies.

"Then I'm not going either," Anna said and smiled sympatheti-cally at her friend.

"Yes, you are," Kelsey said. "There's no reason why both of us should miss out."

"But it won't be fun if you aren't there with me."

"You'll still have fun. Besides, you have to go so you can tell me all about it." Anna stubbornly shook her head but didn't say any-thing else.

Later that night, I tucked the covers around Anna and kissed her cheek. "I love you," I said.

"I love you too." I walked to the door and turned off the light. "Mom, how can I help her?" she asked. I opened the door wide to let in light from the hallway and sat beside her on the bed.

"What do you mean, honey?"

"How do I help her have a happy life? Her life is so sad." Anna sat up and wrapped her arms around her knees.

"Honey, I think you already help her. I think you help her be happy every day."

"I know, but I mean all the time. I want her life to be happy, not just when she's here."

"Anna, I'm not sure anyone is happy all the time. Life is full of hard things."

"I know, Mom." There was an uncharacteristic hint of impatience in her voice. It was clear she had no intention of simply accepting her friend's misery.

"Honey, I don't know why Heavenly Father sent Kelsey to be Stan's daughter. Maybe Stan needed her. Maybe Kelsey needed to have certain experiences in her life, so she needed to be in Stan's family. I don't really know or understand. I just know that it is important that we love her and try to make her life as happy as possible, and I think we're doing that, don't you?"

Anna didn't speak for a long time. She continued to hug her legs and rested her chin on her knees. She looked into the distance, lost in her thoughts. "What are you thinking about?" I asked her gently.

"Someday I'm going to help her get out of there."

"Anna, someday she'll be grown up and able to decide for herself where she lives and what kind of life she'll live. I think you're a gigantic blessing to her, and I think the more time she spends with us, the better able she'll be to decide she wants a better life."

"It isn't fair, Mom." Anna looked at me, her eyes large and intense. "She deserves a good family and parents that love her and want good things to happen to her. Her dad gets mad if anything good happens to her. He's a terrible father."

"Maybe he doesn't know how to be a good father," I said. It made me angry that for the second time in one evening, I found myself sticking up for someone I found despicable.

"Then he should learn." Her voice had an edge I wasn't used to hearing. She lay back down and turned toward the wall. I could think of nothing else to tell her, nothing that might make her feel better. The truth was, I felt as frustrated about Kelsey's father as Anna did. I sat there a moment and rubbed her back. I knew Anna wasn't satisfied. I kissed her cheek and left the room.

In the end, Anna went to Denver and Kelsey stayed behind. It was a difficult two days for both girls. Kelsey put on a brave face both days I picked her up, but I knew she longed to be on the trip and missed her best friend. I still brought her to our house after school every day, and she kept herself occupied by helping me with dinner and a few odd jobs. I admired her good attitude. Anna called the first night she was gone. Before she'd even reported on the exciting events of the day, she asked how Kelsey was. It touched my heart that they were so concerned about each other. I'd never had a friend as close as these two except my sister, Bev. I was glad that since Anna didn't have a sister, she had Kelsey.

The next day Anna came home bearing souvenirs—a perpetual motion toy from the museum and a signed book about government from the representative who had taken them to lunch. She handed these to Kelsey and then gave me a photo of herself with the governor in the capitol building. Kelsey wanted to know every detail of Anna's trip, and instead of feeling sorry for herself, she seemed genuinely excited to hear about Anna's adventures. And thanks to Kelsey's attitude, Anna felt comfortable sharing her experiences with all of us.

✦

One Monday, Brent called the family together for family home evening. The lesson was about love, and we were each assigned to look up two verses in the scriptures on that subject. Brent showed Anna how to search in the back of the scriptures for a topic, and we each looked for scriptures we wanted to share. "There's too many to choose from," Anna said.

We each chose two scriptures and marked them. When everybody was done, Brent asked me to read my scriptures and explain why I had chosen them and what they meant to me. "I really like the scripture in Mosiah where King Benjamin tells parents to teach their children to walk in the ways of truth and soberness, to love one another, and to serve one another. I think love is talked about so much in the scriptures because it's what makes us most like Jesus."

"Anna, what do you think this scripture means for you?" Brent asked.

"I think it means that I need to love and serve my parents and friends." She looked at Brent to see if he agreed with her answer.

"That's right. We are all each other's brothers and sisters, so we need to extend our love and service to more than just our own little family. Good. Anna, do you have a scripture about love?"

Anna opened her Bible. "I found a scripture in John. It says 'Greater love hath no man than this, that a man lay down his life for his friends.' " She looked up from her book. "That means to die, doesn't it?"

"Jesus was talking to his disciples here, and I think that's what it means. What did Jesus do for his disciples? And for all of us?"

"He died on the cross," Anna said.

"So he did just what this scripture says, didn't he? He laid down his life for his friends. He did that because of how much he loves all of us."

"I'd die for you and Mom and Kelsey," Anna said to Brent.

"I think sometimes it's different for us," Brent said. "Instead of dying for someone, sometimes we live for them. I probably won't have to die for my family or friends, but I try to live for them every day. I try to make them happy and help them with what they need. I think that's what you do for us. You don't have to die for us. You can live your life in a way that makes us happy and that blesses us. That also makes Heavenly Father and Jesus happy. Does that make sense?"

"Yes."

"You make Kelsey's life better because of the nice things you do for her and because you treat her just like she's your sister." I reached over and squeezed her hand. "Kelsey is lucky to have a friend like you."

We finished our family night lesson and had a lemon bar for the treat. Brent turned on Monday Night Football, I folded a load of clothes, and Anna got ready for bed. "I hope I always do things that make you and Dad happy," Anna said when I went in to kiss her good night.

"We sure are lucky you're our girl," I said.

From Anna's journal:

> *In family night we talked about love, and I found a scripture about loving our friends so much that we would die for them. Dad said that Jesus did that for us because we're his friends. I wonder*

if Jesus had a best friend? I hope he did. I'm glad Kelsey is my best friend. I hope he had a friend as good as Kelsey. Sometimes I forget Kelsey's my best friend because it seems like we're sisters. If Jesus had a best friend like that, I think it would have made all the hard things he had to do a little, tiny bit easier. I wonder if one of the disciples was Jesus's best friend.

One evening, just before dinner, the doorbell rang. I opened the door to find a young man standing on the porch. He slouched into a parka, his hands in his pockets in an effort to stay warm. Even though he slouched, I still had to look up at him. His messy hair hung nearly to his shoulders, and his chin was covered with the scruffy fuzz of a teenager. "Can I help you?" I asked. He looked familiar, but I couldn't remember where I'd seen him before.

"Um, yeah, is Kelsey here?" He shifted from one foot to the other and stared at the ground.

"She is." As I said it, I realized this was Kelsey's brother, Dusty. "Do you want to come in?" I stepped aside and opened the door wider.

"Um, no thanks. Could I just talk to her?"

"Sure, but it's cold out there. Are you sure you don't want to come inside?"

"That's okay." I could tell he was uncomfortable, and I didn't want to scare him away.

"I'll go get her."

"Thanks." I left the door open, not wanting to shut him out in the cold. The chilly air followed me inside as I went up the stairs to get Kelsey. The girls were in Anna's bedroom, studying science.

"Kelsey, your brother's at the front door. He'd like to see you."

"What?" She was obviously surprised but quickly jumped up and hurried out the bedroom door.

"He doesn't want to come inside," I said, grabbing her coat off the end of the bed and following her to the front door. Before I could hand it to her, she and her brother were hugging each other tightly, and I felt like an intruder. "Here's your coat, Kelsey." She took it from my hands, and I quietly closed the front door to give them some privacy.

"Why is he here?" Anna asked from the bottom stair.

133

"I don't know. He probably just wanted to see his sister."

"He probably didn't want to go to their house. His dad hates him," Anna said. I couldn't argue with her. I'd heard Kelsey say many times that her father was mean to Dusty. Brent, who had heard us talking, joined us. "Kelsey's brother is here," Anna told him.

Brent looked at me questioningly. "He didn't want to come in," I said. "They're on the front porch."

"Is he hungry?" Brent asked.

"I wouldn't be surprised."

"I'll invite him to eat with us." Brent opened the door to find Kelsey and Dusty sitting on the top step, talking. He extended the invitation, which was politely declined. "Let's make him some sandwiches to take with him," Brent said after he'd closed the front door. "He looks cold and hungry."

Brent and Anna helped me make several sandwiches, which we put in a bag with some cookies and a couple of bottles of water. Brent took it out and gave it to Dusty.

"Thanks," Dusty said. He looked embarrassed.

We held off on dinner until Kelsey came in a half an hour later. She was smiling. "Thanks for giving him that food. He hasn't eaten all day."

"He was welcome to stay and eat with us," I said.

"He would have felt too stupid. His friend came to Grand Junction to visit his parents, so Dusty caught a ride with him. He said he wanted to check on me." Kelsey looked happy.

"That was very nice of him," Brent said. "Where is he living now?"

"In Boulder. He hasn't found my mom, but he said he's living with some friends in an apartment there. He got a job at a video store."

"You miss him, don't you?" I said and put my arm around Kelsey's shoulders. She nodded and swallowed hard before she could speak.

"It's better that he doesn't live here, though. He's happier there. He said he'd check on me again when he can."

"He must really love you," I said. She nodded.

❋

Mildred, the girls' piano teacher was now ninety-six years old. I knew I might have to find a new teacher at any time, and yet every week, there she was with a smile on her face and a hug for the girls. While both girls played the piano very well, it was Anna who Mildred said was the most musical. Kelsey could hit all the notes right, but Anna made the music come alive.

"Susan?" I recognized Mildred's crackly voice.

"Hi, Mildred, how are you?"

"Fine, dear, just fine. I wanted to talk to you about the girls."

"Okay," I said, silently praying she wasn't going to tell me I needed to find another teacher.

"I want to enter Anna in the Rocky Mountain Youth Piano competition that's going to be held in Denver in May. I'd like her to compete in the Sonata and Sonatina categories."

"Wow, that's fantastic," I said.

"Now, I want Kelsey to be ready for the festival this summer, but I think this competition is better suited to Anna. When she plays, she makes me cry. I just want to be sure Kelsey won't feel bad. Do you think she'll be disappointed?"

"I don't think so," I said. I thought of how nervous Kelsey was whenever she played, even if I was the only one listening.

"Good. Anna will need to practice very hard, but I think she can do well."

"That sounds wonderful," I said.

"Now, Susan," she said, her voice all business, "there's an admission fee of fifty dollars. But if that's a problem, I can pay it."

"No, that won't be a problem," I said.

"All right, then. One more thing. I want to go. I know I'm an old woman, and I'll slow you down some, but I'd like to ride along to the competition and be there to hear her in the winner's concert." I smiled. Mildred had already placed Anna in the winner's concert.

"Of course you can go with us."

"Wonderful. I already have her music picked out, so she can start it this next lesson."

"What do we owe you for that?" I asked.

"Oh, dear, please. I've had most of this music longer than you've been alive. Just be sure you encourage her to practice. I think she's going to do fine, just fine."

Anna was excited about the competition, and just as I'd

suspected, Kelsey let out a huge sigh of relief that she wouldn't have to participate. The months leading up to the competition were filled with the sound of the piano. I couldn't play the two songs, but I soon knew them by heart and often caught myself humming them during the day when Anna was at school. Anna improved week after week, and I was in awe of the emotions she was able to evoke as she played. She really was a natural. I was so grateful we'd found Mildred.

The second weekend of May, Brent, Anna, and I picked up Mildred and Kelsey and were on the freeway to Denver by 5:30 a.m. The girls slept in the car while Mildred shared stories about her years of teaching and the competitions she'd participated in as a young lady. "You know, they didn't have anything like this when I was young. I remember a couple of competitions in school, and once or twice we competed at the college, but this is a wonderful opportunity for Anna. I'm so glad I can go watch her play."

We arrived at the Denver Center for the Performing Arts just before ten and found a small practice room where Anna could run through her pieces. An hour later, Anna performed them in a larger room for two judges, one from Denver and one from Manhattan. The rest of us waited outside in a long hall. Brent and Mildred sat on a little bench while Kelsey and I stood with our ears pressed to the door. It was hard to hear, but the muffled music that came through the door sounded good to us, and we gave each other an enthusiastic high five when the playing stopped. Now it was out of our hands. At 3:30 that afternoon, a list of finalists would be posted. Those who made the list would perform in the evening competition, after which the awards would be handed out.

Anna felt happy with her performances. She couldn't remember any mistakes and was hopeful she'd make it to the finals. We left the concert hall and found a cute little diner not too far away called the Eggshell Café. As its name implied, it served breakfast all day, so some of us ordered sandwiches while others had pancakes and eggs. It was a cozy, cheery little place. It had red brick walls, comfy booths painted a glossy hunter green, and big front windows that let in lots of light. It was difficult for Mildred to get in and out of the car, and the restaurant was uncrowded, so we sat in the café eating and talking until almost three.

When we got back to the center, Brent waited in the car with Mildred while Anna, Kelsey, and I went to check the list. Anna was nervous and didn't want to look. "You just look and tell me." She covered her eyes dramatically.

Kelsey pulled on her arm. "Come and look with us."

"I can't."

"Baby," Kelsey said. We left Anna standing across the wide hall and walked up to the list. Kelsey's finger slid down the list. I realized right away it was in alphabetical order, so I glanced immediately to the bottom of the list and saw her name—Anna Weller. I breathed a quiet sigh of relief. I waited for Kelsey to reach Anna's name. She let out a squeal and started jumping up and down. Anna's eyes got big, and her expression went from anxious to hopeful. "You made it! You made it!" Kelsey crossed the hall to Anna, and together they skipped out of the marble lobby to the car. I hurried to keep up with them.

Mildred was so happy she couldn't wipe the smile off her wrinkled face. We parked the car and went back into the center. Mildred was tired, so we found her a couch to rest on in one of the dressing rooms, and Anna found a room where she could practice for a little while. I could tell quite a few people were from out of town with nowhere to go because the auditorium filled up well before five. We found a good place to sit during the concert and took turns saving our seats while the others took walks. At 6:30, I helped Mildred freshen up a bit and guided her back to our seats.

Anna was the fifth performer. She played beautifully, and I had a big lump in my throat the whole time. She looked so pretty on that stage at the grand piano but much too grown up in her simple black dress, and I felt a stab in my heart as I realized she was already twelve years old. How had that happened? It didn't seem possible, and I felt the pain mothers everywhere feel when they realize their children have grown up much too quickly. We cheered wildly as she bowed and joined us in the audience.

Fourteen children under the age of sixteen performed. A few suffered from stage fright, and their public embarrassment was hard to watch, but most of the finalists were composed and played beautifully, and I wondered how the judges could possibly choose the winners. After the last girl had left the stage, we were told that the winners would be announced in fifteen minutes. Most of the audience got up to attend to one thing or another, but I knew that would be difficult for Mildred, so we remained in our seats until the ceremony began.

First the winners for the sonatinas were announced. Anna's name wasn't called. Then it was the sonata winners. Again, no Anna. I was disappointed as I looked at her hopeful face. I looked over at Mildred to see her reaction and saw that she was beaming. My initial thought was that she must not have understood what was happening. Then I realized that this was Mildred, and I wondered what she knew that I didn't. Then the announcer clued me in.

"The grand prize winner has achieved the highest score of any contestant since this competition was first instituted in 1983. And she will be eligible to enter this contest four more times. With a combined score of 98.9 out of 100, the grand prize goes to . . . Anna Weller, taught by Mildred Thompson." The room thundered with applause. Anna stood and walked to the stage. I glanced at Mildred and saw she was grasping the sides of her seat in an effort to stand up. I took her arm and helped her to her feet. She stood there, giving Anna a standing ovation as tears streamed down her cheeks.

When Anna came back from the stage, she went right up to Mildred and gave her a hug. "That was fine, dear," Mildred said. She hugged Anna tightly and patted her back.

Mildred slept most of the way home, a satisfied and happy look on her tired, lined face.

✦

One afternoon the phone rang. "Hello, is this Mrs. Weller?"

"Yes, it is."

"This is John Crandall, Mildred Thompson's brother."

"Hi," I said. I was filled with dread. "Is Mildred all right?"

"She fell last night and broke her hip. She's in the hospital right now and won't be able to teach lessons this week. She wanted me to let you know."

When Anna and Kelsey got home from school that afternoon, we drove to the hospital to see Mildred. We stopped at Enstrom's on the way for a box of her favorite English toffee. We found her room, and I knocked softly on her hospital door. John, her younger brother who was in his eighties, opened the door. Mildred was awake and reached her arms out to the girls. They ran to her and hugged her gently.

"We brought you some English toffee," Kelsey said, and Anna handed her the box.

"Now how did you know I needed some chocolate?" Mildred said. She opened the box and popped a big piece of the candy into her mouth. Then she held the box out for the girls and me to take a piece.

We talked with Mildred until I saw that she was getting tired. Mildred motioned for the girls to come stand beside her.

"Now you listen here, young ladies." Each of her hands held one of the girls' hands. "I'm sorry I'm such a clumsy old lady and can't make your lessons this week, but you have to promise me that you'll keep up with your music no matter what. The music will stay with you long after anything else will. My goodness, I've been able to teach 'til I'm an old, old lady. Don't you dare give it up, either one of you." She squeezed their hands, and they made their promises before they hugged her good-bye. She held them close for a long time, and then I stepped forward and gave her a hug. "Thank you for bringing me these girls," she said quietly into my ear.

"Thank you for teaching them and loving them," I said.

Mildred died that night, just nine days after Anna had competed in Denver. Anna, Kelsey, and I cried and hugged each other when I told them the news. They spent the entire evening reminiscing about all their experiences with Mildred. They both worried about her cats and insisted that I call her brother and make sure they were cared for. They were relieved to learn that her great-granddaughter had taken the cats home with her.

Mildred's funeral was held the following Saturday. We drove to Kelsey's that morning to pick her up for the service. Stan was waiting for us in the front yard. Kelsey stood at the door, her face streaked with tears.

"She ain't going," Stan said. "She don't do nothin' around here, and I need her to help me clean up this mess." He swung his arm out wildly in a gesture that took in the entire house and yard. I looked around. It didn't look any different than usual. We looked at Kelsey in the doorway. She gave us a sad little wave and then turned around and disappeared inside the house. Stan followed her inside and slammed the door. More than ever before, I wished that Anna's dream of our family adopting Kelsey could become a reality. We sat in the car in front of the house for a couple of minutes and hoped that something might change Stan's mind. Finally, Brent started the car, and we drove to the funeral. As I looked at Anna crying softly beside me in the church, I knew there was more than one reason for her sorrow.

"She should have been here. She loved Mildred," Anna whispered.

"Mildred knows that," I said.

The summer before junior high flew by. Anna couldn't wait for seventh grade. Kelsey was nervous. We found a new piano teacher, but she took summers off, so the girls had more free time than ever. We bought some supplies, and they each made a scrapbook in anticipation of all the fun pictures and accomplishments that would come with junior high. I taught them to sew, and they spent hours at the fabric store picking out material for pillowcases and skirts. They both learned quickly but had very different styles. Kelsey was quick and efficient while Anna was slow and careful.

We shopped for school clothes together, but the girls worried that Stan might get angry, so we bought just a few basic items. Anna didn't want to have a lot more clothes than Kelsey, and they knew if Kelsey brought home too many new things, Stan would get defensive and make life hard. Still, they looked cute on the first day of school.

Junior high was surprisingly easy. They had each other, so they weren't much bothered by the cliques and politics that can make those years difficult. Their grades were good, and much to our relief, the weeks went on with no indications that we'd face some of our earlier problems with regular public school. Of course, I knew it helped that they now moved from teacher to teacher throughout the day.

One evening in September, Brent and I were getting ready for bed when the phone rang. Surprised that someone would be calling at such a late hour, I answered the phone with trepidation.

"Susan?" It was Kelsey. She sounded scared.

"Kelsey, what's wrong?" I asked.

"Nobody's here. Do you think I can come back over to your house?"

"Where are they?" I asked.

"I don't know. No one was here when I got home."

"You've been there by yourself all this time?" I asked. I looked at the clock. She'd been home alone for nearly five hours.

"Yes. I thought they'd come home or I'd have called earlier."

"Did you look for a note?" I asked. I was stunned. This was shocking, even for Stan.

"I looked, but I didn't find anything," she said. "Sorry it's so late. I just don't want to stay here alone."

"I'll be right over. Get some clothes together for school tomorrow and your schoolbooks, okay?"

"Okay."

"And don't worry. It's no trouble at all."

"Thanks, Susan." She sounded relieved. I hung up and told Brent what was happening as I put on my jeans.

"Let me go," Brent said. "I don't want you over there alone if Stan suddenly shows up." I let him go, and fifteen minutes later, Brent and Kelsey were back with her pillow and blanket, a plastic bag of clothes, and her backpack. I helped Kelsey get settled on the trundle bed in Anna's room. Anna woke up at the commotion and was thrilled to have Kelsey spend the night.

"Thanks, Susan," Kelsey said.

"You're welcome, Kelsey. We love you. You know you're welcome here anytime."

"What do you think is going on?" I asked Brent when we were alone in our room.

"I don't know. There was no sign of them. No note. Nothing. We left a note telling them she's here and to call when they get back. I may have to run her back over there at three in the morning if he throws a fit," Brent said. I got the portable phone and put it beside the bed in case Stan called. Even though I was exhausted, I had trouble falling asleep. The thought of a parent leaving a twelve-year-old girl alone overnight made me angry.

Stan didn't call that night. Or the next day. In fact, we didn't hear a word from him for six days. I drove by their house every morning after I took the girls to school, and the house was silent. Even the dog was gone. I was outraged that Stan had taken the dog with him wherever he'd gone but had left his daughter behind. Brent drove by each afternoon on his way home from work, but there was no sign of Stan or Starr. Fear of what might happen to Kelsey kept us from calling anyone. We knew if Stan didn't get back soon, we'd be forced to let someone know, but we wanted to put it off until the last possible second. If Family Services got involved, we might not be able to see Kelsey or even contact her. So we waited anxiously to see what would happen.

Anna wasn't nervous at all. For her this was a dream come true. She loved having Kelsey around all the time, and for the most part Kelsey didn't seem to mind it, though I'd sometimes see a worried look on her face.

"Are you okay, honey?" I asked her one evening as the girls were going to bed.

"I just don't want to be in trouble," she said.

"Oh, Kelsey, you're not going to be in trouble. They're probably worried that they'll be in trouble."

"But if they're in trouble, they'll be mad at me," she said.

"Try not to worry. Everything will be okay. Have you prayed about it?"

"No," she said.

"Would you like to?"

"Will you pray with me?" she asked. So I sat down with my arm around her as she said a short prayer, asking Heavenly Father to keep her father safe and to help him not be mad at her when he got home.

Late the next night, Anna slipped into our room after Kelsey had fallen asleep. "Mom?"

"What is it, sweetie?" I asked.

"I'm just wondering, if Stan and Starr don't come back for a long time, can we adopt Kelsey?" Her face looked so hopeful.

"It isn't likely they'll be gone forever, Anna. And when they come back, I'm sure they'll want Kelsey back."

"But they don't deserve to have her anymore. They abandoned her," Anna said.

"We'll have to see what happens," I said. Sometimes I felt like I never knew what to say or do. I'd always figured that when I was the grown up, I'd have all the answers, but it felt like I knew very little for certain. I hugged Anna and kissed her cheek.

"I just really want her to come live with us," she said from the bedroom door.

"I know you do." I was all the more sympathetic to her feelings because I felt the same way.

Sunday came, and we took Kelsey with us to church. On the ride home, the girls decided to make cookies and take a plate to their Sunday School teacher, but as soon as we turned onto our street, we saw Stan's truck in the driveway. Stan was pacing back and forth beside it. I'd known this time would come, but I felt sick. My stomach did flips as we pulled in beside the truck. I was concerned about Stan's temper, so I was surprised when I saw that his face wore a sheepish expression. There was no sign of his usual belligerence. He looked at the ground and kicked at a couple of little rocks on the driveway.

"Hello, Stan," Brent said. I loved how confident his voice sounded.

"Hello, Brent," Stan said.

"Where you been?" Brent's question was direct, but his voice was friendly.

"I had some, uh, problems I had to go work out." He stumbled through the words and refused to make eye contact.

"We weren't sure if you were ever coming back," Brent said. "Kelsey was scared. You left her all alone."

"I know," Stan said. "I figured she'd come stay with you. I knew she'd be all right."

"You should have asked us," Brent said. "You know we'd have said yes."

"I know. I shoulda." Stan looked at Kelsey. "I'm here to take you home now."

Kelsey nodded. "I'll go get my stuff." We went inside to help her gather her things together and then walked her back out. She hugged us good-bye, and we all tried not to cry.

"Be brave," I whispered in her ear, and she nodded. "Call us if you need us." She walked to the truck, put her bag on the floor of the cab, and climbed in.

"Thanks," Stan said. He got in the truck and roared out of our neighborhood. We stood in the driveway and watched them disappear.

Starr was gone for about two months. Then just after Thanksgiving, she was back in the house again. We worried about how this whole incident would play out for Kelsey and were happy to find that Stan was a little less difficult to work with. No one ever said another word about that six days Kelsey was left on her own, but Stan seemed to want to smooth things over. I suppose he didn't want to make us angry. We had some pretty damning information against him, and I think he didn't want to provoke us into sharing it with the authorities. We considered that a little silver lining to our otherwise cloudy relationship with Stan and Starr.

Brent and I decided to take advantage of Stan's more agreeable state of mind. A few days before Christmas, Brent called him.

"Stan—hi, it's Brent."

"Hi." Stan said.

"Listen, we're going to give Anna a trip to Disneyland for Christmas. We won't go until spring break, but we'd like Kelsey to come with us. We'll take them the week they're out of school. That's March 17th through the 23rd. We're going to pay for everything, so you don't need to worry about it." Brent wasn't leaving any room for Stan to balk, and I was proud of him for it. There was a long pause as Brent waited for a response. "All right then. You can mark it on your calendar. Merry Christmas, Stan," he said.

"What did he say?" I asked.

"She's coming with us. I think he wanted to say no, but he didn't have the guts." I gave a cheer.

"What are you smiling about?" Anna asked me at dinner.

"Nothing really," I said.

"You look really happy," she said.

"I guess I am."

Kelsey joined us for Christmas Eve, and we gave the girls Christmas cards with Mickey and Minnie on the outside and news of the trip on the inside. Anna jumped around the room. Kelsey just looked at us with wide, questioning eyes. We explained that we'd already cleared it with Stan, and she joined Anna in her celebration.

Chapter 9

We quickly learned that a trip to Disneyland with two cute thirteen-year-old girls is a much different experience than the same trip with one eight-year-old. We left on the last day of school and drove six hours with two happy girls who talked and giggled in the backseat. We spent the night in St. George, a cute town nestled among magnificent red cliffs in southern Utah. Unfortunately, it was too dark to see any of those red cliffs when we pulled into the parking lot of the modest little mom and pop hotel called Inn by the Cliffs. The room looked like it had been decorated by the owner's grandmother. There were lace doilies and antique quilts everywhere.

The next morning we drove around St. George for about an hour and ate delicious omelettes and pancakes at a little diner before we headed southwest into Nevada. We didn't stop in Las Vegas, but the girls oohed and aahed at the sight of the huge hotels visible from the freeway. "Can you imagine sliding down the sides of that black pyramid?" Kelsey asked.

"You know I hate heights," said Anna. "I'd probably die of fright."

"I'd love it," Kelsey said. "Think what the people inside would think when I slid across their window." By early evening, we were in southern California and were searching for our hotel. The brochure had said "walking distance to the Magic Kingdom" so we were pretty sure we'd be able to find it once we reached the vicinity of Disneyland. Forty-five minutes and two phone calls later, we found the hotel. It was three and a half miles from Disneyland, not exactly our idea of walking distance before or after a day at the park. The next morning, we noticed a little laundromat called "Magic Kingdom Laundry" about a half block from the hotel. We decided maybe that was the Magic Kingdom referred to in the literature. In the end, we drove to the park each day.

Sunday was a beautiful, southern California day. We attended church in the morning and then drove out to Newport Beach where we spent the afternoon. The girls hunted for seashells and waded out to their knees in the cold water. It was definitely warmer here than Grand Junction, but the water was still much too cold for me to do anything more than get my feet wet. Kelsey looked out at the vast ocean in amazement. This was the first time she'd seen it. In fact, she'd never been out of Colorado before. The four of us played along the edge of the water for a while, but soon Brent and I retreated to a log and sat down to watch the girls run and play and explore.

"Anna's growing up way too fast," I said. I watched as she tried to outrun the waves that soaked the hem of her rolled-up pants. The ocean breeze whipped her hair into her face, and after a few minutes, she pulled a ponytail holder off her wrist and put her hair into a messy bun. There was no help for Kelsey's hair. She had nothing to pull it back with, so she kept turning toward the breeze to blow it away from her face.

"Do you ever stop to think how lucky we are her family chose us?" Brent looked out across the sand at Anna.

"I wonder what it was about us that made her choose us."

"I'm sure it was my dashing good looks," he said.

"I bet you're right," I said.

"Really, though, whatever it was, we're very lucky."

"Lucky and blessed," I added.

"Life would be so different without Anna."

"I wonder what we'd even be doing with ourselves. Probably not going to Disneyland."

"Do you ever wonder what it would be like if she wasn't different?" he asked.

"I used to. I used to wish she was like everyone else. Some things would be so much easier if she was like all the other kids. But every time I think that, I wonder how it would change things. I love our lives. I don't know if I'd really want to change anything." He nodded, and we sat quietly for several minutes.

"I don't think I'd change a thing." Brent finally said. "Do you think the world changes for other people when she's around? I mean the way it looks, like it does for us?"

"Sometimes I've wondered that, but we can't mention it, so all we can do is wonder. Since other people learn faster when she's around, I think they must sense her other gifts too. They probably just don't know why things are different."

"The difference is so huge," Brent said. "I go to work and everything is normal, but then I come home and everything is peaceful and clear. I look forward to coming home every day."

"I'm excited for her to get home from school every day." A family with two small children walked by, and the father and Brent nodded at each other. "Imagine the difference for Kelsey when she leaves Anna and goes home to her house. It must be so hard."

"I'm glad she has Anna," Brent said. "That girl definitely needed some beauty and goodness in her life."

"I'm amazed at how much Anna cares about her and worries about her and wants to help her. It seems so unusual for a girl her age to be so unselfish. I know I wasn't that way," I said. "Look how pretty they are." Kelsey was so tall, and Anna looked so petite next to her. Everything about them was different, from the color of their hair to their height to the color of their eyes. Anna's eyes changed so much—usually they were a deep blue, but today they looked green—while Kelsey's eyes were always dark brown. The girls looked so grown up out there in the afternoon sunshine.

"Do you think we'll ever understand it?" Brent asked.

"I hope so. I still wish we had someone to talk to about her birthparents. I can't help wondering if maybe one of them was like Anna and would have known better how to handle things. Sometimes I just want to open that letter and see if it says anything that would answer our questions. There are so many things I want to know."

"I don't think that would be fair to Anna," Brent said.

"I know." I paused. "Do you think they'd be happy with the way we've done things?" I often worried about that but had never said it out loud before.

"I think they'd know we did the best we could. Maybe someday they'll be able to tell us," he said, matter-of-factly. "You know, maybe we were never meant to understand it. Maybe we're just supposed to love Anna and help her take care of her gifts and use them for good things."

"What do you think they're all for?" I asked. "Her gifts, I mean. Don't you think there must be some purpose for them?"

"I don't know. Maybe. Maybe we just don't know yet, and someday it will make sense."

"I'd love for it to make sense someday," I said. "It seems like something so special would be there for a reason."

The girls were making their way toward us now, and we stopped talking.

"Hey, Mom and Dad, can we get Mexican food tonight? Fish tacos sound so good," Anna said.

"Sounds good to me," Brent said. He stood and reached down to pull me up. "What do you think?"

"I'm always in the mood for Mexican food." I grinned.

"What's so funny?" Anna asked.

"Nothing, really," I said. Unable to resist the urge, I put my arm around my daughter as we walked to the car. For some reason, something about my very unusual daughter asking for something as normal as Mexican food put a smile on my face. In some ways, she was just a regular girl.

Monday was the first day of our Disneyland experience. When we'd brought Anna five years ago, we thought she was too young to enjoy California Adventure, but on this trip, we'd bought tickets that let us go back and forth between Disneyland and California Adventure for three days. That proved to be the right move. We spent three days jumping back and forth, enjoying the rides, shows, shopping, and food.

Kelsey was astounded. The closest thing to this she'd ever seen was when she'd attended the county fair. She'd ridden a small Ferris wheel and a ride that looked like spaceships spinning out of control, but nothing to compare with this. She got the giggles and couldn't stop laughing as she listened to Anna sing "It's a Small World" in every language. I could only remember the English and Spanish versions.

I was happy that the girls seemed content to hang out with Brent and me. I saw so many kids about their age in groups without parents that I had suspected they might want to take off on their own for a while. That only happened when they wanted to go on California Screamin' about a hundred times, and Brent and I were only good for the first ten. So we left them to it and went to find other things to do.

Disneyland turned out to be a bit of an eye-opener for me. I found a shady table across from California Screamin' and sat down. I was hot and sweaty even though it was only April, and I was grateful for the umbrella that provided some shade. Across the walkway, Anna and Kelsey made their way through the line to the ride. They didn't see me, so I watched them unobserved. In line was a group of young people about their age, maybe a school or church group. There were three girls and six boys. Of course, I couldn't hear their conversation, but it was pretty apparent that a few of the boys were paying a lot of attention to Anna and Kelsey. That really didn't surprise me. What did surprise me was that both of the girls really seemed to enjoy the attention. As they talked and smiled, it occurred to me that the days of playing with Jacob in the backyard or thinking boys were yucky were probably gone for good.

"What are you looking at?" Brent asked. He handed me a paper cup of frozen lemonade.

"Check that out." I nodded at the kids in line. Brent turned to look. "I'm not sure I'm ready for this," he said. "We're going to have to lock the doors. We might have to make a rule about no dating until they graduate from college." I smiled, and we watched them until they disappeared behind a barrier.

Anna had brought her camera on this trip and took so many pictures it became a joke. "Stop teasing me. You'll be glad I took all these pictures when we have a fun scrapbook to look at."

"But do you think you might be getting a little carried away?" Brent asked.

"I just want to remember everything about this trip. It might be the only time we're all here together," she said. "Besides, you'll never be this young again," she said as she took another picture of Brent.

"Or this handsome," he said.

On Thursday, we drove back toward Newport Beach to an IKEA store we'd seen from the freeway on Sunday. The girls were like Alice in Wonderland. Every couple of steps brought new things to admire—dishes, flowered bedspreads, cute lamps, and colorful rugs. As we walked through the enormous store, the girls found dozens of things they would have loved to have taken home to redecorate their bedrooms.

"Should we give them a fifty dollar budget and let them get what they want?" Brent asked me. Just then they threw themselves onto a round bed with a hot pink mosquito netting over it.

"They'd be in heaven," I said.

"All right girls, you can each spend up to $50 on anything you want." They shrieked with delight. "But remember," Brent said, "we have to be able to get it home in the car without crowding ourselves too much, so don't get too carried away. Nothing too big and bulky."

We started to regret the offer when, after four hours of indecision, the girls still didn't know what they wanted. After much encouragement and then a firm fifteen-minutes-or-you-lose-it time limit, Anna finally picked a yellow and red floral bedspread—much more grown up than the princess one she had now—and a set of red, stackable cubes, hollow inside, that could be configured in a variety of ways. She wanted to use them stacked on top of each other like a bookshelf.

Kelsey picked a set of apple green dishes with a blue flower border and matching green glasses. "I love these," she said. "We've never had dishes that match before."

"Look at this." I picked up a blue tablecloth with embroidery around the edge that matched the flowers on the dishes and showed it to Kelsey.

"Oh, I love it. Do I have enough for all of this?" she asked.

We worked it out. "With two dollars left over," I said. We loaded the purchases into the car.

"This was as much fun as Disneyland," Anna said. Now that the purchases had been made and I was off my aching feet, I had to admit, it had been pretty fun.

The trip home from California felt much longer than the trip there. To give ourselves a break from the road, we stopped in Las Vegas. We parked the car at the Bellagio hotel and walked around the water to the street. The fountain in front of the Bellagio was dancing to the music of Frank Sinatra's "Luck Be a Lady," and we watched the show, enthralled by the intricate waterworks. The girls pleaded with us to wait another twenty minutes for the next song, so a short time later we were watching "Hey Big Spender." The girls looked so happy as they watched the water show. We walked across the street and ate at a buffet with more food than any of us had ever seen in one place. As we were leaving, we walked through a shopping arcade under a painted sky. The girls jumped as the sound of thunder roared through the market, and then they realized it was a sound effect and had a good laugh.

I always feel a little blue when a fun trip is over. The planning and anticipation of a vacation, and then the trip itself, are always so much fun. Getting home and back to real life always makes me feel a little empty. The feeling was magnified this time because Kelsey would be leaving us again. We all felt a little sad when we dropped her off at her little house.

"Thank you so, so, so, so much for taking me with you," Kelsey said as we unloaded her things from the car.

"We're glad you could come with us," Brent said.

"It's the most fun I've had in my whole life." Kelsey threw her arms around me and hugged me tightly and then hugged Brent and finally, Anna. "I'll never forget this. It was so nice of you to take me." We all stood there smiling.

The summer after seventh grade was the summer we called "the growing summer." Anna outgrew everything she owned. She was three inches taller when she started the eighth grade than she had been at the end of seventh grade. She was nearly as tall as me, and Kelsey now looked down at me.

Eighth grade started out much like seventh with mercifully few complications. We soon discovered another big difference between the girls. Kelsey loved PE, while Anna could barely tolerate it. She dramatically shared her dislike at dinner one evening. "I'm not good at anything in PE. I'm the slowest runner, and when we play sports, I'm always the worst player."

"She had six turnovers today when we were playing basketball," Kelsey said.

"My poor team! I looked ridiculous out there," Anna said. She didn't mind that we all enjoyed a laugh at her expense. "Did you see the ball bounce off my knee?"

"It went right through the gym door into the hall!" Kelsey said. "A boy brought it back in and said, 'Did somebody lose this?' and about six girls turned and pointed at Anna."

"It was the most humiliating moment of my life," Anna said, smiling.

Kelsey laughed. "That would have been a great move if we were playing soccer." Soon the girls were laughing so hard they could barely eat. I was glad that Anna could laugh at herself—I'd been too insecure to do that when I was a teenager.

One evening as we emptied the dishwasher, Anna said, "Mom, I think Kelsey wants to play basketball this year."

"She's tall enough. She'd probably be a very good player," I said.

"You should have seen her in PE. The teacher said she's a natural and told her she should try out for the team."

"She should do it."

"I don't think she will, though."

I put the last clean dishes into the cupboard and closed the dishwasher. "Why not?"

"She doesn't want you to have to run her back and forth to practices, and she doesn't think her dad will."

"She knows we wouldn't mind," I said.

"But Mom, she knows you're not her real mom, and sometimes she feels bad that you have to do so many things for her."

"Did she say that?" I asked.

"Yeah, several times," Anna said quietly. "Don't feel bad, okay?"

"I don't, honey. What do you tell her when she says that?"

"I tell her she's like my sister, which makes her like your daughter, and that she should talk to you if she wants to do it. I told her I thought you'd say yes."

"I would say yes," I said.

"I knew you would." Anna's eyes looked like beautiful gray clouds, and I noticed, as I often did, how pretty she was as she smiled at me. "Too bad she's not your daughter. I wish she was," she said.

"I know." There had been times when I'd worried that it might bother Anna that Kelsey spent so much time with us. Some children would be a little jealous of a friend being treated so much like a part of the family, even a best friend. But when Anna said something like this, I knew everything was okay. I felt proud of her.

✦

"So, Kelsey," I said the next day after school, "I think you should try out for the basketball team. I'm sure they could use a girl with your height." Kelsey shot Anna an accusing look. Anna shrugged her shoulders and smiled innocently. "I actually love watching basketball, and since Anna's not the least bit interested, it would give me someone to come and cheer for. Brent loves it too, and if you were playing, we might be able to persuade Anna to go to a game or two."

"I'd go to more than a game or two," Anna said. "I'd go to all of them. You should do it."

"Did your dad play basketball?" I asked Kelsey. "He's pretty tall."

"He played in junior high, but then he quit in high school."

"I'll bet he'd like to see you play too."

"You'd have to make two trips to the school in the afternoon if I did. I wouldn't be finished until about 5:30 every day," she said. I smiled. She already knew when practices were.

"Kelsey, don't be ridiculous. The school is only a couple of miles away. I really don't mind."

"Really?" she asked.

"Really. I want you to play."

So Kelsey tried out for the team, and just as her PE teacher had predicted, she proved to be a natural. By the time the season began, she was the starting center for the junior high team. Brent and I loved going to the games, and Anna, who had never really liked sports, became Kelsey's biggest fan. True to her word, she never missed a single game.

✦

"Susan, does Anna do any babysitting?" Lucy Conrad, our neighbor whose husband was a dentist, asked one day at the mailbox.

"She really hasn't done any, but I think she'd like to."

"Doug's receptionist is going to have a baby, so I thought I'd fill in while she's gone so he won't have to hire a temp. It would be for about an hour and a half each day after school for about six weeks. Do you think she'd be interested?" Lucy asked.

"I think she probably would. I'll talk to her." And that was the beginning of Anna's babysitting career. Each day after school, Anna would look after Lucy's six-year-old, Grant, either at our house or at his. Anna was a patient and fun babysitter. She didn't mind getting down on the floor to play cars or dinosaurs with him. Grant thought she was the best babysitter ever, and I think he even had a little crush on her. He always wanted to hold her hand when they walked back and forth between the houses.

"Let's play school," Anna would say, and Grant's homework would be finished before he even realized he was doing it. "Okay, we played what I wanted to play. Now it's your turn," she said.

"I'm afraid he likes Anna better than he likes me," Lucy said after the first week was over. "I think she's got quite a bright babysitting future ahead of her."

Anna genuinely liked little children, and they liked her. Watching her play with Grant made me wish she had a little brother or sister of her own. With just her enthusiasm, Anna was able to get him to do whatever she wanted, and Grant never seemed to feel bossed around.

Eventually Doug's receptionist returned from maternity leave and Lucy came home to Grant. But Anna continued to babysit Grant every other Friday. The arrangement suited everyone involved. Lucy and Doug got to go out on regular dates, Anna got a little spending money, and Grant got to spend time with his adored Anna.

✳

Anna and Kelsey turned fourteen that school year. One day in May, just a few weeks before school ended, the girls walked into the kitchen and sat down at the counter. After a minute, I noticed they were unusually quiet, and I could tell when I looked at them that they had something to say.

"What's going on?" I asked. I leaned on the counter opposite them.

They glanced nervously at each other, and then Anna summoned the courage to ask. "Can we go to the spring dance?"

I knew eventually we'd be faced with this kind of question, but I wasn't sure I was ready for it. "Hmm," I said. "Why don't you tell me about it?"

"It's just a dance for the end of the school year," Kelsey said.

"When is it?"

"May 21st," Anna said.

"It's not like a date or anything," Kelsey said. I raised my eyebrows. "I mean, you don't go with boys or anything." She hurried on. "Everyone just goes, and then sometimes you dance. Some people just stand around."

"What time is the dance?"

"From seven to nine," Anna said. "We probably won't even get asked to dance. It would just be fun to go."

"What would you be wearing?"

"The poster just said 'nice clothes.' Girls can wear dresses, but they don't have to," Kelsey said.

"Dad and I will talk it over." I bit the sides of my mouth to keep from smiling at their nervousness. Brent and I decided it would be fine if they went, as long as they behaved themselves and kept track of each other. They assured us they would, and on May 21st, I dropped off two pretty, nervous, fourteen-year-old girls. Anna wore a blue skirt with flowers around the bottom and a white cotton blouse. Kelsey wore a denim jumper with a yellow T-shirt underneath. They looked very cute in their "nice" clothes. They waved nervously as they got out of the car.

"I'll be right here at nine," I said.

Two hours later, two very different girls returned to the car. Their earlier anxiousness had been replaced by laughter and smiles.

"How did it go?" I asked.

"It was okay," Anna said. "We only danced once."

"Once was enough," Kelsey said and elbowed Anna.

I took Kelsey's cue. "Who did you girls dance with?"

"I danced with Mitchell Blackman," Kelsey said. "He's about three feet shorter than me. Anna danced with Sam Kielver."

"Was he shorter than you?" I asked.

"No, he was about the same as me," Anna said.

"Yeah, just right," Kelsey said. Her tone was mocking and dreamy.

"Is there something I should know about this Sam Kielver?" I asked.

"You'll have to ask Anna," Kelsey said.

"He's just a really nice boy," Anna said.

"Did you have fun?" I asked.

"Yes," they answered together.

Yearbooks came out the last day of school. Anna and Kelsey sat at the counter and ate cookies as they looked at the pictures. When Brent got home, he looked over Anna's shoulder at the pictures she wanted to show him. "Did lots of people sign it?" he asked.

"Lots," Anna said.

"Sam signed it," Kelsey said, a swoon in her voice. Anna blushed and elbowed Kelsey hard. Kelsey giggled and elbowed Anna back. What had this Sam written, I wondered, that would provoke this pink-cheeked reaction.

"Sam, huh?" Brent said. "Is he a nice guy?"

"Yeah," Anna quickly said.

"Well, that's good. But just remember, girls," Brent said, "no one—and I mean no one—who lives in this house or spends a lot of time here . . ." he looked directly at Kelsey, "will date before she's twenty-eight." Both girls burst out laughing.

Later that night, I looked through the yearbook. I found pictures of Anna and Kelsey and a few of the kids I knew. At the bottom of the page was Sam Kielver's picture. He was a cute boy with freckles and a crooked smile. Scrawled in his boyish handwriting was a simple message.

> Anna,
> Hopefully I'll see you around this summer.
> Sam

That was it? *That* had prompted the blushing embarrassment? It was obvious. Anna was experiencing her first real crush. If it were someone else's daughter, I'd have thought this was all very sweet. As Anna's mother, I found it terrifying.

Chapter 10

From Anna's journal:

Mr. Lark, one of the English teachers at school, challenged us to read about important women in history this summer. He will be our teacher in the fall. He said he'd give extra credit to anyone who could come back to school with a finished report about an important woman who made a difference in history. It's been pretty great reading about some of these women. I've read about Joan of Arc and Harriet Tubman and Florence Nightingale. They all did such amazing things. I don't know who I want to choose for my report. Maybe I'll do one on all of them. I wonder if Mr. Lark would give extra credit for all three?

The thing I liked about all of those women was that they each made such great sacrifices for others. They didn't worry about them-selves. They only thought about the people who needed them. Joan of Arc led her people in war, even though she was just a teenager. She inspired them and encouraged them and then she died for them. Harriet Tubman could have escaped to freedom and then just lived a happy life, but instead she went back over and over, helping other slaves escape to freedom, even though if she had been caught, she would've been put to death. Florence Nightingale gave up almost everything to work in the hospitals and help save people's lives. She sacrificed a comfortable life with plenty of money to help those in need and even suffered horrible sickness because of her hard work.

I wonder if I'm supposed to do something important. Sometimes I think maybe I'm weird because there's something special for me to do.

I feel like that sometimes. I don't know what important thing I could do, though. It's not like there's a war where I could lead my people to victory, and there aren't slaves that I need to guide to freedom. I guess I could be a nurse or a doctor, but that has never really interested me, and seeing blood scares me a little. Okay, it scares me a lot.

*

Everything felt normal that summer. Brent worked a few days every week with his friend, Dave. They remodeled Dave's master bath and painted the exterior of his house. Then in August, they set to work on our house. They replaced the scarred and stained linoleum in our kitchen with ceramic tile. They also painted almost every room in the house. Anna chose pale green walls with white trim. Everything looked fresh and new, and I loved the results.

Brent asked me if I could help him get his classroom ready for school. We decorated bulletin boards, cleaned desks, and organized books. It wasn't until we got home that I realized it had all been an elaborate plan to get me out of the house. On the table was a birthday cake and a card—quite a surprise, since my birthday wasn't for three more months.

"Happy birthday!" Brent, Anna, and Kelsey said.

"What's this all about?" I turned to Brent and said, "You do know when my birthday is, don't you?"

"I know when it is. But this gift couldn't wait," Brent said. He handed me a card and kissed my cheek.

"So we decided we might as well celebrate the whole thing now," Anna said. I opened the card. I glanced up and smiled at their excited faces as I unfolded the paper inside. It was an enrollment form. My gift was a writing class at Mesa State that started the first week of September. Now it made sense.

"Wow," I said. "Thank you."

"We know you've wanted to take a class, and you said you wished sometimes that you were better at writing down your thoughts, so we thought this would be perfect," Anna explained. Kelsey lit the candles on the cake. "Do you like it?"

"I love it!" I couldn't decide whether I was more excited about the class or nervous that I'd be going to college again. Excitement won out. I blew out my candles and made a silent wish that I wouldn't feel ancient and frumpy and out of place on a college campus after all these years. We enjoyed the delicious chocolate cake that Anna and Kelsey had baked. It was a happy early birthday.

"Thank you for the class," I said to Brent that night. "It was a very thoughtful gift. There are so many things I want to write about. Someday, I'd like Anna to be able to read about her life and the things we've felt about it. Maybe after this class, I'll be able to do it justice."

"I can't wait to read what you write," Brent said. "It'll sound more like fiction than reality, I'm afraid."

That fall we all went back to school, and I had more homework than the girls. The class only met twice a week, but I worked on assignments almost every day. I enjoyed the challenge of putting my thoughts and ideas down on paper. The first time I had to read something I'd written out loud to the class, I thought I'd pass out. But after I'd finished, several people, including the professor, said good things about it. Writing in my journal, which I'd done haphazardly since I was twelve, became part of my routine, and I filled up pages every day. The professor pointed out things I could do to improve my writing, and I embraced his every suggestion. Anything that might help me improve excited me. By the time the course was over, I felt almost like a real writer. It helped that I got an A.

I kept writing. I wrote about our lives, our adventures, our day-to-day experiences. I didn't realize that someday in the not-too-distant future, I'd look back at that class and those journals with gratitude, and I'd long for the happy humdrum of those times.

Early one morning in February, Kelsey called. "Susan, I'm not feeling good at all. I think I'm going to stay home from school today." Her voice was raspy, and she sounded congested.

"Are you okay?" I asked. I knew she had to be pretty miserable to miss school. She loved school, and she especially loved basketball practice.

"I'll be fine. I'm just going to sleep all day."

"Do you need anything? I could bring over some medicine or some soup. Have you eaten anything?"

"I'll find something to eat," she said. "I really mostly feel tired. I'm just going to try to rest."

"If you want to come over here, I can come and get you after I take Anna to school."

"I don't really feel like moving. Thanks, but I'll just stay here and sleep. I'm sure I'll feel better tomorrow."

"All right, but if you need anything, call me. I won't call you, just in case you're sleeping." I wasn't so sure she'd be better by tomorrow. She sounded terrible, and I worried about her all day.

Wednesday morning, she called me again. She was worse. "I think I'm going to stay home again," she said.

"What do you feel like?" I asked. "Tell me your symptoms."

"I keep sweating and then I freeze." She paused and coughed for several seconds. "This cough really hurts, and once I start coughing, it's hard to stop."

"It sounds like you've got a fever. Have you had any medicine?" I asked.

"No, but I slept all day yesterday."

"Is someone going to be there with you today?"

"No. Dad's gone to Durango on a job, and Starr has to work."

"I'll come and get you. You can spend the day here, and we'll get you some medicine. I'll stop by after I drop off Anna."

"Are you sure you don't mind?"

"I'm sure. I'll see you in a little while."

"Thanks, Susan," Kelsey said.

"Should I stay home too?" Anna asked from the doorway of the kitchen. "I could help take care of her and keep her company."

"I think she'll be fine. Besides, don't you have to give your speech today?"

"Yeah, but I don't mind missing it if she needs me. I'm sure Mr. Dayle would let me reschedule it."

"I think you should go ahead and go to school," I said. "Kelsey will be here when you get home."

When I pulled up to the curb at the high school, Anna opened the door and then turned to me. "Mom, thanks for taking care of Kelsey. We're really all she's got."

I reached over and tucked her hair behind her ear. "You're welcome," I said.

"I love you, Mom." She leaned over and gave me a hug before she got out of the car. She waved, and I blew her a kiss.

Kelsey's house looked cold and forlorn as I pulled up. The maniac dog was gone, probably in Durango with Stan. I was relieved not to have to deal with it. I knocked on the door, and a minute later Kelsey opened it. "Honey, you look terrible." She was wearing the pink plaid, flannel pajamas we'd given her for Christmas. Her hair was dirty and tangled, and her eyes were sunken and tired. She had dark circles under her eyes, and her skin looked pale and clammy. She had her arms wrapped tightly around her, and she shivered against the cold outside air. "Let's get a few things together and take you home." I'd never been inside Kelsey's house before, and what I saw felt like a punch in the stomach. I followed her through a cramped front room with a broken recliner that faced a big-screen television—the only expensive thing in the house. The couch had holes worn down to the foam. A coffee table was covered with beer bottles and an ash tray that overflowed with cigarette butts. A bag of Alpo sat just inside the front door, and bits of dog food crunched under my feet as I walked across the floor.

The kitchen was no better. The air was thick with the smell of burnt bacon and cigarette smoke. Dirty dishes filled the sink and covered the counters. My shoes stuck to the dirty linoleum and made sucking noises as I walked. As I passed by the cluttered table, I saw one of the pretty green dishes with blue flowers that Kelsey had chosen. It was being used as an ashtray. The once-pretty flowered tablecloth underneath was stained and crusted with food. Just off the kitchen was a wide hallway, and a twin bed was there, pushed up against the back door. An old dresser stood at the foot of the bed. Two of the drawers had no handles, so they were left partly open. On top of the dresser sat Belle, the doll Anna had given Kelsey years ago.

The whole house was cold, but the hallway felt even colder. I could see daylight between the door and the door frame and could feel the cold draft that blew through the cracks.

"Is there anything you want to bring with you?" I asked. She took her coat off a hook beside the bed, slowly shrugged her arms into the sleeves, and pulled on a pair of sneakers.

"Just my pillow, I think," she said, tucking it under her arm. We made our way back through the house and out the front door.

"Where's your dog?" I asked.

"Dad took him to Durango." Just as I'd suspected.

When we walked through the front door at our house, I appreciated its warmth and coziness in a way I never had before. "Why don't you go take a quick shower? That always makes me feel a little better."

While Kelsey showered, I changed her pillowcase and made up a bed on the couch. When she reappeared a few minutes later, she looked better, and she smiled weakly when I gave her some cold medicine and some warm, fuzzy socks. She watched television for a little while before drifting off to sleep. She slept until just before Anna got home. They worked on a math assignment Kelsey had missed, but Kelsey soon got tired and fell asleep for several more hours. "Do you want me to call Starr and see if you can spend the night?" I asked after she woke up. I couldn't stand the thought of her sleeping in that cold, drafty hallway.

"I'd better not. Starr doesn't like to be alone at night. I should probably go home," she said.

"Okay, but you call me if you need anything," I said.

"I will, but I'm really feeling much better." Kelsey smiled. "Thanks for letting me come spend the day."

I stroked her hair. "You know we don't mind."

Kelsey went back to school the next day, but the cough persisted. She looked tired and lacked her usual energy. She insisted she was fine and wanted to finish the last two weeks of basketball, but I worried about the cough and the lack of color in her cheeks. The night of her last game, I drove her to the school early. "Are you going to be okay tonight? Your cough is sounding pretty nasty."

"I'll be fine. Dad said he'll be here tonight, so no way am I missing it." I smiled and hid my annoyance that he hadn't been to a single game all season. She reached in to grab her gym bag, and I noticed that the skin around her eyes looked especially dark and hollow.

"You go have a great game. We'll be back in a little while." I watched her walk through the gym doors. I could tell she'd lost weight in the past couple of weeks, and she looked weak in spite of her long stride and bouncy ponytail.

An hour later, I sat in the stands with Brent and Anna as the announcer introduced the teams. "In at center—wearing number six—Kelsey Davies." We cheered, and I searched the crowd. I wanted

Stan to be there and prayed that this time he wouldn't let her down. I noticed that Anna was looking too. She even stood up to get a better look at the people in the bleachers. By halftime, we'd given up.

"He's not coming, is he?" Anna said with a bitterness in her voice I'd never heard before.

I reached over and took her hand. She held my hand tightly and stilled her trembling lips between her teeth. Then Kelsey rebounded the ball, and Anna let go of my hand to clap and cheer loudly as if she could somehow make up for Stan's absence.

In spite of her sickness, Kelsey had a good game. She scored eight points and brought down seven rebounds. She scanned the crowd during warm-ups and time-outs, but always ended up looking back at us. On the way back to her house after the game, Brent asked. "Do you want to stop and get ice cream or pie or anything?"

"Thanks, anyway," Kelsey said. "I'm really tired. I think I'm just going to head to bed."

"All right, another time then," he said. We pulled up outside the chain-link fence, and the crazy dog immediately started his fence-destroying routine. Stan's truck, a newer model he'd purchased a few months earlier, was there in front of the house.

"Thanks for coming to the game," Kelsey said. There was a little quiver in her voice.

"Thanks for playing," Brent said. "We had a great time watching you." When Kelsey opened the door, I could see the light from the big television and Stan in the recliner with his feet up. Kelsey turned and waved good-bye before she closed the front door. I turned at the sound of a sniffle. In the glow of the streetlight, I saw Anna brush away the tears that were streaming down her cheeks.

"Don't be sad, sweetie," I said.

"I'm not sad, Mom. I'm angry. I don't know why I'm crying. All she wanted was for him to come to one game. He really doesn't care about her at all," she said.

"Some people don't know how to show they care," Brent said.

"You don't show it by sitting in the house watching TV when your daughter is playing in her last game of the year," Anna said. "Why can't she just have parents like you?"

Kelsey was worse the next day. Brent called Stan that evening
after Kelsey had excused herself from the table to go in the bathroom
and have a terrible coughing spell. "Hi, Stan, this is Brent. I'm calling about Kelsey. She doesn't seem to be getting better, and we're a
little worried about her. Is there any chance you could take her to
the doctor?" Brent sounded uncomfortable, but Kelsey needed to see
a doctor. "Well, I understand that, but I think she's really sick. Do
you mind if we take her to the nighttime clinic before we bring her
home?" He paused, and his voice became quieter so that Kelsey and
Anna couldn't hear him. "No, Stan, I'm not asking you to pay for it.
If we take her, we'll pay for it. I just think she needs to see a doctor."
He listened. "Fine then. We'll take her before we bring her home."
Of course, we'd take her, and of course we'd pay for it. A movement
at the doorway caught my attention, and I looked over to see Anna
shaking her head.

A short time later, Kelsey and I sat on a couch at the nighttime clinic. I flipped through a two-year-old *People* magazine as we
waited. "Susan?" Kelsey asked, "Will you come with me when they
call my name?"

"Of course I will," I said.

She let out a sigh of relief. "Thanks. I didn't want to go back
there alone." I laid the magazine down and took her hand.

"I'm sorry you had to bring me."

"Don't be sorry. I'm glad I can be the one to bring you. Now
don't worry about a thing. I'll be there the whole time."

An hour later, Kelsey and I waited on the cracked vinyl seats of
the pharmacy while the pharmacist filled her prescription. A blast of
cold air blew through the drive-through window behind the counter, and she shivered. She leaned back against the wall, too tired and
weak to hold her head up, and closed her eyes against the bright,
harsh fluorescent lighting. "Kelsey, I'm going to borrow their phone
and call Brent," I said quietly. She nodded but didn't open her eyes.

"Hi, Brent," I said. I picked up a tube of Chapstick from a dis-
play by the phone. "She has pneumonia. We're at the pharmacy waiting for her prescription."

"Wow, I'm glad you took her," he said. I swallowed hard. I was
so angry I wanted to cry, which made me even madder. I rolled the

Chapstick between my fingers. "Susan?" Brent said. "What's wrong?"

"Brent, I don't want to take her home. She doesn't even have a room. She sleeps in a drafty hallway." I tried to keep my voice quiet. I looked across the room to be sure Kelsey couldn't hear me before I continued. "Please call Stan. Ask if she can stay with us," I said. "Just until she gets better."

"I'll call him," Brent said. "But Susan, he wasn't happy about our conversation tonight. We're stepping on his toes, and he doesn't like it. I don't think he'll agree to it, so don't get your hopes up."

"Just try. Please," I said. "I don't want to take her back there. I don't know if anyone even checks on her, and she's got pneumonia. It's serious."

"Susan," Brent interrupted me. "I'll call."

"Thanks, Brent. I'll check back with you when the prescription is filled." I sat back down by Kelsey. She opened her eyes, leaned over, and then rested her head on my shoulder. I put my arm around her, and she snuggled in closer. For the next ten minutes I sat there simmering in my unpleasant thoughts about Stan as I twirled the stubby tube of Chapstick with my free hand like I used to twirl a pencil.

"Kelsey Davies?" the pharmacist said, and I left Kelsey to pay for the medicine. Then I called Brent.

"Can I bring her home?" I asked. I crossed my fingers like a little girl.

"Sorry, honey. He said you can pick her up in the morning since they have to work, but if she's sick, she needs her family." I laughed bitterly.

"Swing by the house," Brent said. "I'll bring the down comforter out to the car. She can take it with her." I was fuming. I gathered up the medicine and Kelsey and returned to the car, only to reach for my keys and discover I still had the Chapstick in my hand. I dropped it off along with my apologies at the drive-through.

Brent came out the front door as I pulled into the driveway. He was carrying a large, black garbage bag with the comforter rolled inside. "Suze, let me take her home?" he said as he opened the back door and put the bag on the backseat.

"I'm going to do this," I said. Brent didn't try to change my mind. He closed the back door and then opened the front door where

Kelsey was sitting. "Susan will come get you in the morning, okay?"

"Okay." She didn't lift her head off the back of the seat.

"You bundle up in that blanket and stay warm tonight." He reached in and felt her forehead tenderly. "We love you, Kelsey," he said.

"I love you too," she said.

Brent closed the door and stood on the porch as I backed out of the driveway. As I drove to Kelsey's, I took deep breaths in an effort to control the anger and frustration I was feeling. I didn't want to burst out crying or start screaming at Stan. So I said a silent prayer that I'd be able to maintain my composure. When we pulled in front of her house, I helped Kelsey out of the car and retrieved the garbage bag from the backseat. There was no outdoor light on to greet us, but as we walked through the gate, the front door opened and light spilled onto the uneven, cracked sidewalk. Stan's lanky form was a silhouette in the light from the television as he waited for Kelsey to get to the door. Was this some lame attempt to play the doting father? It would have been funny if it weren't so sad. The dog was nowhere to be seen, so I walked with Kelsey all the way to the front door. I fought to keep my voice steady as I explained what medication she should have before she went to bed. I gave her a hug, kissed her cheek, and handed her the garbage bag as she went into the house.

"What's that?" asked Stan. His tone was defensive.

"It's a down comforter. She needs to keep warm," I said in my iciest voice. I guess he could tell it would be a mistake to challenge me any further because he stepped aside and let Kelsey through with the bag.

"Kelsey, I'll be back in the morning," I said.

"Thanks, Susan." She carried the comforter and disappeared into the darkness of the house.

"Yeah, thanks," Stan said.

"Please, just take care of her," I said. Stan just stood staring in the doorway as I walked away, and I had to force myself to walk steadily to the car instead of running like I wanted to. I glanced back, and he was still standing there watching me as I pulled away.

"Are you okay?" Brent asked when I walked through the front door.

"No," I said. He walked over and put his arms around me. I leaned into him and let myself cry while he hugged me for a long time.

A little while later, I walked into Anna's room, tucked the blankets around her, and kissed her forehead. She stirred and looked up at me. "Is Kelsey okay?" She leaned up on her elbow.

I sat down on the edge of her bed. "She has pneumonia, but she's going to be okay."

Anna let out a long sigh. "That's good. Thanks for looking out for her."

"We have to," I said. "She's family."

Anna smiled. "Good night, Mom. I love you." She turned over and snuggled back under the covers.

"I love you too, Anna."

✸

Kelsey stayed at our house during the day, and then we'd take her home at bedtime. After a week of medication and rest, she felt much better. Anna brought home schoolwork, and Kelsey stayed caught up in school, with the exception of a couple of tests she would take once she returned. One night when I got back from dropping off Kelsey, I found Anna sitting up in her bed waiting for me.

"Mom . . ." She nervously picked at a piece of thread on her bedspread. "I need to talk to you."

"All right." I sat down on the bed and scooted my back against the wall so I could see her. "What is it?"

"Remember a long time ago, when Stan and Starr quit fighting, and you told me that I had a gift for being a peacemaker?"

"I remember."

"Remember how you said I had other gifts that you'd tell me about someday?"

"Yes."

"Can you tell me about them now?" I knew this day would come, I'd even expected it a bit sooner, but it still caught me off guard.

"Do you have any idea what they are?" I asked.

She thought for a moment. "Well, I definitely know about people not fighting around me. Sometimes I see things at school, and I know that people have quit arguing because I'm there. But there are other things that are strange, aren't there?"

"What other things?"

"I don't get sick, do I?"

Part of me hesitated. Acknowledging her special gifts made them impossible to ignore. From now on, they would be a conscious part of her life. "No, you don't. You've never been sick."

"Kelsey's been so miserable. I don't even know what that's like. What does it feel like to be sick?"

"Well, it depends on the kind of sickness. Sometimes your head hurts, or your body aches, or you feel like you're going to throw up. Your nose can get stuffy, and it's hard to breathe."

"When Kelsey kept coughing, it looked like it hurt," she said. "It's not like I want to get sick, but I wish I knew what that felt like."

"You don't get hurt, either," I said. "Like cuts and scrapes and broken bones—you've never had any of those."

She thought for a minute, and I waited quietly. "Do you think I'll ever get sick or hurt?"

"I don't know. If things stay the way they are, probably not."

"Why am I like this?" she asked.

"I really don't know, honey. I've never known anyone else that's like you. I guess it's just a blessing that you have. Lots of people would love to never get sick or hurt."

"I'm sure that's true. But I don't want to be a freak or something."

"You're not a freak, Anna. You're different, but you're not a freak. Your difference is a gift. It's a blessing to you and everyone around you. A long time ago, your dad and I decided to just enjoy and love the things that are different about you. They're what make you Anna. There is nothing, nothing, nothing about you that should make you feel bad," I said. "We couldn't love you more than we do—special gifts and all." Anna scrambled down to where I was sitting and hugged me. Then she sat by me, with her back against the wall, and we held hands.

"Do you think Kelsey has noticed anything weird about me?"

"I'm sure Kelsey knows you're special, but she's never said anything to me. Has she said anything that makes you think she knows?"

"Not really. Once she said something about the room looking different, but that was a long time ago. Do you think I should tell her? We've never had secrets from each other."

"I think that's up to you. Give it some thought. Pray about it and be sure before you do anything, but Anna, this is your decision. And you're getting old enough that you should decide who knows about it."

"When did you first know about it?" I told her about the day she and Jacob had fallen out of the wagon. She smiled. "Too bad I couldn't share it."

"We'd probably all like a little of that. I know I would." We sat quietly for several minutes. "Do you have any other questions?" I asked.

Anna hesitated and then spoke quietly. "Why didn't you ever tell me?"

"Because we were trying to protect you. We didn't want you to feel different."

"But I am different." We were quiet for almost a minute, each of us lost in our own thoughts. "Mom, if I have a gift, shouldn't I use it instead of hiding it?"

I felt like the wind had been knocked out of me. All these years we'd thought we were doing the right thing by protecting her. But to protect her, we'd hidden her gift. We'd hidden her talent under a bushel. Had we been wrong all this time?

"I don't know, Anna. We've wanted you to feel normal and happy. I don't know if you're supposed to use it for something or not. I think if you are, you'll know what you should do." I tucked the blankets around her. "You know, honey, you might not get sick or hurt, but you do get tired."

"That's true," she said and smiled. I kissed her good night and touched her cheek. She reached up, grabbed my hand, and pressed it against her face. "You're the best mom I could have asked for. I love you."

"I love you too. So much." I quietly left the room and started down the stairs. About halfway down, I sat down and leaned my head against the wall, suddenly weary. What if Anna was right? What if she *was* supposed to do something with her gifts? Who was I to stand in the way if Anna had a special purpose?

Chapter 11

From Anna's journal:

I think Caleb Sanders likes Kelsey. In fact, I'm sure of it. I've seen him looking at her in English, and today in Science, when we split up for labs, he actually asked her to be his partner. We were surprised because he's so shy. I think it's the first time he's ever spoken to her.

Mr. Nelson asked me to stay after class for a minute because he wanted to talk to me. He wants me to take an advanced chemistry class next year. He said I'm so good at science that he thinks I should think about a career in science. He said I'd make a good biochemical engineer. He explained that if I had that career I'd be working on a cure for cancer or some other sickness. I've never thought about studying science in college, but it might be fun. I like figuring things out. That would be ironic, me doing research to find cures when I don't even get sick. I wonder what he would have thought if I told him that. I'm sure he wouldn't believe me.

That spring, Anna turned fifteen. Kelsey had turned fifteen a couple of months earlier, and they added a driver's education class to their fall schedule. All summer, they talked about driving and pointed out cute cars they'd like to own after they got their driver's licenses. I smiled at that. They'd be lucky to have any car at all to drive.

"Susan?" I turned around in the hallway at church to see Lora Sims approaching me. "I'm so glad I caught you. I've been meaning to talk to you about something."

"Hi, Lora." Lora was a heavyset woman in her late fifties. She was one of the busiest women I'd ever met. Not only had she owned a large day care center for many years, but she also was one of the first people to volunteer for a church committee, or anything else, for that matter. She loved children and usually sat close to an overwrought young mother so she could help care for a couple of children. She linked her arm through mine, and together we walked outside.

"Do you think Anna would be interested in a job this summer? I have a couple of ladies who'd like to take the summer off and stay home with their kids but want to have their jobs back at the end of the summer. I know Anna's good with kids, so I was wondering if she'd like to fill in at the day care."

"I bet she'd love it."

"Do you mind if I give her a call about it then?"

"No, that would be fine."

Lora smiled and gave my arm a little squeeze. "I just wanted to check with you first and make sure it was okay. No sense putting ideas in her head if she can't do it."

I smiled at her consideration. "I think she'd enjoy that. You should definitely call her."

That afternoon, Sister Sims called for Anna. They talked for nearly half an hour, and then Anna came into the kitchen with a huge smile on her face.

"We've got a job this summer."

"We've?" I asked.

"Kelsey and me. Two of Sister Sims's ladies want to take the summer off, so she asked if I wanted a job and then asked if I had a friend who might want to work too. I've got to call Kelsey." Immediately she dialed the number. I hoped Stan would agree to the idea. You just never knew for sure how he was going to react. A few minutes later, she was beaming as she announced that Kelsey had permission and they'd be working all summer for Sister Sims.

I should have known Stan would be fine with the idea. Kelsey bringing in some extra money so he didn't have to cover any of her expenses was just exactly the kind of thing he'd approve of, I thought bitterly. Then I remembered our Relief Society lesson this morning on charity and felt just a little bit bad for judging him harshly.

School got out on a Wednesday. Anna and Kelsey couldn't wait for Monday to arrive. I was a little conflicted about the day care job. The girls would be much busier this summer than we were used to, and I knew I'd miss their company during the day, but their enthusiasm was contagious, and by the time I dropped them off on Monday morning, I was almost as excited for them as they were for themselves. I picked them up at 5:30 that evening. They were exhausted but talkative and excited about the day.

"Mom, you should have seen this little boy named Caleb. He has the curliest blond hair, and he sang all day. He even sang on his cot during nap time. I didn't think he would ever fall asleep, so I started stroking his nose and forehead with my finger, like you used to do to me, and pretty soon he stopped singing and fell asleep. But as soon as he woke up, he started singing again. He is so cute!"

"That trick always worked on you. I could probably do that to you right now, and you'd fall asleep in minutes." We laughed.

"You probably could. I'm so tired," Anna said.

"How did it go for you, Kelsey?" I asked.

"It was great. I held babies all day long. It didn't even feel like a job. There are two little babies there, and that's what I got to do almost the whole day. I fed and rocked a baby girl named Samantha until she fell asleep, and Mrs. Sims said I did such a good job she asked me to feed and rock a baby boy named Jez. I fed some of the other kids snacks too, but by far my favorite part was taking care of the little babies."

"Sounds like it's the perfect job for two nice girls," I said.

"Mom, they call us Miss Anna and Miss Kelsey," Anna said. "Isn't that the cutest thing ever?"

"It's cute, but it makes you sound too old," I said.

That summer was like a dream for Anna and Kelsey. Their nurturing instincts surprised me. Lora said to stop by anytime, so I did a few times that summer. One day, I stopped by at nap time. I was confused as I walked in the door because there were no lights on. I picked my way around the center by the light that came through the partially blinded front windows. Sleeping children on cots lined the walls. I found Anna sitting against the wall, knees up, holding a little boy of about three. She was rubbing his back as he fell asleep. Her other hand was being held tightly by a little girl lying on the cot next to her. The little girl was asleep, but Anna hadn't moved her hand.

"Hi, Mom," she whispered. I sat down on the floor a few feet from her.

"How's it going?" I asked.

"Good."

"I just wanted to stop by and see you in action. Is that Caleb?" I reached out and touched the curly, blond head resting on her shoulder.

She nodded. "Isn't he cute?"

"He sure is."

"They're all cute." She looked lovingly around the room.

"These two look pretty comfortable." I nodded toward Caleb and the little girl holding Anna's hand.

"I love nap time because it's a challenge. Some of the kids don't want to go to sleep without their parents—like Lizzy and Caleb—so I try to make them happy and help them fall asleep. It only took twenty-four minutes today," she said proudly. I smiled. She was so sweet with the kids, and so patient too. My little girl was growing up.

"Kelsey's back in the nursery with the babies if you want to go see her. The babies are really sweet. You won't believe how tiny the new one is."

I nodded and blew her a kiss. She kissed the air in return, and I walked through the darkened room to the nursery. Four cribs were lined up against the wall, and to my right was a rocking chair. The room was unlit except for a little lamp on a table beside the rocking chair. In the chair, rocking a tiny baby wrapped in a yellow, giraffe-covered blanket, was Kelsey. Her face lit up when she saw me, and she smiled as she continued rocking.

"Oh my, what a tiny baby," I said.

"She's only two months old. Her name is Grace."

"She's sure pretty."

"We keep Kelsey back here with the babies," Lora said quietly, walking over to stand beside me. "She has a real knack for keeping them happy." Kelsey blushed but looked pleased at the compliment. "I'm not sure if we're going to let these girls go back to school this fall. The kids adore them."

"I'm glad," I said. "I know they love the kids too." I turned to Kelsey. "I just wanted to stop and say hi. I'll see you after work."

"Bye," Kelsey said. Lora walked out with me. I waved at Anna, who still held Caleb.

"It's like they're magic," Lora said when we were outside. "I've been running this day care for fifteen years, and I've never had a more peaceful and pleasant summer. The kids don't fight. They play nicely. They're happy. I wasn't kidding when I said I didn't want them to leave at the end of the summer. We're really going to miss them."

"Thanks for giving them the chance to work together. They're excited to be able to buy some of their school clothes this year, and it's nice for them to have a little of their own spending money. They talk about the kids all the time. This has been great for them."

"I really wasn't sure about hiring Kelsey without ever meeting her, but I'm glad I trusted Anna's instincts. They're two amazing young ladies. They're already hired for next summer if they want the job," she said.

Anna and Kelsey's summer became a comfortable routine. They worked all week, went swimming or bicycling on Saturday afternoons, and sometimes saw a movie on Saturday nights. I took them to the bank, and they both opened savings accounts. They were so responsible that a couple of times I was actually glad to see them blow some money on something like a CD or a piece of jewelry.

From Anna's journal:

> Yesterday at the day care, Caleb fell off the side of the slide and broke his arm. We had to call his mom and have her take him to the doctor. He cried and cried and wanted me to hold him, so I held him until his mom got there. Today he was excited to show me his new blue cast. He handed me a black marker and asked me to sign it. After a little while, he came up to me and said his arm hurt, and he wanted me to hold him. I held him almost all day. He cried a few times and said it was hurting inside. It was so sad. He's so little, and I felt so bad for him.
>
> It bothers me that I don't know how he feels. I know it sounds strange, but I want to know how it feels for something to hurt. It's

not like I want something huge. I just want to know what other people feel. I want to know what pain is like. I guess I should be thankful that I don't get sick or hurt, but sometimes I just want to be like everybody else. Sometimes I don't want to be special or extra blessed. I couldn't even say, "I know how you feel," because I don't.

"Susan, where are you? Susan?" I heard the front door hit the wall as it flew open. I hurried down the stairs to find Kelsey frantically running through the house looking for me.

"Kelsey? What's wrong?" I asked.

"Susan, Anna's hurt. She crashed her bike, and she's bleeding." I stood on the stairs and tightly gripped the handrail, stunned. "Susan, you've got to come," Kelsey said. I realized it was my mind that was racing, not my feet. I forced myself to follow Kelsey as I tried to fathom what was happening. Kelsey led me out the front door and down the street. I felt numb. Anna didn't get hurt. What was going on? Just around the corner, I saw her. She was sitting on the curb, holding her leg. Her knee had a huge gash. Blood was running down her leg and tears were streaming down her face. She looked up at me with an odd expression on her face. She almost looked guilty. But other, more pressing concerns filled my mind.

"Anna, what happened?" I did my best not to sound panicky.

"I didn't see that skateboard," she said. I looked a few feet away and saw a skateboard in the gutter. "I came around the corner and ran right into it."

"She flew over the front of the bike and hit her knee on something," Kelsey said. "It scared me to death."

"Well, let's get you home and see if that needs stitches." I helped her up. Questions flooded my mind, but I knew this wasn't the time to ask them. I put my arm under hers, and she limped home while Kelsey walked behind us with Anna's bike. Once inside, Anna sat on the counter, the same counter that Jacob had sat on all those years ago, and I began to clean her knee. The gash was long and deep, and I knew right away she needed stitches. I wrapped a clean dish towel around her leg, helped her out to the car and drove to the emergency room. Anna had stopped crying, but her eyes were still red. I looked at her intently, but she wouldn't look me in the eye. Everything felt new and strange. I wished Brent was home and not at an overnight scout activity. I felt very alone and scared.

A businesslike woman walked in and introduced herself as Dr. Limone. After a few questions and a quick examination, she got right to work. Anna's knee needed six stitches. Anna held my hand tightly and watched the doctor work, her eyes glued to the injury on her knee. Kelsey sat in a chair several feet away and turned her head so she wouldn't have to watch what was happening. Dr. Limone wasn't a very warm and fuzzy woman, and I felt a little sad that Anna's first, and hopefully only, injury was being treated with so little tenderness. I whispered encouraging words and held her hand.

Dr. Limone finished the stitches and wrapped the injured knee in a gauze bandage. "There you go," she said. "Keep an eye on that and try to keep her from bending her knee much for the first few days. A lot of bending and straightening, and she'll have those stitches worked loose. If she can keep it straight, she may be able to avoid a nasty scar. I'd like to see her back in ten days to remove the stitches. If you notice any heat or redness around the wound, bring her back in. We don't want an infection. Okay, hang tight here until the nurse comes." She exited through the curtain and left us there in the little partitioned area to wait for the nurse to bring Anna's check-out papers. A short time later, a nurse was wheeling Anna through the big double doors of the emergency entrance and to our waiting car. Anna and Kelsey talked about the accident, the doctor, and the stitches while I silently drove, completely absorbed in my thoughts. I had questions for Anna, and I couldn't wait to talk to Brent about what had happened. I knew it wasn't his fault, but I was upset that he was gone for our daughter's first emergency and that I wouldn't be able to talk to him about it until tomorrow afternoon.

Kelsey enjoyed playing nurse. She helped Anna get situated on the sofa, put pillows under her leg, and loaded the little side table with milk and snacks. I didn't want to leave Anna home alone, and I wanted her to keep her leg up and straight, so Kelsey called Stan and asked him to pick her up that evening. To my surprise, he did it. I felt guilty that I was eager for Stan to get there. It wasn't that I wanted Kelsey to go home, it was just that I couldn't talk to Anna with Kelsey there, and it was testing my last bit of patience to go on waiting for the answers I'd wanted to know all day.

I waved to Kelsey at the front door and then hurried back to the family room and sat down in a chair across from Anna. She looked at me and turned off the television with the remote. I didn't say anything. I just waited as she glanced at me uncomfortably and then fidgeted with the bandage on her knee. Finally she said, "I'm sorry, Mom."

"Sorry for what?" I asked.

"I'm sorry I got hurt." She still wouldn't look at me.

"How did it happen?"

I waited in silence while she continued to fidget a little longer. Finally she looked at me. "I didn't mean to scare you or upset you. I just wanted to know what it felt like."

I stared at her, dumbfounded. "You mean you did this on purpose?" I asked.

"Not exactly."

"What do you mean?"

"I didn't crash on purpose. I really didn't see the skateboard when I came around the corner. When I ran into it, the bike really did throw me."

"Okay."

"The thing is . . ." She paused, and I waited. "The thing is, it felt like everything was happening really slowly, like slow motion in a movie or something. I could feel myself falling off the bike, and I thought to myself, 'I want to know what it feels like to get hurt.' And then I was on the ground, bleeding." Anna's voice was soft, and I leaned forward to hear her. "Mom, it was like it happened because I wanted it to happen. Like it was my decision."

"You decided you wanted to be hurt?" I was overcome by a mixture of feelings. I was both relieved and troubled that she'd consciously chosen to go through this.

"Mom, please don't be mad. I didn't know I'd need to go to the hospital and have stitches. I just wanted to feel what it's like to get hurt, to get scraped or bruised or something. I've never felt it before, and I just wanted to be normal for once." Anna's chin was quivering, and I felt sorry for her. All her life, Brent and I had wanted her to feel normal and happy. I was torn. I was horrified that Anna would hurt herself, and yet, how could I begrudge her desire to feel what normal people experience? I moved over beside her and held her hand.

"And how did you like it? Feeling normal?" I asked, my annoyance gone.

"I didn't like it very much." We both laughed a little. "It really hurt. And when I was sitting there and the blood was running down my leg and getting on my hands, I got really scared. I saw all that blood, and it was stinging. And then Kelsey brought you over, and you looked so scared I was afraid for a minute that I was going to bleed to death."

"Oh, Anna." I rested my head on the back of the couch, exhausted. "I'm sorry if I made it worse, but I was so shocked. This is something I thought was never going to happen, a part of being a mom that I wouldn't ever have to deal with, so I was really surprised. Over the years, I guess I've just quit worrying about your safety, as strange as that seems."

"Are you mad at me?" she asked.

"No. I think I understand why you wanted to know what it feels like to get hurt, but I don't understand how it happened."

"I don't either. I didn't know that just by wanting it to happen, I could make it happen."

"I certainly hope you aren't going to make a habit of this," I said.

Anna laughed. "Don't worry. I'm glad that I know what it feels like, but I didn't like it at all, and now I have to be all careful with my knee for a few weeks. I feel so bad for people who go through things like this all the time. It must be so hard. I think I'd always be scared of getting hurt." She paused a few moments. "I guess it was kind of a dumb thing to do."

"I don't know about that. Physical pain is part of life for just about everyone on this planet. I can see how you'd want to know what it is. But now that you know, can you keep your curiosity in check? For me?"

"Just for you, Mom." She smiled, and I gave her a hug and then carefully helped her to bed. I'm not sure if I slept at all that night. I was glad Anna seemed satisfied with her new knowledge of pain, but my sense of security had been deeply shaken. I tried to rationalize away my fear with the knowledge that this had happened because Anna had chosen it, but now I knew that Anna wasn't physically invincible.

Now I was like every other mother who had to worry about her child's safety. I hadn't asked for Anna's unique gift, but I'd definitely benefited from the peace of mind it had given me. I felt strangely afraid.

I had planned to tease Brent about his absence during the family emergency, but one look at his face when he saw Anna's injury let me know that wasn't a good idea. I thought my peace of mind had been rocked, but Brent seemed almost unable to cope with what had happened. He asked me to describe the event so many times that I began to grow impatient. He quizzed Anna about her choice and about how it had felt as she fell. He made her promise him that she'd never let curiosity get the best of her again. The more he fussed, the more uncomfortable she seemed.

"Brent, could you come help me flip the mattress," I said from upstairs. Reluctantly, he joined me in the bedroom. "Brent, you've got to stop," I said. "You're driving us all crazy."

"I can't help it. I don't understand this. How could this happen?"

"Because she wanted it to happen. Brent, she wanted to know what other people feel. It isn't really a bad thing," I said. "Now she knows."

"But now we know she can get hurt. What if now that it's happened, it can happen any time? What if this just opened a door that was supposed to stay closed?"

How was I supposed to answer that? I had the same fears. "What if it does?" I asked, surprised at both my calmness and the words that were coming from my mouth. "Then I guess we'll be like all the other parents in the world." Oh, I hoped that wasn't true. I hoped that everything could go back to how it was before. I missed the security I'd felt. I didn't want to be like all the other parents in the world in *this* way. But Brent needed to get control of himself. This frantic fussing was too hard on Anna.

"Why are you so calm about this? I can't believe you're happy about it," he said.

"I'm not happy about it. I couldn't breathe yesterday. I've never been so scared. But when Anna explained it to me, I understood. Just imagine how she feels, Brent. She sees other people getting hurt and sick, and she has no idea what they're going through. She feels like an alien from another world. We can't really blame her for wanting to feel normal. It's what we've always wanted for her."

"Not like this. Not downstairs with stitches in her leg."

"If it makes you feel any better, she didn't enjoy it." I smiled, and he finally smiled back.

"That's a relief. Our daughter didn't enjoy getting stitches in her leg. I guess she really is normal." It wasn't easy, but over the next few weeks, Brent and I began to feel a reserved peace about Anna. She healed quickly and only missed a couple of days of work at the day care. Once or twice, she joked about her choice as she tried to reassure us. It wasn't long before we stopped talking about it altogether. Brent and I grudgingly accepted that Anna was more normal than we really wanted her to be, and Anna seemed to have satisfied her desire to feel like everyone else.

★

The two Saturdays before school was to start, I took the girls shopping for school clothes and supplies. They each got a couple of pairs of jeans and a few shirts. At Famous Footwear, Anna and Kelsey both found boots that they really liked, but when they looked at the price tag, they hesitated. "If you want the boots, I'll pay half on them," I said.

"Thanks, Mom," Anna quickly said. But Kelsey still hesitated. She stood there thinking as she looked down at the angled mirror by her feet and admired the boots from several angles.

Finally she made her decision. "I'd better not."

"Why not?" Anna asked. "You've saved lots of money for school clothes. You should get them." I walked away and looked at a sales rack of shoes. I didn't want to influence Kelsey one way or the other. I glanced at the girls and could tell Kelsey was whispering something serious to Anna. Anna got a serious look on her face, and then both girls took off the boots and placed them back on the shelf.

"You should still get them," I heard Kelsey say as I walked closer.

"I don't really want them. Even my half would be a lot. Let's go find something else."

"What happened at the shoe store today?" I asked later that

evening, when it was just Brent, Anna, and me.

"It was no big deal. The boots were too expensive anyway."

"Was it just the money Kelsey was worried about?" I asked. Anna nodded, her mouth shut tight as though she was working hard to keep quiet. Finally she gave up and leaned forward in her chair.

"Stan made her give him five hundred dollars to pay the rent this month. He told her they wouldn't have anywhere to live if she didn't give him the money. That's why she didn't have enough to pay for the boots." I was surprised at Anna's outburst. She let out a long sigh and fell back in her chair. "Poor Kelsey," she said. She sounded weary, as if the confession had worn her out.

I reached over and rubbed her arm. "I'm sorry, honey."

"It's okay. She just doesn't deserve to be treated like that."

"Life isn't about what we deserve," Brent said. "It's about what lessons we need to learn. I'm sure God doesn't think Kelsey deserves a hard life. I think he just knows she can handle it and will learn some valuable lessons from it."

"What does that say about me?" she asked. Her voice was quiet, and she looked down at her hands in her lap.

"What do you mean?" Brent asked.

"God must not think I can handle very much, 'cause he sure made my life easier than hers."

"Anna, your challenges are different than hers," I said. "God loves you both and knows that both of you are amazing. Have you ever told Kelsey about any of the special things about you?" I asked.

"No."

"Did you decide not to?"

"I just didn't want her to think I had all the good luck in the world when sometimes she has such bad luck. Maybe I'll tell her someday, but not now."

"That makes sense," I said.

"That's just it, though," Anna said. "It doesn't make sense to me. If my challenge is that I don't get sick or that people around me don't fight, what kind of challenges are those? They don't sound very hard to me. I don't get it." I didn't have the answers for her, and she didn't seem to expect any.

Naturally, I wanted to break down the door of Stan's little house and insist he give Kelsey her hard-earned money back, but Brent, ever the voice of reason, calmed me down and reminded me why we had to remain civil. Fighting with Stan would only make things harder for Kelsey. She already faced so many hard things. It didn't make any sense to add to the contention and strife in her life if we could avoid it. That was sometimes easier said than done. A little while later, I went upstairs, closed the bedroom door, knelt down, and prayed. I prayed for answers for Anna, peace for Kelsey, and patience for me.

Driver's education was by far Anna and Kelsey's favorite class that fall. They told me numerous stories about near-accidents and teachers afraid for their lives. I thought many times how glad I was that someone else was teaching them to drive. They did have to practice their driving, however, and once they got their permits, we'd sometimes take short drives with one of them behind the wheel and me in the passenger seat. They did a good job most of the time, but once, as Kelsey approached a stop sign a little faster than I liked, I nearly put my foot through the floor of the car as I tried to step on some imaginary brake. They both thought that was hilarious and laughed so hard that Kelsey had to pull over until she regained her composure.

They finished the class in December. Now they just had to wait until Kelsey turned sixteen in January, and Anna in March.

Christmas that year seemed extra festive. It helped that there was an unusual amount of snow. It started the second week of November and didn't stop. About every other morning, I shoveled a few inches of snow off the sidewalk and driveway. It piled up higher and higher until the house looked like a Christmas card. The snow made it feel more like Christmas than some years and caused us to spend more time in the cozy comfort of our house. We decorated the tree the Monday after Thanksgiving, and Brent decorated the house with strand after strand of lights. It was so beautiful that it nearly took my breath away every time we turned onto our street.

The baking bug bit, and Anna, Kelsey, and I made so many Christmas cookies and candies that we took plates of goodies to neighbors, friends, people from church, and school teachers. We made little pink and white candy-cane shaped cookies, fudge, toffee, peanut brittle, and caramel popcorn. Anna suggested we leave a box of candy with a big, red ribbon on top of the garbage can on garbage day. Since Anna and Kelsey were in school, it was my job to spy out the window and check out the garbage man's reaction to the gift. I was happy to report that he looked very pleased. The next week, when I pulled the garbage can back to the garage, there was a nice thank you note taped to the top of the can.

We baked enough for Brent to put a huge plate of Christmas cookies in the teachers' lounge at the high school. Kelsey took a plate of candy home, and Stan loved the peanut brittle so much that we made a whole batch just for him. I could tell it made Kelsey happy that he liked her peanut brittle, and I was glad he'd given her this little bit of approval.

Several times, I noticed odd behavior from Anna and Kelsey. They'd suddenly get quiet when I came toward them. At first, I wondered what was going on, but soon I realized it probably had something to do with Christmas, so I tried not to sneak up on them. They asked if I'd drop them off at the mall at noon on a Saturday and not pick them up until at least four. I agreed but wondered what they had up their sleeves. When I picked them up, they were empty-handed and didn't seem to have anything at all to show for their four hours of shopping. I didn't ask questions, but curiosity gnawed at me.

Brent and I wanted to get something special for the girls for Christmas that year. They were getting older, and we wanted to give them something a little more grown up. I had noticed that during the summer they'd become more interested in jewelry, so we decided to get them "best friends" necklaces with their birthstones. The necklaces were sterling silver with silver heart pendants. Each heart had an aquamarine and a garnet to represent the girls' birthstones. On the back of the heart were engraved the words "forever friends."

Stan wouldn't let Kelsey come to our house on Christmas day or spend Christmas Eve with us, so we had our Christmas Eve with Kelsey two days before Christmas. We listened to Christmas music while we enjoyed soup, biscuits, and cinnamon rolls. After dinner, we gathered in the living room and took turns reading about Jesus's birth from the Bible. The girls asked if they could save their present for last, so we handed them their little gift boxes and told them they could open them at the same time. I watched them carefully remove the wrapping paper and open the little boxes, knowing they were going to love them. Their faces lit up as they realized the significance of the gift, and both immediately came to give Brent and me a hug. I was glad we'd decided on this gift as I watched them help each other clasp the necklaces. They really were beautiful, and the girls were thrilled that they had both of their birthstones on them. "It's like we're really sisters," Kelsey said, and Anna smiled at me.

After the girls had each opened their warm flannel pajamas, it was time for them to give us our gift. Anna went to her room and came back with a large box. "You have to open it together," she said, so Brent came and sat beside me. Together we tore off the wrapping paper, and then Brent lifted the lid. Inside was a big, framed portrait of Anna and Kelsey together. They were sitting outside on two big, red boulders. Anna sat on the taller rock and Kelsey sat to her right on a shorter one. Behind them, the sky was vivid blue with fluffy white clouds. Both girls wore jeans and sweaters. Their hair was gently blowing in a breeze, and they both looked relaxed and happy.

"This is beautiful," I said, touching the antique-looking wood frame.

"What a perfect present," Brent said. We looked at the portrait for several minutes as the girls told us about the day the picture was taken. The photographer and his wife had driven them up a canyon until they found the perfect spot. I'd never seen the girls look prettier than they did in the picture. Brent stood and walked to a framed print on the wall and took it down.

"You don't have to put it in here." Anna sounded embarrassed. "You can put it in your bedroom or something."

"It's too beautiful to put anywhere else," Brent said. He straightened the picture and stepped back to admire it.

It was a wonderful "Christmas Eve" celebration—probably the best we'd ever had. We drove Kelsey, along with another plate of peanut brittle, home at about 11:00 p.m. We all got out of the car and hugged Kelsey good-bye, glad she'd been part of our family on this special night.

We spent Christmas morning in our pajamas. We ate our

traditional sausage and egg Christmas casserole and opened presents from grandparents. In the afternoon, we went to a movie. It was a pleasant, happy day.

I found myself gazing at the portrait many times in the coming days. Sometimes I'd stand in front of it and take in every detail—Anna's honey-colored hair and long fingers or Kelsey's long legs and dark brown eyes. Other times, I'd sit in my favorite chair and stare at it from a distance, looking at the pretty girls, their happy smiles, the perfect, puffy clouds, and the beautiful red rocks. I loved that portrait and couldn't think of any gift in the world I could have loved more.

★

Kelsey had a great time playing basketball that year and made the varsity team as a sophomore. She was healthy and steadily improved as the season progressed. Many times, we found her name listed in the newspaper. Anna took pictures and clipped articles to put in a scrapbook for Kelsey. About halfway through the season, we were sitting in the stands cheering for Kelsey's team. I glanced to the door of the gymnasium and was astonished to see Stan. I grabbed Brent's arm and nodded toward the door, just as Stan looked in our direction. Brent waved. Stan gave a little nod but didn't come and join us. Instead, he found a spot in the opposing team's section. I tried not to stare, but I found myself glancing at him often during the game. I never saw him look our way again. His expression never changed throughout the game and, with two minutes left, I watched him get up and quietly leave. "Did you know your dad was coming to the game?" I asked Kelsey in the car after the game.

"No. Was he there?" she asked.

"He was."

"I didn't see him. Where did he sit?"

"He sat across the gymnasium."

"Really?" she asked.

"I'll bet he loved it when you brought down that rebound and put it up for a score at the end of the third quarter," Brent said.

"I can't believe he came," she said quietly.

"Maybe he'll come more now," Anna said. "How can he stay

away now that he's seen how good you are?" Kelsey smiled hopefully. But that was the only time Stan ever saw her play.

✦

There was something easy and relaxing about that winter. We all felt happy and calm. Though I was a worrier by nature, I was surprised to notice that I wasn't really worrying about anything. School was going smoothly, Stan seemed a distant figure, and the girls were growing up to be beautiful and bright. I know it sounds silly, but I actually opened my notebook one day and tried to make a list of things I should be concerned about, sure I was missing something that needed my attention. But nothing came to mind other than trying to fix healthier meals. Looking back, I should have realized there's usually a calm before the storm.

March came, and the weather got warmer. On Anna's birthday, I took both girls to the DMV. They passed the written test and then took a turn at the driving portion. We walked out of the building with two new driver's licenses and two very happy girls. Anna drove us to Cold Stone, where we celebrated with ice cream, and then Kelsey drove us home. They'd been talking about getting their driver's licenses together for about a year, and now they'd reached that milestone together. Later that night, we gave Anna her other birthday present—a cell phone.

"Now, this isn't for a bunch of texting," I said.

"And we don't have a ton of minutes on the plan," Brent said, "but we decided that since you now have a driver's license and will be out on your own sometimes, we want you to have this, in case there's ever an emergency."

"Okay," she said. She looked excitedly at the little, electronic gadget. Before Anna went to bed that night, she'd read the instruction book and programmed in the numbers for Kelsey's house, our house, and Brent's and my cell phones.

✦

Something happened to Kelsey when they reached the driver's license goal. She finally started to believe that maybe she and Anna really could go to college together on scholarships. Up until that year, she'd been reserved and quiet whenever Anna mentioned any plans for the future. I'd worried that Kelsey believed Stan when he said she'd never be able to go to college. I encouraged this talk of college and reminded the girls that there were scholarships for students with good grades like theirs. They sent away for information packets for various colleges and talked about being roommates. While the thought of them leaving made my heart hurt, I was excited for them. They were dreaming big, and I knew that was something Kelsey had never dared to do. I did put in a plug every now and then for Mesa State College and the advantage of both of them living with me and Brent, but mostly, I just let them dream and plan.

★

"Mom, you'll never guess what happened at church today," Anna said on the way home. "Elizabeth Smithson asked if I'd play the piano at her wedding reception. She said she heard me play at Festival last year, and she wants me to find some romantic piano music to play. She even said she'll pay me."

"Wow! A professional pianist," I said. "That's great."

Weeks were spent preparing beautiful music for the wedding. It seemed that everything I did was accompanied by the sound of lilting, romantic piano pieces. By the time the wedding arrived, Anna had enough music ready to play for hours. I was amazed at her confidence. She sat at the piano in a pretty, yellow dress and played for nearly two hours.

"That was so much fun," she said on the way home. "Maybe I want to study piano at college."

"I think that's a great idea."

"Maybe I'll get a doctorate in music just like Mildred."

"Maybe you can teach piano until you're nearly a hundred years old too."

★

From Anna's journal:

> Sometimes I don't know what to do. I hate keeping secrets from Mom and Dad, but today Kelsey told me that her dad lost another job and he started drinking hard. She said that last night he got

drunk and beat up Starr. He hit her and knocked her down and then kicked her. Kelsey was really scared. I asked if he hit her, and she said no, but he threw an ashtray across the room at her when she told him to stop. It hit the wall right by her head.

I want to tell Mom and Dad, but she made me promise not to. Stan told her if she ever says anything, he'll just take her away to Texas, and she'll never see us again. I don't want that to happen, but I don't want anything to happen to her either. He's a terrible person. I wish even more that she didn't have to live with him. I always pray for Kelsey, but I guess now I'm going to have to start praying that I'll know what I can do to help her.

After dinner one evening, Brent and I were watching television when I was startled by loud chattering at the front door. I hurried into the front hall to see what was going on, and there were Anna and Kelsey, bent over something on the front porch. "What is it?" I asked.

"A cake. It's a cake," Anna said.

"Bring it in," I said. I thought we should examine it more closely. Who would leave an uncovered cake on a front porch after dark? Anna carried it into the kitchen and carefully laid it on the counter. It looked like a cake for a toddler. It was made in the shape of Cookie Monster's face. In a speech bubble on the cake board were the words "Will you go with me?" written in icing.

"Where did it come from?" I asked. I didn't want to eat a cake left by a stranger.

"I think Anna's being asked to the spring formal," Kelsey said. "The name of the guy asking her is probably somewhere in the cake." They cut the cake into small pieces, at first cutting neatly and carefully placing each piece on a separate plate, but soon it disintegrated into a mess as they hurriedly looked for whatever was inside. When they'd cut the entire cake into small squares, they still hadn't found anything. So they started over and cut each piece into even smaller pieces. About halfway through, they found a square of folded tin foil that had been baked into the cake.

"Oh please, oh please, oh please," Anna whispered as she unfolded the paper. I hoped it would be what she wanted. When she finally unfolded the foil, she found a note that read, "Anna, I'd be a happy monster if you'd join me at the Spring Formal, Reed."

Instantly, both Anna and Kelsey started laughing and jumping up and down. "I take it you're happy about that?" Brent asked.

"Yes," Anna said. I listened to Anna and Kelsey chatter while they nibbled some of the crumbs of cake at the kitchen table. I smiled as their lips turned blue from the garish icing. They talked about the dress Anna should wear and even pulled out a notebook so that Anna could draw a picture of what she hoped the dress would look like. I watched Kelsey carefully, concerned that she hadn't been asked to the dance, but I saw no sign of sadness or envy. She seemed to be just as excited about this as Anna. That was the beautiful thing about these two—what made one happy made them both happy. I was thankful for that.

Before Anna went to bed, she pulled out her yearbook and showed me a picture of Reed Cox. He looked young and cute and had a wide, friendly smile.

"How do you know him?" I asked.

"We have Honors English together. He's funny. He writes really funny poems. Miss Downing says he needs to take his writing seriously, but she laughs at the poems anyway."

"Do you like him a lot?"

"Kinda," she said. She looked embarrassed. "He's really nice." I kissed her good night and left the room, sure she would probably lie there and daydream late into the night.

"Do you know this boy who asked Anna out?" I asked Brent later as I washed my face.

"Reed is a nice kid," Brent said. "I had him in Algebra last year. He's a bit of a joker but very nice. I approve."

"Good." There were definite advantages to Brent teaching at Anna's high school. Even though he had never been her teacher and probably never would be, I was glad that he was there with her as she started dating. "Are you ready for this?" I asked and patted my face dry on a towel.

"Ready for what?" he asked with a smirk on his face.

"Ready for her to start dating," I said.

"Not really," he said. "But ready or not, it's starting."

Chapter 12

From Anna's journal:

Seriously, I can't believe how lucky I am! If I had to choose anyone in the whole school I'd want to go to the Spring Formal with, it would be Reed. He's the nicest, funniest guy I've ever met! Okay, he's really cute too! He has an adorable smile and dimples! I've had a crush on him all year! I can't believe my first date is actually going to be with him. I hope we can find a gorgeous dress for me. I want to look amazing!

We went to several stores, looking for Anna's dream dress. Anna carried the picture she and Kelsey had drawn into each store, but we found nothing that even resembled what she wanted. Finally I suggested we go to a fabric store and look at patterns. Maybe we'd find something there that she'd like. That was the answer. We purchased a pattern and some pale lavender fabric, and I began sewing. I'd never made a dress for Anna before, and with every stitch I imagined how beautiful my little girl would look. When it was finished and Anna put it on, I felt a happy sense of satisfaction. It was exactly what she'd wanted, and it meant so much more than if we'd bought a ready-made dress.

"It's so pretty," Anna said and twirled around. The lavender dress fit perfectly. It had an empire waist and tiny cap sleeves, with varying lengths of sheer ruffle on the skirt. Under the dress was a darker lavender sheath. She looked like she'd stepped out of the pages of a Jane Austen novel while still being stylish. As she modeled it for me, I was suddenly struck by a happy, frightening realization. My little girl was a young woman. And she was beautiful.

"Wow," I said.

"I didn't know you could make something so beautiful," Anna said. "Will you make my wedding dress when I get married?"

"Of course I will. But that has to wait a few years. Okay?"

"We'll see. Maybe if the dance goes well . . ." she said and gave me a mischievous smile. We laughed, and she twirled as she looked at the dress in the mirror. "I'm going to go show Dad," she said. A minute later I heard Brent let out a whistle.

Reed looked handsome when he came to pick up Anna. He looked tall and elegant in his gray suit. He was almost a foot taller than Anna's five foot three inches, and they made a cute couple as I took pictures of them in the living room. Reed behaved like a perfect gentleman as they left and offered her his arm as they walked out the front door. I peeked through the curtains as they walked to the car. Anna laughed at something Reed said, and he opened the door for her. As he walked around to the driver's side, Anna smiled and waved at me. I grinned and waved back, unconcerned that I'd been caught.

The evening stretched on. I wished that Kelsey could have stayed and kept us company. Brent graded papers and watched a Denver Nuggets game. I cleaned the kitchen, folded a load of clothes, and then sat down in the living room and forced myself to read a book. I was nearly a hundred pages into it with no idea what I had read when I heard voices on the porch. I tried not to strain to hear what was being said. After a few minutes, Anna walked in the front door with a smile on her face.

"How was your evening?" I asked.

"Oh, Mom, it was so much fun." She twirled before collapsing into the chair closest to mine. "We danced a few times, but mostly we just talked and laughed. He's so funny."

"Where did you eat?"

"We went to the Grand Vista Hotel. It was so good. Have you and Dad ever eaten there?"

"Once, a long time ago."

"You should go again. The food was delicious. I had salmon with almond butter sauce. I wish you could taste it. You'd love it." Anna described the date in glowing detail, and I enjoyed her excitement. "Mom, he's so nice. When we left here, he asked if we could drive to his house so we could show his mom how pretty I looked. Isn't that the sweetest thing ever?"

"That's very sweet," I said. "And he was right. You looked very pretty tonight." Anna was quiet for several seconds.

"I have a good life," she said looking at me. "I felt like a normal girl tonight."

I reached over and squeezed her hand. "I'm glad."

"I know I'm supposed to do something important with my gifts, but tonight it was nice not to worry about it. I just got to feel pretty and happy." It was nearly one in the morning when we finally stood to go to bed. I kissed her good night, and she hugged me tightly. Sixteen was such an exciting age—the beginning of so many wonderful things.

From Anna's journal:

Okay, I think I'm in serious like. Reed is amazing! He was so funny and so nice. Two times I laughed so hard I almost cried. We didn't run out of things to talk about all night. We talked about our families and about school and about our plans after high school. He's going to go on a mission. He wants to go to somewhere in Europe. I felt so comfortable with him I almost said too much. He was telling me about how he missed basketball tryouts this year because he caught the flu, and I almost told him I don't get sick. Crazy, huh? I've never almost told anyone that. Not even Kelsey.

He held my hand after dinner and kissed me on the cheek when he dropped me off. I can't believe how much I like him! I think he's almost perfect. I'm saying almost because I know no one is perfect, but so far I don't know anything about him that isn't. He said we should go out again. I sure hope we do.

May was unusually hot that year. Most days were as hot as mid-summer, and we turned on the air conditioning earlier that year than we ever had before. The school didn't have a good air conditioning system, so Brent was especially happy to get home from school each day, and he was eager for the school year to come to a close.

School ended the last Wednesday of May, so Anna and Kelsey had four days to play before they started working at the Little Charmer's day care for the second summer. They were both very excited. We'd arranged for them to have a week off at the end of June for a trip to the Oregon coast. Stan had already agreed to let Kelsey go with us, and we'd rented a little cottage on the beach. It was going to be a good summer.

Thursday, we all worked in the yard for most of the morning. Brent mowed the lawn while Anna and I dug up the flower beds and planted a few flowers. By noon, it was miserably hot. Brent went to the school to clean up his room for the summer and Anna, Kelsey, and I went to a matinee. The air-conditioned theater felt like heaven.

On Friday afternoon, my cell phone rang just as I was walking out of the dentist's office. I looked at the screen and saw Anna's name.

"Hi, Anna. I'm on my way home right now."

"Where are you?" Anna asked.

"I'm over at Dr. Klein's office. I had a dentist appointment, remember? I'll be home in about ten minutes."

"Okay. Dad went for a run, and I'm not sure where he is, so I'm just taking his car to go pick up Kelsey."

"I thought we were picking her up later," I said.

"We were, but she called, and she sounded pretty upset. Stan and Starr were having some knockdown, drag-out fight, and Kelsey just wants to get out of there."

"I can go by and pick her up on my way home," I said.

"That's okay. I'm already in the car. I told her I'd be right over. I'll just see you back at the house."

I didn't like the idea of Anna interrupting one of Stan and Starr's fights, but I was worried about Kelsey too. "Okay," I said hesitantly.

"Love you, Mom. Bye."

"Love you too," I said. My hand fell to the steering wheel, my phone still open. The air conditioning didn't seem to be cooling the car. I was hot, and the sun was too bright. Something wasn't right. A sense of foreboding came over me. I closed and reopened my phone and called Anna back.

"Hi, Mom," she said.

"Anna, don't go over there," I said.

"Why not?" She sounded puzzled. "I'm just going to pick up Kelsey."

"I just don't want you to go over there. I'll stop and get her. If Stan and Starr are fighting, I don't want you over there."

"Mom, think about what you just said. If Stan and Starr are fighting, and I go over there, they'll stop. Then I can get Kelsey, and I'll be home before you know it." It made perfect sense. They would stop when they saw her. She sounded so confident. So why did I have this shadow weighing on my heart? What was I so worried about?

"Honey, I really think you should wait."

"But I told Kelsey I'd come. She was really upset. I'll just get her and come home, Mom, I promise. She's waiting for me, and I'm almost there." I didn't say anything. I was thinking.

"Mom?"

"At least wait for me. I'll go with you."

"I'll be there in like two minutes."

"I can be there in three." I realized I'd been speeding toward the Davies's house.

"All right, I'll see you there. Mom, relax, everything's okay," she said.

The next few minutes are burned in my memory. They will be with me for the rest of my life. Details that would usually go unnoticed are as vivid as photographs, forever nailed to the walls of my mind. It was so hot that the road in the distance looked liquid and distorted. I sped down the street toward Kelsey's house. I turned a corner, and ahead I saw Brent's gray car in front of the chain-link fence. Funny, I'd never realized the car was the exact same color as the fence. I watched the red brake lights go off and the driver's door open. I watched Anna as she got out of the car and walked toward the gate, the car door still open. She must have heard my car because she looked over at me as I drove up and waved. Her long ponytail bounced as she walked toward the front door.

As I pulled my car behind Brent's, I saw Starr standing in the front yard between the gate and the house. Her arms were spread out, and she was leaning forward, yelling at someone I couldn't see. I put the car in park and opened my door at almost the same moment. As I took a step toward the gate, I heard Stan yelling from the side yard. "You can't just walk out on me," he screamed and called Starr a filthy name. I watched as Stan came around the corner of the house. His arms were flailing wildly. Terror overtook me as I realized that there was a gun in his hand. I heard Starr's scream mingle with my own. Then I heard the shot. Time froze. I looked at Anna. Her eyes held mine as she slowly crumpled to the ground.

Kelsey and I reached Anna at the same time. Kelsey was screaming and crying. Anna's eyes were open, her face was white. She looked from me to Kelsey and then back to me. "He didn't see me, Mom." Her voice was barely audible.

I sat down in the dirt in the Davies's front yard and pulled Anna onto my lap. Every movement sent up a little puff of dust from the hot, dry ground.

"Call an ambulance," I said to Starr, who was standing stupidly above me. Her shadow didn't move. I looked up at her and screamed through my tears, "Starr, go call an ambulance." She hurried into the house. Anna's breathing was quick and shallow.

Anna closed her eyes slowly, as if she were very tired. Then she opened them wide. "It's okay, Mom. It's okay." She was so calm and quiet, and I wondered how I could hear it so clearly with Kelsey sobbing beside us. Anna's eyes looked into mine, clear and filled with understanding. Then they became distant and unfocused. Finally she closed them.

"Anna, we're getting help," I said. "Someone's coming to help you." Kelsey held Anna's hand with one hand and reached for mine with the other. She held my hand so tightly that it hurt, but I didn't pull it away. Kelsey's body shook with the increasing force of her sobs, but Anna's was quiet and still. "Anna, it's okay, honey. Be strong." I heard sirens in the distance. I continued offering words of encouragement. "Everything's okay. Don't worry." Then something happened in my mind, almost like someone had flipped a switch, and I knew that Anna wasn't going to be okay. "Anna, I love you. I love you. I love you. You beautiful, precious girl, I love you."

Kelsey either sensed the same thing I had or she noticed the change in my words. "No, no, no," she cried. Her voice was filled with panic. "You can't leave me. You can't leave me. What will I do without you?" she said between her sobs.

From somewhere I heard a deep moaning sound. I looked around to see where it was coming from. After a moment, I realized the sound was coming from me. I forced myself to be quiet, but the tears continued to come. I looked down and saw the darker pink spots my tears were making on Anna's pink T-shirt. Somewhere in my mind, I remembered my tears landing on a soft, flannel baby blanket, many years ago in a beautiful hospital room in New Mexico.

Across the yard, I saw Stan. He was on his knees, his hands on his thighs propped himself up. The gun lay in the dirt in front of him. His sweaty baseball cap was sitting back on his head at an awkward angle that made him look like a really tall little boy. "What have I done? What have I done? What have I done?" he wailed over and over. If I hadn't been holding my dying daughter, I might have felt sorry for him. But here I was, in his filthy front yard, surrounded by weeds and empty beer bottles, holding Anna. My Anna. The Anna who would have made him stop fighting if only he would have seen her. The Anna who made the world a beautiful place. The Anna who had made my life complete. My sweet girl who wasn't supposed to get sick or hurt, who lay dying in my arms.

The sound of sirens got louder and louder until it was deafening and I wanted to scream for it to stop. A man and a woman in uniform came and gently moved Anna out of my arms. I sat there for a moment reaching for her and then slowly got to my feet and pulled Kelsey up from the ground with me. She hugged me. She stooped over slightly to bury her face into my shoulder. We clung to each other as I watched the people work on my daughter. I prayed out loud, begging Heavenly Father to help them make her okay again. It was hot. Heat boiled up from the ground, from the cars around us. I felt sweat running down my back. The air was too fiery and dry to breathe. I tried to take a deep breath, but the air seemed to scorch my throat and lungs. Somewhere to my right, two police officers put handcuffs on Stan and led him away. He was a full head taller than either of them even though he was slouching, and his head drooped forward. The baseball cap was gone. Strangely, I looked for it and found it crushed on the ground by the gate. Starr was standing in the little sliver of shade made by the ambulance, talking to another officer. I looked back at the paramedics. The woman was shaking her head. The man looked at his watch and said something. I tried to read his lips but couldn't. I really didn't need to. I knew what he was saying.

A policeman came to me and told me where they were taking Anna. He asked if I needed help getting there, and I told him no. He nodded to the paramedics, who then loaded Anna's stretcher into the ambulance. The officer stood by me for a moment, holding onto my arm, as the ambulance carrying Anna made a U-turn and drove away. After a few moments, he let go of my arm and walked away. As I watched him get in his car, I realized I couldn't remember what he'd told me. I needed to get out of this hot and dusty yard. I took Kelsey's hand, and together we walked to my car. I closed the door and felt the heat press in on me. Kelsey was beside me. I stared at Brent's car in front of us. The door was still open. I got out and walked over to the door Anna had left open not very many minutes ago. As I closed the door of the car, I felt the low, steady vibrations of the engine. The car was still running. I reached in, turned it off, and took out the key. Then I closed the door, walked back to my car, and drove home to tell Brent.

It's strange to me that I can so vividly remember every word, every shadow, and every thought I had in that twenty minutes or so, but I can remember so little about the following days. I know that Brent cried like a little boy. I know that by the end of the day, my parents and Brent's parents were there at the house with us. Sometime in the next couple of days, Dan and Bev arrived. I know that Kelsey came home with us. Someone from Family Services came to talk to us about her, and somehow our home became her home. Brent took her back to her house to get some clothes, her necklace, and Belle. She never returned there. I know that they took Stan to jail and that Starr disappeared. I know that somehow there was a lovely funeral with flowers and kind words. I know that generous people made sure we ate and slept. I know these things happened, I just don't know how they happened.

Chapter 13

That summer, life took on a new and terrible quality. Nothing felt right. We were all suffering. The beauty and peace and clarity that Anna brought to the world were missing, and I felt adrift and confused. Each gray day turned into a gray night that turned into another gray day. I'd always associated gray with cool—clouds, storms, rain showers. But that summer's gray was synonymous with heat—a gray, oppressive, stifling heat that filled each day. I couldn't get cool. I couldn't sleep with anything over me because it was too hot. The air conditioning didn't seem to cool the house. No matter where I was, I felt hot and sticky and claustrophobic. I looked around for something of beauty to cling to, but all I saw were bleak rooms—rooms that now looked as dreary and old as I looked on the outside and felt on the inside.

One day as I walked woodenly in front of the mirror in the family room, I stopped short, shocked at the disheveled stranger that stared back at me. Her eyes were vacant, her face drawn and gray. *More gray*, I thought.

Brent didn't want to be in the house and spent hours doing little time-consuming tasks in the yard. He planted new flowers and then, disappointed, he'd rip them out and start over. He combed the lawn with mind-numbing diligence, slowly and patiently removing every clump that didn't look right and every little weed that dared pop up. He edged and groomed and mowed and trimmed and then started over again.

I sat. Occasionally, somehow, I'd do a load of laundry or load the dishwasher or sweep the floor, and then, exhausted by the effort, I'd sit again. I couldn't open a book; I couldn't watch television; I couldn't write. I'd just look at the portrait on the wall or Anna's bedspread or her hairbrush. I'd sit until I fell asleep at night and then sometime in the night, Brent would come and guide me to bed. Some nights, he didn't come, and I'd sleep sitting on the couch with the lights on all night long.

Kelsey didn't want to work at the day care without Anna, so she called Lora Sims. But two weeks after the funeral, sad and lonely and aching for her friend, Kelsey changed her mind and went back to work. Lora told me later that Kelsey rocked and cuddled the babies and cried by the hour. Lora just let her cry. The babies were providing something Kelsey desperately needed.

We didn't go to the Oregon coast that summer. The cottage was never used. We never even called them to cancel our reservations. The owner of the cabin left several messages on the machine, but we never returned them. The cabin just sat there empty. The summer dragged on forever. Every day felt endless.

Sometime during the summer, Stan made a plea. Brent and I went to court because we were supposed to, but because of his plea, we didn't have to say anything. I don't know what I could have said. As vivid as my memories of that day were, I couldn't bring myself to talk about it. I sat through the hearing, lost in my own head. I just held Brent's hand. I can't remember any of the words that were spoken, but I remember I looked down and saw Brent's hand holding mine. I stared at the little scratch on his wedding band the entire time.

About the same time school started that fall, two important things happened. Stan was sentenced to five years for manslaughter, and we were given permanent guardianship over Kelsey. Despite our loss, we were thankful that Kelsey was able to live with us now. This was what Anna had wanted for so many years. I replayed the conversations over and over in my mind as I thought of Anna's wish to have Kelsey be part of our family. The irony was not lost on me. Anna's greatest desire had come about only because she was no longer here. It felt cruel and unfair. We moved everything from the sewing room and office to the unfinished room in the basement and set up the room for Kelsey. We all knew that none of us were ready to change Anna's bedroom.

The Saturday after school started, Brent busied himself in the yard. All summer I'd watched him do yard work. I knew this was his coping mechanism, but for some reason, that day it infuriated me. I stepped outside and stood over him while he fiddled around with a sprinkler head. "What are you doing?" I asked.

"The sprinkler's not aiming the right direction."

"And?"

"I want it to hit the lawn, not the sidewalk."

"Are you serious?"

He looked up at me, squinting into the sun. "What?" he asked.

"Is this all you can think of to do?" I heard my voice getting shrill. I didn't recognize it, even though I knew it was mine.

"Did you have something you wanted me to do?" he asked. I could see the confusion on his face.

"Anything! Absolutely anything but wasting your time out in this stinking yard. Can we *go* somewhere? Can we *do* something? Anything?" My voice rose higher.

"What do you want to do?"

"Surely you could think of something besides this?" I threw my arm out in a sweeping gesture that took in the entire yard.

"You want to complain, but you don't have any ideas? You want me to think of something else to do?" His voice was bitter.

"A perfect yard isn't going to bring her back, Brent." My voice was laden with sarcasm, and I felt ashamed. But somehow I couldn't stop myself. "No matter how many times you plant flowers or pick weeds out of the lawn, Anna will still be gone."

He stood up straight. "You think I don't know that?"

"Well, do you?"

Brent shook his head. "What exactly are you trying to accomplish by picking a fight with me?" he asked. His words stopped me cold. We hadn't fought for more than sixteen years, and now here we were, in our backyard, fighting because Brent was doing more yard work than I thought was necessary. I burst into tears and fell to my knees. "What?" he asked helplessly.

"We're fighting."

"Yeah?"

"We're fighting!" I said again, and he understood. His defiant shoulders sagged, and he knelt down beside me and reached for me. We cried together for a long time.

So much had been lost when we lost Anna. What had been easy was now so hard. We had to work to be peaceful. We had to make an effort to get along. Sometimes it felt impossible, but we tried hard. To fall into a pattern of arguing and bickering would have been to disrespect Anna's memory. She would have hated to see us fight. We couldn't allow that to happen.

★

With Brent and Kelsey gone to school each day, I found myself with too many empty hours. I got up each morning and sent them off but then usually ended up back in bed for a few more hours before I'd force myself back up to wander the house, doing my daily chores with robotic indifference. I trudged through the long, empty hours with no direction.

One day shortly before noon, I awoke with a start. The letter. I hadn't thought of the letter from Anna's great-aunt in many years, but now that Anna was gone, we could open it and see what her great-aunt had known. I grabbed the key from a hook in the kitchen cupboard and hurried to the small, locked firebox in the basement. I shuffled through the contents of the box, but there was no letter. I searched it again. I carefully removed everything and then put it back in the box. There was no pink envelope. Had Brent already looked at it and not told me?

I locked the box and went to the bedroom. I searched through the drawers by the bed. Nothing. I looked through the paperwork in the office. I couldn't find it. It was gone.

"Brent, the letter from Anna's great-aunt is missing," I said to him later that day.

"What do you mean, missing?" he asked.

"I mean it's not in the box. Did you take it out?"

"No. I haven't even thought about it for ages," he said.

"I've looked everywhere I can think of. Where do you think it is?"

"I have no idea." Together we looked again in the places I'd already looked, and Brent suggested a few more places to check. But there was no letter. I knew it didn't really change anything, but I went to bed that night disappointed that we'd probably never know what Anna's great-aunt had wanted to tell her.

✦

"I just don't get it," Kelsey said. She was sitting at the counter doing her homework. "I understood how to do this last year, and now it's like another language." I walked over and looked at the math she was working on. Of course, it made no sense to me.

"Maybe Brent can help you when he gets home," I said.

"But why can't I just get it? Last year I was doing problems a lot harder than these." She didn't know. She didn't understand why it was suddenly harder to learn. I walked over and sat down by her. She looked at me with an expression of confusion. I felt for her, but math was not a subject I could help her with.

"Kelsey, you're dealing with some really hard things. Sometimes a terrible thing like we're going through makes it hard to do even the simplest things. Sometimes I can't even remember how to turn on the washing machine or make the meatloaf I've been making for more than twenty years. Sometimes I open a bill and try to read it, but nothing makes sense to me. I don't even understand what it's saying, and I feel completely lost." Kelsey nodded as tears ran down her cheeks. "Be patient with yourself. You're smart and you'll get it. Just work hard and be patient with yourself." We hugged each other and cried on each other's shoulder.

That night I met Brent on the porch when he got home. We sat on the front steps together, quietly talking. "I almost told Kelsey about Anna's gift today, how she made it easy to learn and understand things, but then something stopped me." I stared across the street at the neighbor's leaning mailbox.

"Did you think she wouldn't believe you?" Brent asked.

"Actually, I was afraid she would. I don't want her to go through the rest of high school and college thinking that the only reason she's had good grades is because of Anna. I want her to know she's smart, and I want her to take credit for being smart. The last thing Anna would want is for Kelsey to be lost without her."

"I think that was wise. But we're going to have to help her, or she might feel that way anyway."

A breeze blew a leaf across the sidewalk in front of me, and I realized I felt cool, even a little chilled. I looked at my arms and saw goose bumps. It was the first time I'd felt cool since that day.

Brent worked with Kelsey on her math, and I helped quiz her on her other subjects. She really was a good student, and by working hard, she kept her grades up. Sometimes she joked that she was working harder than she ever had before, but she didn't complain, and we were proud of her for her accomplishments.

★

November was cold, and I loved it that way. I was so tired of feeling hot that I refused to put on warm clothes or wear a coat. Brent finally insisted that we turn on the heat. Some days I'd walk out on the deck and stand in the cold air until I'd get goose bumps or my teeth would begin to chatter. I welcomed them as signs that I was still alive.

One morning Bev called me. "Are you going to be okay for Thanksgiving?" she asked. "I know it was Anna's favorite."

"It'll be hard," I said. "I'm glad we're all going to Mom and Dad's house. I don't know if I could stand being here."

"When you went through Anna's things, did you find that gratitude list she made in seminary? You should bring that. It was so sweet. If you felt like it, you could read it to everybody. Maybe it would help us all feel like she's there with us." I heard Bev's voice catch, and I knew she was trying not to cry. I couldn't speak. Just remembering that list made a giant lump grow in my throat. "Susan, are you there?"

"Yes," I said.

"Sorry, I didn't mean to upset you."

"You didn't. I should see if I can find it." I paused. "Bev, I haven't gone through her things yet."

"Oh, Susan, I'm sorry. I wish I was there to help you. Do you want me to come home with you after Thanksgiving and help you do that? I'm sure Dan wouldn't mind. Or maybe I should come before."

"Thanks, but I'll be okay. Maybe I'll see if I can find the list." It would be so nice to have her there with me, but I knew I couldn't. There would be things in there that would be difficult to explain without revealing Anna's unusual gifts. I wondered why that mattered now that she was gone. What would it hurt for people to know how special she had been? But there were two things holding me back. I didn't know if Brent and I would ever feel comfortable sharing the details of Anna's life, and I wasn't sure how Kelsey would react. I just couldn't. Not yet.

A little while later, I stood in the doorway of Anna's room. Her little bulletin board was still unchanged. A scripture she was memorizing hung there beside a picture of our family and Kelsey. Her desk was tidy and organized with a couple of little notes to remind her of things she wanted to do before the trip to Oregon. In the top drawer were pens and notebooks. In the side drawer was a box with letters from her grandparents. On a shelf in her closet, I found what I was looking for. There were seven journals, six of them full, the seventh a little more than half filled. I carried them to the bed and sat down. I looked around the room that was so Anna. Then I opened the first journal and started reading.

I sat there for hours, stopping only long enough to get a box of Kleenex out of my bedroom. I read each entry from her life. The journals began when she was eight. Her primary teacher had given her a journal with a picture of Jesus being baptized on the front. The entries matured as Anna got older and changed from the writings of a little girl to the thoughts of a young lady. There were funny stories mixed in with all her thoughts and feelings. I cherished each accomplishment, each worry, each tender feeling.

When I reached the journal from her first year in seminary, I found the gratitude list. I unfolded the paper and read through the things that Anna was thankful for.

My Blessings

1. *That Mom and Dad somehow found me and love me like their own.*
2. *That I know about the Savior and what he did for me.*
3. *That we have a nice home.*
4. *That Dad works hard so that Mom can be home when we need her.*

5. *That I ignored the kids that were making fun of Kelsey and invited her to play.*
6. *That I have the best friend in the world.*
7. *That Mom and Dad love Kelsey as much as they love me.*
8. *That I don't get sick or hurt.*
9. *That people are happy around me.*
10. *That I can play the piano and that Mildred was my teacher.*
11. *That I have wonderful grandparents.*
12. *That I'll get my very own pumpkin pie on Thanksgiving.*

I smiled at that. Anna loved pumpkin pie so much that Grandma had baked one especially for her since she was about seven years old. I would copy most of the list and share it with the family. I was glad Bev had suggested it. I folded up the paper and laid it on the bed beside me and then continued to read the journals.

As I opened the sixth journal, a pink envelope fell into my lap. I picked it up and found myself looking at the shaky handwriting of Anna's great-aunt. The envelope was empty. I thumbed through the pages of the journal, held the book up and shook it, but the only thing that fell out was a ticket stub for a movie. Where was the letter? I looked through the last journal and then searched her desk and the shelf in her closet that had held her journals. There was no letter. After a thorough search, I sat back down to read, hoping to find a clue. As I read, I came across a couple of entries that surprised me. I read them again and again and then slipped paper in to mark the places so I could share them with Brent.

Tucked in the last journal was a birthday card from Kelsey. In it she thanked Anna for sharing her family. A folded sheet of lined paper was a note from Reed. He thanked Anna for the fun date and reminded her that they would see a movie sometime during the summer. So many lost possibilities, so many things she'd never do. The journals were tender and emotional, but when I was finished, I felt good—better than I had in nearly six months. I put five of the journals back in the closet and took the list of blessings and the two bookmarked journals to my bedroom.

"Brent, there's something I want to show you," I said as we were getting ready for bed. "Today I went through Anna's journals, and I found a couple of interesting things. She found the letter." Brent gave me a puzzled look as I pulled out the journal and opened it to the first bookmarked page.

> *March 11—Today I found a letter addressed to me. I needed a copy of my birth certificate to get my driver's license, and when I opened the box in the basement, I saw a pink envelope that said "Our Sweet Baby on her 18th Birthday." I didn't know who it was from because I could tell it wasn't Dad's or Mom's handwriting. I knew I wasn't supposed to read it until I'm eighteen, but I was so curious, I couldn't help myself. I brought it to my room and opened it. It's from my birth mother's aunt. It was amazing. I'm not the only strange one. It said my grandmother had special gifts too. She said to use my gifts to bless the people I love and not to use them in a selfish way. I'll have to tell Mom and Dad that I found it. I hope they won't be upset.*

"There was no letter. Only the envelope. I looked everywhere," I said. "But that isn't all." I turned to the other marked page and began reading aloud, but after a sentence or two, I couldn't continue. I pointed to where I was on the page and silently we read the entry together.

> *April 1—Today in seminary we talked about the Atonement and the resurrection. Brother Meyers had us read the scripture "Greater love hath no man than this, that he lay down his life for his friends." I love this scripture. I've loved it ever since we talked about it in family night a long time ago. It shows me how much the Savior loves us and what he was willing to do for us. I think that to lay down your life for your friends, you'd have to really love them. I mean really love them a lot. It wouldn't be the kind of feelings you'd have for people you just sorta hang out with. It would have to be the kind of love you'd have for friends that were really close. Close like your family. That must be how Jesus loves us.*
>
> *I've thought about this scripture so many times. I love Dad and Mom enough that I would definitely lay down my life for them. I'm sure they would lay down their lives for me too. I can tell they would do anything for me. I'm so lucky that they adopted me. As I was sitting in seminary, I started to wonder who I would lay down my life for. I felt a little guilty because as I looked around the*

room, I saw people I really like, people who I think are my friends, but I didn't know if I would want to give up my life for them. If I gave up my life, I'd be giving up living with Dad and Mom. I'd be giving up getting married someday. I'd be giving up going to college and playing piano and having my own kids. Did I love any of them enough to give up all of that? I wanted to say yes, I would. But I doubted it.

Then at lunch, I saw Kelsey saving a place for me in line. As soon as I saw her, the thought came to me that she is a friend I would lay down my life for. She is a friend that I care enough about that I would gladly die for her if she needed me to. Kelsey is the best friend I could ever have hoped for. I know that we'll be friends forever. It makes me feel good to think that Jesus loves me as much as I love Dad and Mom and Kelsey. And it makes me feel good to know that I have room in my heart to love a few people enough that I would lay down my life for them. I guess I need to work on loving everyone else that much. If I want to be like Jesus, I'm going to have to try.

Brent and I sat there together with tears in our eyes. "Brent, I think she did it on purpose. Like when she chose to get hurt so she'd know how it felt. I think she chose for this to happen to save Kelsey from her hard life." Brent was nodding. "When she was dying there in that awful front yard, she looked at me and told me it was okay. How many times did she tell us she wished Kelsey was in our family? Dozens. It was what she wanted more than anything in the world. She probably thought it was the only way to make it happen." For the first time since Anna had died, I fell asleep that night with a peaceful heart.

Epilogue

I think of my daughter, Anna, every day. She changed our whole lives and left a big hole behind. I don't understand everything about our life with her. I don't understand her gifts. I don't understand why she was the way she was. I still don't understand why we were the ones blessed to be her parents. I'm starting to accept that I'll never be able to explain the marvelous and magical way she changed the world around her.

Time slowly moves on. Nearly a year after Anna died, I pulled out my diary. Back when Anna was a little girl, I'd had a dream. I couldn't remember the details of the dream, but somehow I knew it was important that I read it. I went through the pages of three diaries before I found the right one.

In the dream, I saw Anna as a baby on the day I first met her in the hospital. I stood in the nursery, looking down at her in the clear, little bassinet. Joy filled my heart as I looked at her pretty face. Then, as I stood there, Anna slowly rose out of the bassinet, and the blanket fell away from her. Her eyes opened as she flitted around the room, almost like a fairy or a cherub without wings. As I watched her fly, incredible things happened. Anna extended her arms, and it seemed that color and light were flowing from her tiny hands. She flew to a painting on the wall. Her little baby hands, streaming with beauty, swept in front of the painting, and it became bright and beautiful. Then she flew to the nurse, a rather drab-looking woman, and sweetly touched her hair. Color and splendor flowed out of her hands, and the drabness was replaced with exquisite beauty. The nurse didn't really change, but as the color flowed from Anna's little baby hands, the features took on a radiant loveliness.

I stood there by the empty bassinet, stunned by what I was seeing. I stepped toward Anna, reaching for her, but she escaped my hands. She flew through the open door of the nursery, and I followed her into the hall. As she fluttered down the hall, she left everything around her brighter and more vivid, almost as if she were an angel, changing the world from black and white to color. I followed Anna to the entrance of the hospital. The doors opened, seemingly magically. Anna flew through the open doors, and then they closed behind her. I tried to push the doors back open, wanting to follow her, but they wouldn't budge. I watched Anna through the glass as she flew away and disappeared from my sight.

I sobbed as I read the entry in my diary from my new perspective. The dream had come true. She really had made the world more beautiful, and then she'd left us. I sat there, feeling overwhelmed with gratitude that Anna hadn't left as a baby, as she had in my dream. She'd made our world better for sixteen years before she'd had to leave.

It had been almost a year since I'd written anything. I hadn't written a story or a poem. I hadn't written in my diary. I hadn't even written a grocery list. I closed my diary, found a new notebook, and began writing.

Kelsey graduated valedictorian of her class. Only Brent and I really appreciated the magnitude of her success. To maintain her grades after Anna left was a monumental accomplishment. It would have been so easy to be discouraged. I had expected to have two girls walk across the stage that day, but instead I only had one. Brent put his arm around me as we sat there at graduation. I thought of the many times in the coming years that my heart would ache just like this. When Kelsey goes to college, I'll wish that Anna could have gone to college. Someday, when Kelsey marries, I'll think of Anna and wish she'd had the chance to fall in love and get married. I'll wish I could have made her wedding dress. When Kelsey has a baby, I'll wish that Anna could have been a mother. I'll long to hold her children and recite "Shiny-eyes" to them. Maybe someday I'll try to explain to Kelsey the sacrifice Anna chose to make for her. Maybe.

As I sat there with Brent, we watched Kelsey walk across that stage and receive her diploma. I saw a confident, beautiful girl, happy and accomplished. I was overcome with emotion as I remembered a gangly little first grader, walking across the lawn with my Anna. She had dirty, tangled hair. She was wearing a dinosaur shirt and camouflage pants that were too big for her, held up by a shiny pink belt. She had no coat on, and she looked cold and scared and skinny.

Anna had given Kelsey a new life. She'd given Brent and me a new life. She'd given us everything she had. Nothing could ever completely fill the void she had left in my heart. I smiled through my tears and offered a silent prayer of thanks for the precious gift of Anna.

Discussion Questions

1. Susan wondered if she was lacking some special intuition with regard to Anna because she hadn't actually given birth to her. Do you think it is possible to have the same connection or intuition with an adopted child? Do you think parental intuition is real or exaggerated?

2. Susan and Brent spend much of the book trying to protect Anna from the disadvantages that might come with her gifts. Do you think that protection was too much? How might Anna's life have been different if her parents had reacted differently to her gifts?

3. When Brent and Susan get the letters from Anna's biological relative, it's a temptation to open the letter addressed to Anna. Would you have made the same decision they did? Do you think things might have turned out differently if they had?

4. The friendship between Anna and Kelsey is a deep one. Have you ever had a friend you would sacrifice everything for? Why do you think Anna felt such a responsibility for Kelsey's well-being? Should we feel that kind of responsibility for those around us?

5. While Anna's gifts caused some unusual concerns for her parents, they also removed some of the concerns most parents feel (physical safety, difficulties learning, and so forth). Which concerns do you think would be more difficult?

6. Anna's choices changed Kelsey's life for the better but were devastating to her parents. Do you think Anna knew that would be the case? If so, do you think it was fair to her parents? What would you do in Anna's situation? If you were one of Anna's parents, would you have understood and accepted her choice?

7. Susan chooses not to tell Kelsey why she is having a harder time learning. Do you think that was a wise choice? Do you think they should ever reveal to Kelsey the things they know about Anna's sacrifice for her?

8. Did the book alter the way you look at your own children's talents and gifts? What responsibility do parents have to help their children find and develop their own talents and gifts?

About the Author

Karey White was born in Provo, Utah. As the oldest of eleven children, her life has been full of useful and often ridiculous experiences. She attended Ricks College and Brigham Young University.

She endures housework; enjoys traveling, reading, and baking treats; and loves spending time with family and friends. She lives in Cedar Hills, Utah, with her very funny husband, Travis, and their four clever children. She is currently working on her next book. Find out more about Karey at http://kareywhite.blogspot.com.